FINDING HOME

ALEXA ASTON

All rights reserved.

No part of this publication may be sold, copied, distributed,
reproduced or transmitted in any form or by any means,
mechanical or digital, including photocopying and recording or by
any information storage and retrieval system without the prior
written permission of both the publisher, Oliver Heber Books and
the author, Alexa Aston, except in the case of brief quotations
embodied in critical articles and reviews.

PUBLISHER'S NOTE: This is a work of fiction. Names, characters,
places, and incidents either are the product of the author's
imagination or are used fictitiously. Any resemblance to actual
persons, living or dead, business establishments, events, or locales is
entirely coincidental.

COPYRIGHT © Alexa Aston

Published by Oliver-Heber Books

0 9 8 7 6 5 4 3 2 1

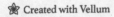 Created with Vellum

PROLOGUE
SOMEWHERE OVER THE MIDDLE EAST

G age Nelson closed his eyes, concentrating on his ritual, one he thought through on each mission.

Eight weeks naval recruit training.

Eight weeks naval special warfare prep school.

Three weeks basic underwater demolition orientation and SEAL training.

Twenty-four weeks demolition and SEAL training.

Five weeks parachute jump school.

Twenty-six weeks SEAL qualification training.

Graduation. Earning the Navy SEAL Trident.

Assignment to SEAL team.

Eighteen months pre-deployment training. Individual. Units. Air operations. Land Warfare. Maritime. Urban and special reconnaissance.

And six months squadron integration training.

Then deployment.

Get in. Get out.

Remember the mission.

Gage repeated the phrase over and over in his head until the words blurred and had no meaning. He allowed himself to float, repeating it, the echo ringing in his head.

Then he cleared all thoughts. His focus became sharp as a knife's edge. His body sensed they were drawing near.

Showtime.

He always thought back on all the training he had undergone in preparation for the task ahead. Fear, a natural instinct, had no place in the world of a Navy SEAL. They were among the most highly-trained soldiers in the world. Eighty percent of those attempting to become a SEAL washed out at some point.

That meant the men on this mission—his mission —had experienced rigorous, thorough training, developing the skills that would make them successful. Make their team successful.

Make their country proud.

A SEAL wasn't in it for the glory. Many of their missions remained classified years after they occurred. But they did it because of their commitment to their country. To the man who stood on either side of them. Gage's SEAL team was an elite unit. Failure was not in the vocabulary. They would follow orders. Complete the mission. Get in. Get out.

And make the world a safer, better place.

Opening his eyes, he studied the faces of the men across from him in the helicopter. Some he had trained beside. Others he had come to know as brothers—his unit was his family. For an orphan who was kicked around the foster care system from place to place, he had never had a family.

But he had had a dream. To be a Navy SEAL. Gage had wanted to serve his country. Push his mind and body to the extreme. Accomplish what few ever did. Make a difference in a world which hadn't cared about him. He had fought for his place among the ranks of these men. He would give his life for the mission. For anyone with him on the mission.

Get in. Get out.

His gaze connected with MCPO Sawyer, the master chief special warfare operator who was head of this SEAL team. Sawyer gave an imperceptible nod. Gage returned it.

He had spent a dozen years as a SEAL and couldn't imagine any other life. Men such as MCPO Sawyer had become an example to him of who and what a leader is. His unit had become his family. His life—his very identity—was wrapped up in being a SEAL.

And he and his fellow SEALs would kick ass today.

Sawyer stood, bringing every man's eye to the front.

"You have your orders. You've studied the layout. You know the role you will play. We get it. We get out —with the subject. We need him alive. Anyone around him is collateral damage."

"Yes, sir!" the men echoed in unison.

The helicopter, flying in silent mode, now hovered in the heavy darkness of night. Quickly, each Seal went to the ropes dropped and slithered down.

Into danger. Inside enemy territory. Into the unknown.

No matter how well they had been prepped, Gage knew not everything could be certain. Established patterns could change. Someone might be sick, changing a rotation. A person might not stick to a routine but act upon a whim, which could throw off the intel. Or the intel might be bad. Going into a mission was as if he voluntarily jumped through the Bermuda Triangle, into a black hole, into a place unfamiliar, strange, uncharted.

Gage touched the ground and moved forward, never hesitating, his night vision goggles making things plain as day. Weapon in hand, booted feet sure and steady, following McLaurrin, Tanner, and Jessop, bringing up the rear, watching their six.

They moved silently through the courtyard, sand at their feet, weapons in hand. His group moved to the right, blazing the way for those behind.

No one awake yet. No sentries. No noise.

And then gunfire erupted, the bright flashes of light blinding him. A bullet hit his flak jacket, knocking him a few steps back. Then lights were switched on. Immediately, he shoved his goggles up, blinking, gunfire still erupting. He saw fellow SEALs falling around him, along with others, the smell of smoke and blood mingling.

"Abort! Abort!" he heard in his earpiece, recognizing Sawyer's voice.

Gage began fighting his way back the way he had come, ignoring the cries and grunts, concentrating on getting through the chaos. He sensed someone close and wheeled, seeing it was Sawyer.

"Go!" the commander shouted.

He whipped around, guiding them through the firestorm, down a long corridor, and back into the open courtyard in which they had dropped. Surprisingly, it was deserted, all the fighting occurring behind them.

The helicopter flew low. Gage yanked his goggles back over his eyes, seeing how the vehicle dropped the ropes, which would be their way to escape. He and Sawyer ran for them, scaling them. Glancing down, he saw no other SEALs followed. His gut churned, hating that they left behind so many. That the mission had obviously had bad intel. That it had failed spectacularly. And they hadn't apprehended the criminal they sought.

A shot sounded, and Gage heard Sawyer's grunt. His commander had been struck in the shoulder. Another shot and Sawyer's right hand was simply gone, a howl erupting from the master chief that pierced the night.

Gage swung his rope and shouted for Sawyer to latch on to him. On the third swing, the commander did, both arms encircling Gage's waist as he continued to scale the rope.

Then he was hit in his upper left arm. Another bullet punctured his left thigh. He fought to reach the top, sensing his own strength waning and aware Sawyer was losing his hold on Gage.

"Hold on!" he hollered hoarsely, feeling the pressure easing as Sawyer's release weakened.

More gunfire sounded and Sawyer's arms fell away, his body falling back to the courtyard.

He watched helplessly, seeing the operator's broken body smash into the ground. A loud wail erupted from him, even as strong hands gripped him, pulling him into the helicopter.

"Anyone else coming?" a voice asked.

"No," Gage said, the most bitter word he'd ever spoken leaving his lips.

"Get us out of here," someone said.

The helicopter rose, the sound of bullets striking it pinging.

"He's been hit."

Gage felt his body being dragged and someone stripping him.

"Nelson, found a bullet hole. Left thigh. Any more on you?"

"Arm," he managed to get out.

"Left bicep," the voice said, poking him and then shaking him violently. "Nelson, two hits it?"

"Yes," he said, floating away as a needle poked him, a delicious darkness swallowing him up.

GAGE PUT in the time for rehab, a sour taste constantly in his mouth from the outcome. The failure of his SEAL team to apprehend the insurgent and gain the necessary intel had led to a bomb exploding at Game Seven of the World Series in Chicago moments after the final out was called and the winning team's players flooded the field. Thousands had been killed in the explosion, with thousands more being injured.

He hadn't seen the mission through. Because of it, all those deaths gathered at his doorstep. He had let his country down. He had lost a good portion of his chosen family. Fellow SEALs, with their high standard of perfection, looked at him with suspicion, as if he were a traitor. At least, that's how he viewed it. His doctors, his unit members, and his superior had told him not to blame himself. The intel had been bad. His team had been set up.

But Gage's guilt weighed heavily on him. He believed others looked at him as tainted because he got out and no one else did. He sat through physical and psychological evaluations. The physical injuries took a little time to come back from. He knew the right things to say for the psych evals. Yet he'd still been called in and questioned at length regarding his fitness to return to duty. One Navy doc told him he bore survivor's guilt. That it was heavy noose about his neck. That his worry and doubt and hesitation could get himself—or a fellow SEAL—killed in the field.

That did it. The final nail in the coffin. Gage wouldn't be responsible for getting another SEAL killed. And as miserable as he felt about himself for letting down his SEAL team members, he wasn't ready to check out himself.

Instead, he asked to be discharged. He got a decent severance package, a clean slate of health, and had absolutely no idea where he might go. The military had been his home for so many years. His mom had died of a drug overdose when he was two. No father had been listed on his birth certificate. His grandmother, who had a bad heart and a two-pack-a-day smoking habit, had given Gage over to foster care. When he was old enough, he had looked her up and found the old woman died two months after she relinquished her grandson to the state. He had no living relatives. No home base. Nothing. No one.

Then he recalled the only vacation he had ever been on. He was ten and living with a foster couple who played fast and loose with the rules, the reason he—and four other children—were later removed from their care. But that summer they had set out from Wyoming for the Oregon coast, a place his foster mom had grown up. They were gone almost three weeks, stopping in little towns up and down the coast, playing on the beaches, eating ice cream for dinner. Gage had never forgotten the rugged beauty of the Oregon coast or the happiness he had known for a short time, swimming in the cold Pacific, running around on the sand, roasting marshmallows over an open fire on the beach.

If he had to go anywhere, it might as well be the one place he had decent memories of. He would rent a car and drive through those coastal towns, and settle in the one that called to him the loudest.

In the end, it was a place called Maple Cove.

CHAPTER 1

FOUR YEARS LATER—
GOVERNMENT STATE
SECONDARY GIRLS SCHOOL,
AFRICA

Sloane Anderson moved among the girls she had featured over the last four weeks. The African school boarded its students, and she had lived in the dormitory with them, getting to know these girls well. It reminded her of her own college days, when she had met Willow and Tenley at UCLA. The three women had remained roommates their entire time in college and still were close friends, though Sloane was usually thousands of miles away on assignment. She decided to call her friends tonight and try to catch up. They hadn't spoken since a few days after Christmas, three weeks earlier.

Knowing both women were extremely early risers, she shot a quick text to them both, seeing if they had time to talk with her, figuring in the eleven-hour time differential. Both responded quickly, and they made plans to chat in two hours. It would be six in the evening her time, while in Oregon, it would be seven in the morning.

"Miss Sloane, come look at my poem," Akachi said, her brown eyes large.

She adored Akachi, whose name meant *God's*

hand. It had been interesting putting names to the faces of all these girls when she had first arrived and then learning what their names meant.

"I'd be happy to." She sat next to the girl. "Read it aloud."

Akachi brightened. "Okay."

The girl read her poem, which Sloane actually thought was quite good. She smiled, complimenting the twelve-year-old on her original work.

"And one day, I will be a writer," Akachi promised. "I will write poems and novels and everyone will read my stories and love them."

"That's a wonderful goal to have. Perhaps I should get your autograph now before you become famous."

Akachi looked blankly at Sloane, and she realized it was just another example of how cultures could be different. Of course, autographs weren't nearly as popular now. Everyone in the US and many places abroad preferred taking a selfie with a celebrity. Even though she considered herself a serious journalist, Sloane had been stopped numerous times in airports and on location and asked if she would pose for a picture with someone. She doubted they were fans of hers. They merely recognized her from seeing her on television.

"It's where you ask someone if they will sign their name on a piece of paper," she explained. "It is something another person treasures, that contact with a person they admire and the physical evidence of the connection they made when they met."

"Ooh, I like that, Miss Sloane. I will sign my poem and give it to you." Akachi scrawled her name in pencil and handed the sheet of paper to Sloane.

"I don't want to take your poem from you," she protested.

"I remember it," the girl said. "It is in my heart. I remember all the poems I write. You keep it."

Sloane would and decided she would also read it on air in a few minutes. She checked her watch and saw her window to broadcast would open soon. Because of the time difference, she had made frequent live appearances, along with these students, on the network's national morning show. The evening national news broadcast called for the taped segments Sloane had put together. All she had to do was a live bookend for the tape that ran, which meant being up to shoot that between two-thirty and three in the morning, African time. She would sleep a few hours before rising and getting as camera-ready as she could and then greet the anchor. The network would run her canned segment, and then she would chat another ten seconds or so with him or her at the end of the story.

Then it was back to bed for a little more sleep before she rose to spend the day with the students at the government-run school, which taught female students between the ages of twelve and sixteen. While she had loved her time with the girls at this school, the odd hours she had to broadcast were beginning to wear on her, physically and mentally, since she had been an international correspondent for close to five years. Part of the stress came from the stories themselves she covered, as well as the countries she broadcast from. Yes, being in her twenties and landing a national correspondent's job at a major network had been thrilling and glamorous.

Until it wasn't.

Everything was starting to get to her. The bad politics and cronyism in every nation she visited. The starvation and lack of basic human necessities she saw on a daily basis. The murders and kidnappings and acts of terrorism. She had lost thirty percent of her hearing in her left ear from a roadside bombing a year ago. All this was enough to have her eager to put in for a transfer. She no longer wanted to be an international news correspondent. She wanted regular hours and to wake up in her own bed most mornings.

But would they want to move her from the field?

Sloane was known for going after a story and keeping at it until she had the truth. She hoped her reputation for producing results and being a team player would help the network decide to let her return stateside. And if they didn't? She might let her current contract run out and see what else she might find. Maybe an anchor job in a Top Ten market would be available. Or a gig on one of the morning shows, which constantly seemed to play fruit basket turnover with their anchors. They might have something open up. She would wait and see. No decision needed to be made just yet. But hopefully, she would get feedback from the network soon. She especially wanted feedback from Tenley and Willow and would bring up the topic when they talked later today.

Tomorrow would be her last day at this school. Sloane had done several general pieces featuring the school as a whole. How they selected their students. The curriculum being taught. What the students' lives were like, both inside and outside the classroom. She had also spotlighted several of the girls, ones who had the greatest potential. She hoped someone out there watching her reports would give those special girls a chance.

Ted Chavez, her cameraman, appeared. "Ready to set up, Sloane?"

"Sure. Let's take this corner of the classroom," she suggested.

Sometimes, they shot outside for her intros, while other times they used the inside of the classroom, the girls working individually or in groups in the background. Since this was the end of the day, however, the students were in cleanup mode. Salana Owusa, their teacher, always stressed how the classroom was the girls' home away from home, and that they should keep it neat and tidy at all times. She had seen this philosophy other places, with students even taking on janitorial duties at their schools, sweeping or washing lunch trays. She hoped when she had kids they would be as responsible as these foreign students were.

Kids...

That was perhaps the biggest reason Sloane was ready to go back to the US. While her own childhood had been one of privilege and angry secrets, she had always wanted to have a family. The way she traveled, though, spending weeks at a time abroad, would make that impossible. What husband would like the fact his wife was gone five out of six weeks, leaving him as a single parent a majority of the time? Besides, she didn't want to be that parent who walked through the door and found her kids didn't even recognize who she was.

No, it was time to return home. Either coast would do. She had grown up in Santa Monica and gone to college at UCLA, but she was based on the East Coast these days. At least she had a miniscule apartment which she shared with a few other journalists. Basically, they parked their stuff in the sixth-floor walkup while they went to the far corners of the globe, wherever the job took them.

Sloane motioned to Salana, with whom she'd become friendly. The teacher came toward her.

"You need me?" she asked in her lovely, lilting voice.

"Tomorrow is my last day, if you recall. I was hoping to get you on camera today to say a few words. The piece the network will run tomorrow is pretty much completed, so if I'm going to get you live, it better be today."

Salana chuckled. "I will never understand this American obsession with having people talk to a camera."

"You make for great TV, Salana. You're beautiful. Educated. Warm. You are a true role model for these girls you teach."

Ted gave her a signal, and Sloane slipped her earpiece into her ear, listening for a minute as Ted passed her a microphone.

"Yes, I can hear you. Ready at your cue. I have the girls' teacher, Salana Owusa. We'll chat for a few, and then I have a poem to read which one of the girls wrote." She paused. "Ted? Can you get Akachi over here."

"Will do."

Two minutes later, Sloane was chatting with the group of morning hosts based in New York, describing her gratitude at having spent the past several weeks at the school. They had asked her to read the poem first and then interview the teacher, so she segued into it.

"I know our audience will be as eager as I am to see what path each of these girls travel in the future. With me now is Akachi, who is twelve and ambitious. She wants to be a writer, and I'd like her to share one of her poems with you."

Sloane removed it from her own pocket, where she had placed the folded sheet.

"No need to give it to me, Miss Sloane," Akachi said. "Remember, I know it by heart."

The girl recited her poem, looking directly at the camera. Ted gave them the thumbs up when Akachi finished.

"Thank you for sharing your work with us, Akachi," she told the girl, and the anchors did their typical ooh-ing and ah-ing.

Then Sloane turned to Salana, who moved into the frame. "Our viewers have already met Miss Salana Owusa, the teacher at the school. I've been fascinated with what the various African names mean. Could you share what yours stands for?"

Salana smiled. My first name is Salana, which means sun. My surname, Owusa, means strong willed and determined. My father told me my will was strong from the time I could crawl and that he never met a more determined person than I."

"It would take determination—and vision—to lead this school," Sloane said. "What are you most grateful for?"

Salana smiled wistfully. "That these girls have a chance when so many others in our country do not. That they are able to study and learn, and in turn, be an example to African girls everywhere."

At that point, a barrage of shots rang out. Salana dashed away, her immediate reaction to protect her pupils. Sloane turned and saw the door flung open. Several men entered, Uzis held high, firing into the ceiling.

Girls began to shriek and scream. Some dropped to the ground, covering their heads protectively.

Others tried to run. Still, others clung to one another, weeping profusely.

What immediately came to her mind was the Boko Haram kidnapping of almost three hundred girls at a similar school to this one. The Nigerian terrorist organization had taken the girls, using them as negotiating pawns in prisoner exchanges, offering to trade girls for captured Boko Haram commanders who were already in jail. While some of those girls had been released or even escaped, a majority of them had never been heard from again.

Sloane turned to the camera, her heart racing. "You are seeing live footage of men who have just entered this government school," she said calmly, letting the journalist in her take over because the woman in her was too frightened to think. "They are heavily armed and rounding up the students, who range in ages from twelve to sixteen."

Ted signaled her, and she glanced over her shoulder before turning back to the camera.

"It looks as if one of their leaders is coming to speak with us. Get everything, Ted," she said, acknowledging her cameraman for the first time ever while on the air.

He nodded grimly at her, causing her to wonder how long either of them might have to live.

Had the network already cut away? Did executives make the decision not to show people eating their breakfast cereal and drinking coffee what would happen next? At least there would be photographic evidence of what occurred here, as long as Ted was filming.

Unless these terrorists burned the camera. And then them.

The man reached her. Sloane had to look up a

good bit to meet his gaze. Since she was five-six, she guessed he was several inches over six feet. His build was strong. A long, white scar ran down his left cheek, stark against his dark skin.

"I'm an American journalist," she said before he spoke.

That earned her a hard slap. She hadn't seen it coming, and stars shone in her vision. Her face also stung painfully.

"You do not speak. *I* do the talking," he instructed.

She nodded mutely, not wanting to draw his ire.

He looked into the camera. "We do not approve of this. Of this school. Girls should take care of their men. Be good wives. We will help them be who they should be."

Sloane couldn't help herself. "You mean you are kidnapping them. Forcing them into marriages they don't wish to make."

He shrugged.

"Take me instead," she offered. "I am a valuable prisoner. My parents are wealthy. They'll pay to get me back."

Actually, she was estranged from her parents and knew her father wouldn't spend a dime for her return. Neither would the US government. But the network was a different story. There might be a sliver of hope that they would pay to see her released. Especially if they had stayed with the story unfolding.

"My men need wives. You cannot marry all of them." Evil shone in his eyes. "One woman would not be enough."

She swallowed. "But the money I could bring would help you, wouldn't it? I will go with you—if you leave all these girls here. Please. I beg you."

"No," he said flatly. "We take you *and* them."

In a casual movement, he raised his gun and shot Ted.

"No!" Sloane shrieked, diving to catch her friend as his camera tumbled from his hands and he fell to the ground.

She wrapped her arms around him. "Ted. Ted. Please," she begged, knowing he was already gone, his frozen stare sending chills through her.

Sloane looked up to the man who had killed Ted and saw the butt of his gun flying at her. She turned her face away but the gun slammed into her temple. Pain rippled through her.

And then darkness came.

CHAPTER 2

Sloane awoke to the swaying of what she guessed was a truck. She kept her eyes closed, trying to ascertain what she could about the situation before she let anyone know she had come around. She could smell the diesel fuel. Felt the press of warm bodies around her. Smelled the fear blanketing the air.

Opening her eyes slowly, she heard a voice say, "She is awake. Miss Sloane is awake."

She looked to her right and saw it was Akachi who spoke. The beautiful tween with the large eyes and round face. The author of the poem Sloane had tucked into her pocket.

Blinking several times, she raised her hand to see the time her watch in order to know how long she had been out. She discovered her wrists were bound together. Glancing around, she saw none of the girls had their wrists tied. That was a good thing. It might help some of them escape when they had a chance. The brave ones. The ones not paralyzed with fear.

She looked at her watch and saw it was over ninety minutes since she had started her broadcast report.

"How many trucks are there?" she asked.

Akachi squinted. "Five others. Six, counting this one."

"Did anyone get away?"

"A few, I think. Right as they came in. Izara and Monifa had gone to the well for water. If they saw the men, they would have run and hidden."

Nausea drifted through her, and Sloane tried to tamp it down. "Did they hurt anyone? Did anyone fight back when they loaded the trucks?"

Akachi averted her gaze. Sloane knew something terrible had occurred while she was unconscious.

"It was Miss Salana," a voice to her left said.

She looked over and saw Kumani—whose name meant Destiny—sitting next to her. She placed her hand over Sloane's and squeezed it encouragingly. At sixteen, Kumani was the oldest of the students at the school. She had told Sloane she had aspirations to be either a teacher or politician, emphasizing that she would be kind and fair no matter which occupation she chose.

"What happened to her?" Sloane asked, fearing what she would be told.

Kumani sighed. "They rounded us up and took us outside. Made us form a circle. Then the leader dragged Miss Salana to the center. He tore her dashiki from her." Kumani's gaze met Sloane's. "She was afraid but did not show it. She stood proudly, even as he berated her, telling her she put nonsense into our heads. That girls should never be educated. That we are meant to serve men."

Kumani paused. Her eyes fell to her lap. "That man hurt her, Miss Sloane. In front of all of us. Then he had other men come up. Kick her. Slap her. Rip out her hair." Her voice grew quiet. "They... they defiled her.

They made us watch. He said they would cut out our eyes if we did not." The girl shuddered, her voice dropping to a whisper. "It was awful. They left her in the dirt. Broken. Bleeding. I do not know if alive or dead."

Sloane was thankful she had not witnessed her friend being brutalized, especially after seeing Ted murdered in front of her. She squeezed Kumani's hand.

"Thank you for telling me."

Closing her eyes again, Sloane tried to think of where they might take the group. What they would do to the girls. What they would do to her. True, in their eyes she would have more value than the kidnapped girls, but if they had raped Salana, they would do the same to her, if only to break her spirit and keep her submissive.

Then she remembered the tracker. Steve Parsons, her immediate boss, had insisted upon it the last time she had returned to New York. She had almost been taken hostage during her last assignment in the Middle East, and Steve convinced Sloane that they would never lose her location if she would agree to the tracker.

The doctor explained it was similar to the birth control implant just beneath the skin in her upper arm, which the same staff doctor had also placed in her. That implant was a small, flexible, plastic rod that was one of the most effective birth control methods available. Being on the road and in remote areas for weeks at a time, she hadn't wanted to rely on something such as a birth control pill. Not that she had sex all that often. Occasionally she did, when in cities where other journalists gathered. Those couplings were little more than one- or two-night stands, more to alleviate the immense loneliness that swelled within her than anything else.

She had agreed to the tracker, which was much smaller than her birth control implant—and wondered if this terrorist group and its leader knew about them, praying they didn't cut it out of her. Praying that it could remain in her long enough to signal her location so that someone might be sent to rescue her and all these poor girls, huddled in the back of the truck as they continued to ride along the bumpy road.

They turned off and headed into the jungle. A small bit of hope died with that. The further away from the little bit of civilization they went, the harder it might be to plan a rescue mission. Still, she couldn't let these girls know how frightened she was. She owed it to Salana to be a brave example for these students.

After another ten minutes, their vehicle began to slow.

"Help me sit up," she told Kumani and Akashi.

They did, taking her elbows and helping her to become upright. Another wave of nausea ran through her. Gingerly, lifted her fingers to her temple, where the butt of the gun had struck her. A huge knot had formed. She wondered if she had a concussion or something worse.

The truck stopped, as did the ones behind it. A teenager no older than fourteen lowered the tailgate, a machine gun in his hand. Another boy close to the same age appeared, demanding the girls leave the truck. She could hear sniffling again, but no one was sobbing outright. They were probably too terrified to do even that.

Kumani and Akashi helped Sloane to her feet and from the truck, where one of the teens grabbed her elbow.

"Stay," he ordered.

She didn't like being separated from the others but had no choice. Akashi gave her a panicked look.

"It's all right. Go with Kumani. She will take care of you. You both will take care of the others."

Though twelve, Sloane always thought that Akashi had an old soul. The girl nodded respectfully and put her arm around two others, leading them away from the truck.

When it was empty, the young man nudged her with his weapon. She didn't protest. Even when he came and stood behind her and jammed the gun into the small of her back, she did not utter a word.

"Mwangi wants to see you. Now. Walk."

She did as asked, being directed to a large tent. Entering it, she saw it was barely furnished, just a few tables and chairs and a single cot. The leader of the terrorists, the one who had murdered Ted, sat in one chair, poring over a map on the table.

Sloane went and stood on the other side of the table. "You asked to see me?"

"Sit."

She took the chair opposite him, taking in her surroundings. A few tables held computers. She also saw some video and sound equipment, which made her wince, thinking of Ted being left behind. He had been a good friend to her over the years, always up for new adventures, and saving her ass a few times along the way. She vowed to get out of here and find his body and give him a proper burial at sea. He had always talked of being cremated, his ashes dropped into the waters of the ocean.

Glancing down, she tried to read upside down and figure out what this was a map to and why Mwangi was studying it. Suddenly, she sensed his eyes on her and not the map.

"What group are you with?" she asked him, ignoring the others who lingered on the perimeter of the tent. "Are you willing to exchange any of the students you captured for your fellow members who are imprisoned?"

His surly look did not bode well.

"I need to use a SAT phone. If you want to demand a ransom for me, I need to contact my network."

Mwangi stroked his chin in thought. "You think you are that valuable? Worth so very much? You are not the typical American with the blond hair and blue eyes. You hair is dark as night. Your eyes green like gems."

"I am very good at my job," she told the terrorist. "I've been in the field a long time. The network values my work. They will pay for my safe return." She paused. "I can give you a number to contact them. Or let me speak to them directly. If they see I am unharmed, it will go a long way in expediting matters. Greasing the wheel," she added, seeing he understood that phrase.

Sloane placed her bound wrists on the tabletop. "You might as well have these removed from me. I'm not going anywhere. I have no idea where we are, and I'm not fool enough to take off into the jungle by myself. Besides, you don't want me to be mistreated. My boss wouldn't like that."

Mwangi frowned deeply. "You sound like a boss, ordering me around. Telling me what to do."

She winced inwardly, not wanting to show any weakness around this man. She knew she could come off too strong, but she had always had to hustle, being a woman in a man's world.

"Forgive me, Mwangi. I will let you make the suggestions in the future."

He nodded approvingly. "That is the way it should be. I will contact your people in a day or two. They need to be fully worried about you before I approach them. In the meantime, you will be my guest."

Sloane glared at him. "And what exactly is expected of a *guest*?"

He laughed. "Guests are to make themselves useful. They are to keep me happy."

She easily figured out what that meant. "I told you I should be unharmed. It won't go well for you if you hurt me." She gently rubbed her temple. "You already knocked me into tomorrow with that gun of yours."

His eyes gleamed. "I have bigger guns than those."

He was not talking about weapons, obviously, because he rubbed his crotch suggestively. She flashed back to a scene in *Last of the Mohicans*, recalling how Daniel Day-Lewis pleaded with Madeleine Stowe, telling her to submit. To stay alive. To be strong and survive. And he would find her.

Sloane had no way of knowing if anyone would find her.

Still, she *was* strong, both physically and mentally. She had trained in Krav Maga, developed in Israel as a fighting and defense system. It took the best of the most effective fighting styles, and she was more than proficient in it. If these other soldiers of Mwangi's weren't present in the tent, she would have already taken their leader out. With so many surrounding them, though, she might be able to kill this murderer —but she would never survive.

Instead she would bide her time.

Journalists were taught to think. To question. To imagine endless possibilities. To come at a situation from various angles. She only hoped Mwangi would leave her alone now so she could think. On how to escape. On how to bring help back for these girls who had come to mean so much to her in such a short time.

"Are you going to cut away the ties?" she asked softly, hoping by tempering her tone, it might convince him to do so.

"No. You are too dangerous. American women do not know their place. We will teach you yours tonight."

He rose. "For now, you will stay here."

The leader left, motioning for the others to follow. Only one soldier stayed behind. He stood at the tent's flap. Unfortunately, he was on her side of the flap and not on the outside. It didn't matter. The others were gone. She had quiet time to think. To plan.

To hope...

SLOANE HAD EXHAUSTED ALL her ideas. She had come up with more problems than solutions. And she knew time was running out. Darkness had come. The tent had one lantern lit. It sat on the table beside the map. She had wondered if she should knock it over, creating a fire, but worried that she might be burned alive if she couldn't escape in time. She had run through endless scenarios in her mind, all coming to a dead end. She had to face facts. She wasn't getting out of here on her own. No matter how courageous she was or how fast she could think on her feet, she was a hostage in the middle of an unfriendly jungle, surrounded by an unknown number of people who brandished weapons.

She would take Hawkeye's advice.

Do whatever it took to survive.

A slight breeze drifted toward her. With the tent only having the one opening, that meant someone had created one somewhere else.

Maybe the cavalry had arrived.

Twice she had stood and walked about the tent. The guard hadn't spoken a word to her. She decided to do so again and came to her feet, stretching her bound wrists high above her head, tipping off the fact she would have a little trouble helping if push came to shove. Of course, she still had her legs and feet and could use them to land some fairly powerful kicks. Her teeth, which could rip off a guy's ear or lip. She would be willing to do her part if someone were here to rescue her.

Sloane turned and begin pacing, immediately seeing the military guy who had cut through the tent. Their gazes connected and since her back was to the sentry, she held up her hands and one finger, indicating who was in the tent. Her rescuer nodded.

Wanting to draw her guard's attention away from this part of the room, she moved closer to him, coming to stand before him.

"Do you know when Mwangi is going to think about feeding me?" she grumbled. "I haven't eaten all day. He said he was coming back. When will he be back?" she demanded.

He frowned at her. "I do not kn—"

His reply was cut off by the guy who had slithered behind him, springing to his feet and slicing the guard's throat from ear to ear, catching him as he fell, gently placing the dead body on the ground.

Her jaw gaped and she forced herself to shut it as

the soldier moved toward her. Sloane raised her wrists, and he sliced through the rope binding them.

He took her wrists and began rubbing them. As the feeling came back and the blood began circulating, they felt as if they were on fire.

"Petty Officer First Class Hill, ma'am. I'm a Special Warfare Operator for Seal Team 5. You must be Sloane Anderson."

"I am, Officer Hill." She sensed others behind her but kept her focus on this man. "I was covering a government secondary school. Terrorists invaded and took most of the girls. They killed my camera operator. Most likely the teacher is also dead."

"We know, ma'am. Your boss gave our boss the ability to read your chip and track your location."

"How did you put together a team so fast? We were only taken late this afternoon. Night only fell a short while ago."

"We were in the area on training exercises. A joint operation with the local government. They gave us permission to come and bring you home."

"And the girls," she insisted. "I can't leave them behind."

"Yes, ma'am, the girls, too. I need you to come with me now. My team will take care of the rest."

He caught her elbow in a firm grip and turned her. She now counted six other men in the room. Quietly, they spoke to one another in some kind of code she couldn't begin to decipher.

All Sloane knew is that she was free—and going home.

CHAPTER 3

MAPLE COVE—OREGON COAST

G age sat up quickly, sweat pouring from him. "You're in the Cove," he told himself. "You're in the Cove."

You're safe.

He rose from his bed, repeating the phrase to himself, calming his trembling body, racing mind, and destitute spirit. He hadn't had any nightmares for almost six weeks, but they crept up on him without warning. He glanced down at the healed bullet wounds, knowing he was lucky to have gotten out that day.

Unlike the others on his SEAL team.

His body might have healed, but his soul had been shattered at losing his friends. He had undergone therapy at the insistence of the navy, but he had discontinued it once he was honorably discharged. He knew a part of him might not ever heal, and he didn't mind carrying those mental and emotional scars in honor of those he lost. He never spoke of them. He never spoke of that day. But it was embedded deeply within him.

Always.

He went through his morning routine, including a twenty-minute session of yoga, which did more to help him than talking to any therapist ever had. Yoga made him feel strong both physically and mentally, helping him center himself and control the sometimes crazy mood swings within him. He had made a new life for himself, away from the navy, in Maple Cove, as well as finding new, loyal friends who had become his family.

He dressed and went to his truck in order to meet some of those friends now on the Cove's town square. A group of the men ran daily, whoever was free to do so showing up. Today as he pulled up, Gage saw Carter Clark and Jackson Martin stretching. Nash Edwards, who usually joined them, had gone with his wife Rylie on a two-day antiques-buying trip. Dylan Martin, the Cove's sheriff, only ran with them occasionally because he and his wife Willow liked to run together to start their day.

Joining his two friends, he also stretched. They started out at a good clip, increasing it. Along the way, they came across Dylan and Willow, who fell in with them, and the group ran for another three-quarters of an hour before returning to the square to cool down. Dylan and Willow waved and turned to head toward home when Willow's phone rang.

She stopped in her tracks, frowning. "Who could be calling this early?"

Dylan circled back to her. "Better see who it is," jogging in place, teasing Jackson.

"Oh, it's Tenley. "Hey, Tens. Just ran some with your lovely husband. Dylan and I are go—"

Gage was always in tune to the others around him. While Jackson and Carter continued their cooldown, he watched Willow's face. The blood drained from it. He went and placed a hand on her shoulder.

"I'll be right there," she said tersely, looking up at Gage. "It's Sloane," she said, her voice quavering.

By now, the other three knew something was wrong. Dylan came to his wife and took her hand. Gage backed away, but he knew the news wasn't good.

Tears formed in Willow's eyes. "Sloane... has been kidnapped," she said woodenly. "It happened... on live television."

She burst out into tears, and her husband enfolded her in his arms.

Gage had never met Sloane Anderson, but he felt as if he knew her. The international correspondent had been the college roommate of Willow and Tenley, Carter's wife. Sloane covered news around the world, often in hot spots, from hard news stories in war-torn countries to human-interest ones. He had watched many of her reports and found Sloane to have a warmth and humanity about her which many reporters lacked, as they bent over backward to be objective.

Willow wiped her eyes and said, "I want to be with Tenley."

Without a word being exchanged, they all went to their vehicles and drove to the Clarks' house, which was only a few minutes away. Dylan and Willow rode with him. No words were exchanged.

As their vehicles pulled up, Tenley appeared in the doorway and ran to meet Willow. The women clung to each other, both weeping. Gage understood how helpless they felt. He knew Sloane had been covering a girls' school in Africa because he had seen some of the stories she had filed. Africa could be a volatile place with all its tribal warfare and superpowers fighting for loyalty of its various countries, if not outright control of them.

Carter ushered everyone toward the house and then he went to his wife and enveloped her in his arms when she released Willow. "Can you tell us what happened, babe?" he asked softly.

Tenley angrily wiped at her tears and said, "I turned on the news while I was eating breakfast. You know the national morning shows are delayed here, but it happened while they were on the air live on the East Coast. Sloane was interviewing Salana, that teacher she's become friends with at the school. Suddenly, gunfire rang out. The girls began screaming. It... it... just... turn on the TV. They'll show it again. That's where I saw it. I can't..." Her voice broke.

"It's okay, babe," Carter reassured her, motioning for everyone to come inside.

The TV was still on, and they gathered around it as the anchor said, "We don't know which group is responsible for taking our reporter, Sloane Anderson, and various pupils at the Government State Secondary School. We warn viewers that the images you will see now are graphic, as this is the moment the terrorists enter the school."

Gage gazed at the screen, seeing Sloane looking confident and polished as she spoke with an attractive African woman who must be the teacher Tenley referred to. Then shots rang out, and the woman bolted, hurrying toward her students. He watched as one of the men, obviously their leader, came toward Sloane, steely resolve in her eyes. Admiration flooded him, knowing even a highly trained SEAL would be fearful and anxious in this situation. He listened to the brief conversation captured by the cameraman and how Sloane offered herself in exchange for the girls being left alone.

Willow gasped. "Her parents would never pay to get her back!"

He thought that an odd statement. Though he never had had parents himself, he couldn't imagine Sloane's parents not wanting to pay a ransom to have their daughter returned safely to them. Of course, even if she were returned, she would no doubt be a different woman from the one pictured on screen, depending upon how long this tribal gang held her. He knew men such as these used rape as a weapon to break and control women. A deep sorrow filled him, knowing what Sloane's fate would be in the hands of these criminals. He would keep silent, however. She was a sister to his two friends, and he couldn't add to the worry they already carried.

Suddenly, the events onscreen shocked even him. The man next to her raised his rifle and fired. The picture went wonky. Everyone in the room gasped, knowing Sloane's cameraman had just been killed, though the event had not been captured on film. She fell beside the man, and the camera picked up a part of it before the butt of a gun appeared, slamming into her temple. Sloane fell directly beside the still-running camera. Then her body disappeared from view, being dragged away.

A tremendous rage filled Gage, one he hadn't felt in a long time. In fact, he tried not to feel any emotions. He had no highs or lows, maintaining an even keel as a middle emotional ground. He didn't become angry. He wasn't really joyful. He merely put one foot in front of the other, each day living his life as the best person he could be and helpful to those around him. Along the way, he had found this group of friends who had taken him in as family, and he occasionally let down his guard in front of them. Sloane Anderson being taken hostage was as if one of these friends had been. They were loyal to her—and he was loyal to them. He wanted to do something to help and yet felt helpless and frustrated.

He turned his attention back to the TV, where the anchor was interviewing some expert.

"Turn it off," Gage ordered.

Jackson found the remote and did so.

He addressed the group. "It won't do Sloane any good, you watching or listening to any of this. It will just make you hurt and worry even more. Some of those experts will be hopeful, while others will sound doom and gloom. You've got to stay in a positive frame of mind for each other and for Sloane."

Tenley tearily said, "We were supposed to talk to her this morning. She had texted us about tomorrow being her last day on this assignment and how she wanted to catch up and talk over something important with us."

"My gut tells me what she was going to say," Willow said. "I've sensed Sloane being unhappy for a while now."

"What do you mean?" Dylan asked.

"She's great at her job, but I think it's been wearing on her lately. The danger. Living such a nomadic life. I think she was ready to talk about coming home and staying stateside."

"I know ever since last year's roadside bombing, she's been on edge," Tenley remarked. "The thing with her hearing."

Jackson asked, "What happened to her hearing?"

"She lost about thirty percent in her left ear. That's what the doctors measured when she came back to New York between assignments. She always wears her earpiece in her right ear now to make certain she picks up everything the network is saying, but she said it makes her a little nervous because she can't quite hear everything around her as well as she could before and that being aware of her surroundings is important on the assignments she takes."

Tenley turned to Gage. "I know you never talk about what you did on your SEAL team, but do you have any idea what could be going on now? Is it true our government will just abandon her?"

"There are always diplomatic channels to go through," he said in an authoritative voice, but then he decided to be frank. "But I have to be honest with you. When you're dealing with these tribal gangs—criminals—they don't listen to any government officials. The people of Africa have good hearts, but they are terrorized by these gangs, which roam their nations, stealing everything they can get their hands on, especially foreign aid sent. Her best bet is if the network cares enough to pay the ransom or possibly hire independent contractors—mercenaries—to go in after her."

He paused. "Why did you say her parents wouldn't pay her ransom?"

Disgust filled Willow's face. "Sloane's parents are the most awful people on the planet. They are incredibly wealthy and two-faced hypocrites. Sloane, despite her privileged background, had a harrowing childhood at their hands. Her sister, who is much older than she is, escaped and lives somewhere up in Canada on a goat farm. She cut all ties with them and pretty much with Sloane, too. Her parents were appalled when Sloane didn't land a rich husband in college and actually wanted to put her degree to work. They literally disowned her when she took the network job to travel and report from around the world.

She hasn't spoken to them in years. Probably ten or more."

Sometimes, Gage allowed himself to have a small pity party, sad that he had never had parents. In his mind, all parents were loving ones. Hearing about Sloane Anderson's, though, made him glad that he hadn't had any and that he'd learned to stand on his own two feet.

"I need to go," he said. "I've got a class soon. But I'll be back here and stay with you whenever I can throughout the day," he promised.

He went and hugged first Willow and then Tenley, telling them, "Prepare yourselves for whatever happens. We'll all hope for the best, but we have to be realistic."

"I understand," Willow said quietly. "Tens and I will keep the faith. Because we're all Sloane's got."

Gage understood that kind of devotion to a friend, one who was family.

He only hoped Willow and Tenley would be able to hold up under the strain if Sloane Anderson were killed.

Or she came back a totally different person.

CHAPTER 4

FLIGHT TO LONDON HEATHROW

Sloane felt the buzz in her pocket and slowly opened her eyes. The shades were still closed on the plane that carried her from Nairobi to London. It also carried Ted Chavez's body.

The last twenty-four hours had been a quick swirl of events. The Navy SEAL team had gotten her out of the jungle, along with all but four of the girls. Unfortunately, those students had been killed by Mwangi's men as they tried to escape. She knew a few of the other girls had been taken and used by the warlord's men, and those girls had received medical attention. Among them had been Kumani. The oldest girl at the school had also been the most beautiful, so it did not surprise Sloane what had happened. It sickened her, but she knew Kumani was strong. Sloane had met with the young woman at the hospital and told her that she had survived a horrific experience, and she would use that to grow stronger and do better in her life. She gave Kumani both her cell number and personal e-mail address and told Kumani to contact her if she needed anything.

Kumani had looked at her with large, liquid brown

eyes, which showed not only the suffering and pain she had undergone, but her strength. Kumani had promised to stay in touch with Sloane and told her that one day she might even come study in the United States.

Fortunately, Akachi had been spared the worst of the brutality. The young girl had told Sloane she would write of this experience and do her best to make certain it never was repeated again.

A few bells sounded, and the lights in the cabin slowly came up. Sloane took the small case she had found after she had boarded her seat in first class, provided by the network. She now took this bag to the restroom and ran the courtesy brush through her hair, trying to make herself a bit presentable, as well as brushing her teeth with the tiny toothbrush provided in the kit. She could do nothing about the large bruise and lump protruding from her temple. An army doctor had looked at it and after checking her out, said that surprisingly, she did not have a concussion. Sloane had known that, because she wasn't fuzzy-headed, as she had been when she received one playing basketball in high school, one of her many activities which had embarrassed her parents.

Returning to her seat, she sat and tried to let everything go, hoping it would calm her mind and body. She knew Steve Parsons, her boss at the network, was meeting her in London with a private jet. She had no idea what she would say to him and hoped she wouldn't blurt out she was quitting the moment she saw him.

The plane landed and taxied to the gate at Heathrow. The moment it stopped and the seatbelt sign went off, everyone sprang to their feet. Sloane remained in hers. She had no clothes other than the ones she wore and only her backpack with her. Her things had mostly been packed since she was to leave the school the next morning. The dormitory where her suitcase sat had been burned to the ground. Her backpack had survived. Though the school had also been set ablaze, Izara and Monifa, who had gone to the well for water when the gang invaded the school, had watched from a distance, seeing the girls loaded into the trucks. Izara said a soldier had thrown a single torch into the school just before the trucks pulled away.

Both girls had quickly entered from the rear of the school, wanting to save a few of their favorite books. Instead, they had discovered her backpack and Ted's body and pulled both from the burning building. Sloane had done a lesson in communications for the girls, talking about computers, cell phones, and social media. She had demonstrated phone calls and texting with Ted, and Monifa had remembered those lessons. She pulled the dead cameraman's phone from his pocket and was able to call for help.

By the time it arrived, the school had been burned to the ground, but the two girls were fine. They had also found Salana, not having seen what had happened to their teacher since the circle of girls and men had blocked their view. They had given their teacher water, washing the blood from her as they held her hands and sang to her. Sloane hoped her friend would live. She had still been unconscious when Sloane left the hospital, and she had left her cell number with one of the nurses, asking that she give it to Salana.

The last person was leaving the cabin. She stood and removed her backpack from the overhead bin. It held her phone and laptop, along with the chargers to both devices. Wearily, she left the plane and moved through the jetway as if she were a zombie.

Upon entering the terminal, her eyes were immediately drawn to a man holding a sign with her name on it, much as drivers did in the baggage claim area. She moved toward him.

He smiled as she approached and said, "Miss Anderson?"

She nodded. "I'm Sloane Anderson."

"If you will accompany me, Miss Anderson, I am to take you to Mr. Parsons."

He led her a few feet away to one of the golfcarts that usually carried the ill and infirm through airports.

"Any luggage?" he asked.

"No. Only my backpack." She held up a hand before he could speak. "I'm bringing back the body of my colleague, Ted Chavez. Before you take me anywhere, I need to make certain Ted is taken care of."

"He is being transported, Miss Anderson," the man assured her. "You have nothing to worry about."

She climbed into the passenger seat as he got behind the wheel, and they took off, with him beeping his horn several times, clearing people out of their way. They went to the opposite end of the terminal and reached an elevator. He stopped the cart and indicated the elevator to her.

"This way, please, Miss Anderson."

"Sloane," she corrected. "Please, call me Sloane."

"Sloane, it is," he said with a smile. "You are famous?"

They entered the elevator and she shrugged. "I'm on TV. I'm not sure if that makes me famous or not."

She had seen a few of the stares as they had passed others in the terminal. She wondered if they gawked at her because they recognized her from the news and had seen what had happened to her, or they were merely jealous she had a ride when they had to walk to their gates.

The elevator doors opened, and she stepped from the car. Her guide led her down a corridor and out a pair of glass double doors, and they emerged outside. She assumed it was the company jet that awaited her on the tarmac.

"This is your plane, Sloane. I wish you the best."

"Thank you," she said, moving toward the stairs which had been pushed up to the plane's entry doors. She climbed them, preparing herself. She had once heard that teachers were like actors upon a stage. No matter how lousy they felt, they put on a bright smile and went and performed in front of their students, much as an actor did for his audience. She had often felt like that when she broadcast, sometimes too weary to string two sentences together, and yet rising to the occasion. This was the same. In moments she would see Steve. She would need to perform. Exude confidence.

And tell him she was done.

She stepped onto the plane and immediately, a flight attendant leaped from the jump seat.

"Miss Anderson, it's so good to see you. May I get you anything?"

"A cup of hot tea would be nice. With lemon."

"Right away. Mr. Parsons is waiting for you."

"I'll find my way. Thank you."

Sloane hitched her backpack up on her shoulder and entered the luxurious cabin. The corporate jet had seating for twenty in this first compartment. Beyond it was an office and conference room. A bedroom was in the rear of the jet.

Steve rose, concern etched on his brow as he stepped toward her.

"Sloane. How are you?"

His kind tone almost made her break down in tears. Steve was as cutthroat as the next network executive, but he had a soft side to him. He used it now, wrapping her in a bearhug and giving her a squeeze. Releasing her, he stepped back.

"I'm so glad to see you." He grinned mischievously. "Happy about that chip now?"

It was just what she needed to release the tension in her body. Sloane belly-laughed, not recalling the last time she had done so. She took a seat opposite him and smiled.

"I'm glad you talked me into it. I'm also glad that the US government had training exercises occurring in the area. Thanks for coordinating with both governments and the military. They found us really fast, Steve. Your speedy actions—and theirs—helped save a lot of lives."

She paused and then asked, "How much was shown on TV?"

His face grew serious. "The first time, it happened so fast that we left the cameras rolling until Ted captured that man raising his gun. We cut the feed immediately, and the morning anchors danced around what was occurring." He hesitated. "Later, we did show the rest of it, with a severe warning. You couldn't see Ted's death, but it was apparent what happened because he dropped the camera. The angle it landed at enabled us to see you trying to help him and then you were pulled from the frame. How is your head?"

Consciously, Sloane, touched the knot with her fingertips. "It hurts like hell, if you really want to know. The doctor said I'm fine. No concussion. Just a rainbow of bruises I'll go through as the swelling subsides over the next several days."

The flight attendant brought the cup of tea, and Sloane thanked her.

A man in uniform appeared and said, "I'm your captain, Miss Anderson. We are certainly glad to be ferrying you back to the US."

"And Ted," she said hastily.

"Yes, and Mr. Chavez. We are waiting for his body to be loaded onto the plane. We can take off once that occurs—and once we file our flight plan." The captain looked to Steve, who looked to her.

"Where do you want to go, Sloane? New York?"

She didn't have to think about it. She was done with New York. She wouldn't go to California to see her parents. All she wanted to do was be with Willow and Tenley, her true family.

"I'd like to go to Portland."

"Maine or Oregon?" the captain asked.

"Oregon."

"Let me go file our flight plan. As soon as it's approved and the body is onboard, we can take off."

She looked to Steve. "Do you mind going to Portland?"

"I may want to get off at LAX. Would you mind a brief stopover there?"

"Not at all."

Steve flipped a switched and told the captain of the slight change, and then he looked to her. "While we're waiting, I have someone on the phone who wishes to talk with you."

"Who?" she asked, puzzled because she didn't think he would have any way of knowing she would want to talk with her closest friends, much less have their numbers.

"It's your parents."

Sloane's blood froze. "They want to talk to me?"

"I contacted them to see if they wanted to fly to London to meet you. They chose to remain in California. They said they wouldn't mind speaking to you when you boarded the plane, however. We have them holding on the line now."

Dread filled her, knowing she had already been on board several minutes. Having her parents wait this long would put them in a sour mood.

"You want to go back to the conference room? They're waiting on line four."

"Thank you," she said, rising and retreating to the mid-portion of the plane, thankful for the privacy she would have for this conversation.

She entered the empty conference room and closed the door behind her. Anxiety filled her as she sat and placed her hand on the receiver. She took a long, deep breath and—like jumping into the deep end of the pool for the first time of the season—she lifted the handset and said, "Hello?"

"How long do you think we have been waiting?" Tish demanded, not bothering to greet her daughter.

"I don't have any idea, Tish. My plane landed in London, and I was brought to one of the network's corporate jets. I just boarded and my boss told me you were on the line and wished to speak with me. Here I am. Speak."

"Well, you still have a surly attitude, don't you?" Thatcher said. "You are a total disgrace," he declared.

Nothing either of her parents said ever surprised her. "How am I a disgrace, Thatcher? Did my being kidnapped by an African gang lord on national TV embarrass you?"

"You know the answer to that," he said gruffly. "We

told you nothing good would come of this so-called career."

"Hmm. I've won both a Peabody and Emmy for news reporting. I think it's more than *so-called*. I believe I've done an excellent job as a journalist."

"Our people simply do not go on television, Sloane," Tish said. "And it was humiliating seeing you that way, lying on the ground, being dragged off by your ankle. The only good that came from it is the sympathy which we have received from our cherished circle of friends. They know how upset we were at the choice you made to gallivant around the world. I hope you will give up all of this nonsense, Sloane. No more traipsing around the world. It's time you took your place in our world. Marry the right man. Have a child or two. Work for the Junior League."

"Tish, your world is not my world," Sloane said flatly. "I live in the real world. You live in a fantasy one. I haven't spoken to you in almost ten years for a good reason, and I hope it's a hundred more before I ever hear from you again. I have no apologies for you or your friends because I don't think I embarrassed you. I think if you were true parents, you would know what I have done and be proud of me. But soulless vipers such as you don't have any feelings, much less ones of love. I'll never contact you again. This is a final goodbye."

Gently, Sloane replaced the handset in its cradle. Her entire body trembled. She remained in her seat a good five minutes, clearing her mind, merely breathing.

When she felt in control of herself again, she returned to the main cabin and sat across from her boss.

"I just heard from the captain. Ted is with us now,

and the flight plan has been accepted. We're about to take off."

They both buckled their seatbelts, and Sloane said, "I need to tell you something, Steve."

Alarm filled his face. "What's wrong, Sloane? No. Don't tell me you're quitting."

She smiled ruefully. "That's exactly what I'm doing. I've had enough of other places. I've lived my professional dream, but it's time now to find a new one. I'm not sure what my next move will be."

"Name it, Sloane," he said, his gaze steady on her. "You want a network job? Done. You can be a national correspondent. The White House correspondent. You can anchor our morning show or one of the Sunday talk shows. I don't want to lose you over this horrible incident."

"I need some time to decide the next move in my career," she said honestly. "Maybe I could take a sabbatical from the network. Six months. A year, possibly. I have a lot to sort out and want to make certain I'm on the right road for the next chapter in my life."

"I'm disappointed only in the fact you want so long, but I respect that, Sloane. I will stay in touch with you. If you want to come back from this sabbatical early, you can. I want you in any capacity possible. If you have a new idea, feel free to run it by me. I'm open to anything you want to try with the network."

"I appreciate that, Steve. I know my contract is up in three months. I don't expect you to pay me for that or during the sabbatical."

"Nonsense. You've earned combat pay and then some, with what you've been through. We'll definitely pay out the remainder of your contract and a bonus."

She offered her boss her hand. "You have a deal."

Turning her head, she watched out the window as

the plane took off. Then yawning, she said, "I think I'm going to grab some sleep."

"I have a ton of work to do. The captain said it's a little over twelve hours to LAX. Sleep as long as you'd like. Take the bedroom. I won't be using it."

Sloane stood, picking up her backpack. I think I may sleep the entire way."

Her boss smiled at her. "If anyone's earned it, it's you, kid."

Retreating to the rear of the plane, she entered and locked the bedroom cabin door. She had always been conscious of her safety and would be doubly so after her recent experience. She set an alarm on her phone for eleven hours from now, thinking she would get up and shower before they landed in L.A.

She could barely hold her eyes open now, but she sent one text.

On company plane. Leaving London for L.A. then will land in Portland. So tired can't talk. Will call once I leave L.A. I need roommate time. XOXO to you both.

Pulling back the covers, she stripped off her clothes, placing them across a nearby chair before climbing into the king-sized bed. The silk sheets felt cool against her skin, and Sloane dropped into a dreamless sleep.

CHAPTER 5

G age finished with his client, encouraging her to
keep up the good work.

"You've lost all the weight you need to," he
told her.

"But I weigh more than I want to," she
complained.

"That's because you've built muscle. You need to
stop focusing on a number on the scale and look at
the changes in your body. How strong and lean you
are. How your clothes fit differently now. You've put in
the hard work, and you need to continue it. I'll e-mail
you a schedule so you can balance aerobic activities
with weight-bearing ones. You've discovered the key is
that balance. Are we going to move to twice-a-week
sessions now that you've met your goals?" he asked.

"I'd rather continue seeing you three times a week
at this same time if that's all right with you. I still need
guidance, and I want to maintain my accountability.
Having to face you three times a week? That should do
it. One scowl from you, and I will stay on the straight
and narrow."

He chuckled. "That's fine. I'll keep you on the schedule as is. And celebrate what you've done—but not with food. Buy yourself something new and pretty to wear. Take a day trip and explore a new place. Buy that new book you've been wanting to read and make the time to actually read it. There are plenty of ways to celebrate besides using food."

"Thanks, Gage." She gave him a hug. "I could never have done this without your encouragement and support. And bossiness," she added.

They both laughed and went to their separate vehicles. He didn't have any more classes or clients the rest of the day, and so he made his way to Boo's house. He was still glad his friends referred to the house as Boo's, even though Dylan and Willow now lived there. Boo had been Willow and Jackson's grandmother—a feisty, creative, passionate woman who was a renowned sculptor. When she died, a bit of the Cove died with her. But Willow had chosen to remain in the Cove, using Boo's art studio as her own for her painting. She and Dylan had married, and Gage believed they would be starting a family soon since they had been married just over a year.

He turned off the main road, pulling into the Taylors' driveway, slowing and then stopping when he saw Tenley's SUV heading in his direction. They both rolled down their windows.

"Hey, Gage. I'm heading home because Carter has cooked several meals that we're going to bring over. Willow and I are thinking since she has more room, Sloane might want to stay here. At least at first. I'll be back in a flash with Carter and the food. I'm glad you're here to keep Willow company. Just go on in."

"See you soon."

Willow had texted him when she and Tenley had heard from Sloane. Frankly, it shocked him how fast she had been freed from the rebels. What didn't surprise him was that Sloane Anderson wanted to be with the women who were sisters to her. She would be arriving later today and would send word when she was to land.

He parked his truck and went inside the house, calling out, "Willow, it's Gage."

She appeared at the head of the stairs and started down the staircase. "Thanks for coming, Gage. I just put fresh sheets on Sloane's bed. I need to run over to Gillian's because she's cut and arranged fresh flowers for Sloane's homecoming. Hold the fort down, if you will."

"Will do."

Gage wandered into the kitchen to grab a glass of water and guzzled it down. Being a good guest, he washed and rinsed it before replacing it in the cupboard. Then he heard a ringtone. Willow's ringtone. He glanced over and saw her phone sitting in its charger. Knowing they would be hearing from Sloane soon, he went to see if it might be her.

It was.

He knew he needed to answer it and lifted the phone from its charger. "Hello?" he said as FaceTime kicked in and suddenly, Sloane Anderson appeared on the screen.

She might have been through hell, but she was a looker. She had a fresh, natural beauty about her, one which didn't need to be enhanced with makeup. He had thought the same when he had watched her field reports, knowing she didn't have access to a makeup artist or hair stylist in the remote locations she reported from. Her raven hair spilled in waves past her

shoulders, and her emerald green eyes were mesmerizing.

A quizzical look appeared upon her face. "Somehow, I've dialed the wrong number," she apologized. "I
was trying to reach a friend of mine."

"Don't hang up, Sloane," he said quickly. "This is
Willow's phone. I happened to answer it. I'm Gage.
Gage Nelson."

She nodded in recognition of his name. "Of
course. Gage. I've heard so many things about you. I
suppose I'll be meeting you in person pretty soon."

"I'm sorry you're getting me instead of Willow or
Tenley. Carter has made a ton of food for your arrival,
and Tenley ran home to help him bring it over to
Boo's. Willow is preparing a guest room for you, and
she just stepped over to Gillian Roberts to pick up a
bouquet of flowers to welcome you. She left her phone
charging, and since I knew it might be you, I thought
I'd better pick up."

Sloane gave him a warm smile. "I'm glad you did. I
was just calling to talk to the girls and give them an
update. We landed at LAX a few minutes ago, and my
boss got off the plane. The pilot says we'll be taking off
for Portland in the next few minutes, and we should
arrive in about two hours or less." She paused. "I do
need some help, Gage. I'm bringing back Ted Chavez's
body. We were close friends, as well as colleagues. He
always said he was a citizen of the world and didn't
want to be buried anywhere. Instead, he mentioned to
me that he would like his ashes scattered over the water. I thought bringing him to Maple Cove and dropping his ashes in the Pacific would be what he
wanted."

Gage heard the emotion in Sloane's voice and
knew she must be suffering. "Not only did you lose a

close friend, but you saw him killed. That had to be traumatic, Sloane. I know that kind of trauma. I saw friends killed in combat. I know we don't know each other, but if you ever need to talk about... anything that happened to you, I'm your man."

Tears glistened in her eyes as she said, "Thanks. You might be the only person I will be able to talk to about this. I know Tenley and Willow will hover over me and blanket me in love, but I don't want the ugliness of what happened to me to touch our friendship. It would be nice to have someone to lean on. Someone objective that might be able to wrap my head around what happened. I've been the talk-therapy route, and it does nothing for me."

He chuckled. "Same. The navy made me go through therapy after... an incident. I found I'm better on my own, doing yoga poses and meditating."

Curiosity filled her face. "You do yoga? I've never tried it."

"I'm a physical trainer. If you'd like, I can teach you yoga. It's the most soul-cleansing, relaxing thing I do."

"I'm going to take you up on your offer, Gage. Thank you." She hesitated. "But back to what I was saying. I have Ted with me, and I haven't contacted anyone about meeting our plane. With Portland being a big city, there must be several mortuaries that could come and claim the body and handle cremation. Do you have any to recommend? I need to contact them before we leave the ground."

"Let me take that off your plate," he offered. "I can make sure someone is there when your plane lands. You can speak with them directly about what you want to do regrading Ted. Do you have an ETA and know where you might be landing at the airport?"

"Let me check with the pilot. They're having to

trade out crews because the current one has been on duty since London. I'll be right back."

Sloane was gone a moment, giving Gage time to reflect upon how she had suffered a traumatic experience as he had. While he had been trained for the eventual possibility of losing comrades in the field, he doubted Sloane had, which meant this experience would hit her doubly hard. Knowing she would be part of the Maple Cove group of friends, at least for a short while, he found his loyalty would be with her and helping her to heal.

She appeared on the screen again. "I've got the information. What's your number? I'll text it to you."

Gage gave her his cell number and then said, "I'm sorry Willow and Tenley weren't here to talk with you, but they'll be at Portland International waiting for you. Those women love you a great deal, Sloane. You're lucky to have them in your corner."

"They are my only family," she said resolutely, causing him to recall the remark Willow had made about Sloane's terrible parents.

"Gage, can I ask a favor? Beyond helping arrange for Ted's remains?"

"Sure, Sloane. Whenever you come to the Cove, no matter how long you stay, you'll be taken in as family with Willow and Tenley's friends. We're a pretty tight group, and we make sure we're always all right."

"Then maybe it's not as big an ask as I think," she said quietly. Sloane's gaze met his and a ripple of awareness of her as a woman passed through him.

"Would you come to the airport with Willow and Tenley and meet my plane?"

He was touched by her words, believing they saw in each other a kindred spirit. "I would be honored to be there, Sloane. I look forward to seeing you in person."

"Thank you, Gage. I have a feeling I may be depending on you a little more than I should."

"But that's okay. It's what friends are for. We may be new ones—but we have a lot in common."

She glanced up as someone spoke to her and turned her gaze back to the screen. "The flight attendant says it's wheels up, so I need to end our conversation. I'll see you in a couple of hours. Bye, Gage."

"Bye, Sloane."

He placed Willow's phone back in the charger and moments later, heard her entering the house. She carried an artfully arranged bouquet of flowers, obviously Gillian's work. The older woman had been Boo Martin's best friend, as well as her next-door neighbor, and Gillian had had a hand raising Jackson and Willow.

"I hope Sloane will like these flowers," she said.

"I hate to tell you, Willow, but you just missed her call."

"Oh, no!" she cried. "Where is she? How is she?"

"I heard the call come in and hope you don't mind that I answered it."

Gage related what Sloane had shared about her ETA and mentioned volunteering to handle arranging for someone to meet the plane and claim Ted's body.

His phone chimed. "Here's Sloane's text."

"We're back," called out Tenley, who appeared with two casserole dishes, followed by Carter, who carried two more.

"I'll get the rest, babe," Carter said, and left after setting down what he carried.

"Sloane called!" Willow said excitedly

"I can't believe I missed her," Tenley said.

Willow gave a rueful smile. "Well, so did I."

"Oh, let me hear her voicemail then," Tenley said.

"No voicemail to hear," Gage informed Tenley. "I was here and picked up Willow's phone from the charger. Sloane will be here in a couple of hours. I need to go make a few calls on her behalf."

"You can use Dylan's study," Willow told him.

Gage left the two women chattering excitedly and pulled up the information he needed on his phone. After a quick check with the Better Business Bureau and reading a few online reviews, he selected the funeral home to contact. He called and gave them the information, with Ted's name and the plane's tail number, along with when and where they would arrive at the airport.

Then he said, "I want to make you aware of the circumstances. It's a sensitive situation."

Briefly, he explained what had happened to Ted and how his colleague had brought the cameraman's body home.

The mortician said, "Yes, I saw this on the news. Horrifying. We are always sensitive to the bereaved, and I promise we will be very circumspect in our handling of Mr. Chavez's body."

"Miss Anderson will want to speak with you directly upon landing. You might go ahead and load the casket into your hearse and then meet with her. I do know Mr. Chavez wanted to be cremated and his ashes scattered over the water. From what I gather, he had no family and these arrangements have been left up to Miss Anderson."

"I understand, Mr. Nelson. Thank you. We will meet the plane promptly."

Gage disconnected the call and sat a moment, mulling what had happened. He knew in talking to

Sloane Anderson about her trauma that he might
have to relive some of his own. If he could help her re-
cover, though, he was willing to do so.

No matter how many old wounds opened and bled
again.

CHAPTER 6

A nticipation built within Sloane as the captain announced they would be landing within ten minutes. She couldn't wait to see Willow and Tenley.

And meet Gage Nelson in person.

It had been a surprise when the former Navy SEAL had answered Willow's phone. Suddenly, the screen had been filled with a rugged, handsome face, tanned and a bit weathered. Dirty blond hair. Unexpected gray eyes.

Her heart had done a crazy flip-flop at his image. She had fumbled an apology, having no idea how she could have misdialed since Willow's cell number was already programmed into her phone. Then he had stopped her before she hung up, revealing his name, one which she easily recognized from her many conversations with her former college roommates. In a way, Sloane felt as if she were coming home, though she had never visited Maple Cove before.

Besides her phone conversations with her friends, Tenley also wrote Sloane long, descriptive letters about her life and those close to her. In them, she told Sloane about their circle of friends and how they were her chosen family. All of them had lost parents, with only Carter having a mother still living, a woman whom residents in the Cove turned to for advice time and again.

Thanks to living in a digital world, both Willow and Tenley sent countless pictures, as well. Though she hadn't been present, she had pictures of both women's weddings and other get-togethers. The homes they had purchased and remodeled. Her mouth had watered at the beautiful desserts Ainsley Martin had created. She viewed antiques brought home by Rylie Edwards, wishing she had a permanent place to come home to, with such beautiful furniture surrounding her. She'd also become a regular viewer of Carter's vlogs and hoped one day the former fire-fighter might even give her a few tips on how to cook.

In all these pictures, Gage had seemed to haunt the background, as if he didn't want to steal attention away from others. Tenley had described the ex-military man as a rock. Quiet. Stoic. Loyal. Independent. A man who would give the shirt off his back to help anyone in need, but mostly likely would refuse help from others. Tenley had said that in a crisis, Gage would be the one who would step up. He was protective and kind, but a bit of a mystery, since he rarely mentioned anything that had happened before he came to the Oregon coast.

Sloane had always been drawn to a mystery. She looked forward to unlocking a few doors within Gage Nelson. She also knew the physical trainer might be the only person she could comfortably unburden her worries to. In him, she had sensed a compatibility. He offered the branch of friendship, and she was more than willing to accept it. She meant what she said. She did not want to taint her relationship with Tenley and

Willow. Yes, they knew of her work and some of the stress of her job, but those hours in which she had been at the mercy of Mwangi and his men was not a topic she was willing to discuss with her friends.

The plane began its descent and she watched as the ground grew closer. She had no plans beyond scattering Ted's ashes. For the first time in more years than she could count, she was adrift. Yes, she had told Steve she was on sabbatical, but what did that mean? She knew it was defined as a break—or change—from a normal routine, usually work. She remembered a professor she'd loved at UCLA, who told her the secret to his success in the classroom was periodic sabbaticals. He would leave to teach in a foreign country or take a semester off to do research and write. Once he had merely traveled, visiting Egypt, Poland, Peru, and ending up renting a cabin at Lake Tahoe.

What would her sabbatical entail?

Would she try and learn new skills that would benefit her reporting? Pursue an interest outside of work? Travel within the US? Write a book about her experiences in the field?

More importantly, would she return to work, rejuvenated with new energy and motivation, the feeling of burnout burned from her?

The weeks ahead would be stimulating. Exciting. Possibly a bit frightening. She had always had goals and plans. She established a routine no matter where she went on assignment. What would it be like to wake up and have nothing to do and nowhere to go?

Hopefully, this sabbatical would help her discover more about herself. What she wanted out of life. What her expectations might be regarding both the professional and personal—and how to achieve them. More importantly, it would give her the time she needed to decompress. To learn to enjoy the small things in life again. To not be in such a rush that she didn't have time to stop and smell the proverbial roses.

The plane landed smoothly, taxiing down the runway. She didn't know the next time she might be on a plane. Work seemed in the distant future. For now, it was simply enough to be on American soil again.

As the plane turned to the left, Sloane glanced out the window and saw the black hearse waiting on the tarmac. Her throat grew thick with emotion. She had told Steve of her plans to have Ted cremated and that she would hold a memorial service for him at a later date. Now, she wasn't certain she would do so. Ted's friends were the people who covered the news around the world. Rarely were they home, much less all at the same time. Ted had been an only child. He'd married right out of college and divorced three years later, his wife complaining that he was always abroad, hopping from story to story. That's why he'd named Sloane on his paperwork with HR and given her name to his attorney to be executor of his estate, if and when the worst happened. She would need to reach out to the attorney once she was settled. The estate would most likely reimburse her for the expenses she incurred in having him cremated.

When the plane came to a halt, she saw the hearse pull closer to it. Then she saw an SUV come into sight. Anticipation filled her and then happiness as she saw Willow emerge from the driver's side. Tenley spilled out from the back seat. Sloane's eyes cut to the passenger's side as the door opened.

Gage Nelson came into view. He closed his door, and she saw he wore jeans and a dark brown pullover sweater. He moved toward her friends, and she was struck by his catlike grace and how tall he was. Willow was five-ten, and Gage looked to be almost half a foot taller than she was. He dwarfed poor Tenley, who stood at five-four.

The flight attendant appeared. "The captain is opening the door, Miss Anderson. Do you need help with anything?"

"No, I've got it. Thank you."

She unbuckled her seat belt and slipped the strap of her backpack over one shoulder. She passed the captain, thanking him again for bringing her home.

Home...

Where was that?

Pushing aside the question, she moved through the open doorway and heard the shouts of her friends. Sloane raced down the stairs, throwing herself into the open arms of Tenley and Willow. They clung to one another. It was a sweet moment which had been a long time in coming.

"We finally got you to the Cove," Willow declared, slipping the backpack from Sloane's shoulder. "Everything is ready for you. Everyone is excited to meet you. And I guarantee you, Shadow *will* be your shadow."

"I've never had a pet. I'm looking forward to being buddies with Shadow."

Tenley laughed. "You'll probably be more than buddies. I suspect Shadow will wind up sleeping with you tonight. He's very protective. Like Gage." She turned. "Get over here and meet Sloane."

Gage approached them and for a moment, Sloane was intimidated by his size. He was several inches over six feet, with an extremely muscular build. He looked as if he could smash a person flat with one blow.

Sloane looked up—way up—as he came to stand in front of her. "You didn't tell me Gage was a mountain," she teased, seeing the slight blush cross his cheeks.

Willow playfully punched him in the arm. "Gage is like a St. Bernard. Huge and loveable. But he doesn't smile very often. If you can tease one out of him, you've accomplished the impossible."

"It's nice to meet you, Sloane," he said, finally speaking, his voice low and sexy.

She offered her hand. He took it, his large one engulfing hers as they shook. It was warm and comforting. And the most delicious tingles danced through at the contact.

"I'm happy we're meeting in person," she told him, her eyes drawn to his deep gray ones.

"You can stop shaking hands now," Tenley teased.

Sloane felt her own blush rise now as Gage released her hand. "I hear you enjoy a good piece of chocolate."

He grinned. "My secret is out. Yes, I'll confess that I'm a chocoholic, although I'll eat pretty much anything sweet that Ainsley bakes. Maybe I can take you to her bakery so you can sample a few things."

She caught a look pass between her friends and knew what it meant. "No," she said firmly. "That's a *no* to these two, but a *yes* to you, Gage. I'd love to go to Buttercup Bakery with you."

Her words made Tenley's eyes grow large. She quickly brought a hand to her mouth and coughed, but Sloane knew her friend was covering laughter.

Gage motioned and a man in a dark suit came over. "This is Mr. Pinkerton. He's the funeral director. Mr. Pinkerton, this is Sloane Anderson."

Turning her attention to the newcomer, Sloane offered her hand. "Thank you for meeting us, Mr. Pinkerton. I know it was short notice."

"It wasn't a problem, Miss Anderson. We are happy to help. Our funeral home is family-run. One or more of us is always available to help others in their time of need." He paused. "Mr. Nelson said that you wished for Mr. Chavez to be cremated."

"Yes, that's correct. Ted was my cameraman. He traveled to all seven continents. He always said he would like to spend eternity floating in the waters of the world. I plan to scatter his ashes in the Pacific Ocean."

The funeral director presented her with his card. "You can reach me anytime at one of the numbers listed there. We will take the best of care with Mr. Chavez. I will call you when his remains are available, which will be this Friday."

Sloane shook her head. "I'm sorry. I've been on planes for almost two days now. What is today?"

"Wednesday," Mr. Pinkerton said. "If Friday isn't convenient for you, we can hold his ashes."

"No, Friday will be fine. Thank you for handling this so promptly."

"Then I will call when he is ready. I'm sorry we are meeting under such sad circumstances."

The mortician took his leave, and Willow said, "Are you ready to see the Cove?"

"She means Maple Cove," Gage interjected. "Only tourists and those passing through call it Maple Cove. That was the first thing I learned when I moved to town."

"What made you decide to set up your business in the Cove?" she asked, curious about this gentle giant.

"I grew up in foster care," Gage said. "The only vacation I ever went on was with a family who took us to the Oregon coast. I was only ten and had such great memories from that trip. When I left the Navy, I knew

I wanted to be near the water. That trip along the Oregon coast came to mind. I drove up and down—and the Cove just felt like home."

"I think that's the longest speech you've ever made, Gage," Willow said. "I never knew you were in foster care."

Sloane saw his eyes go wintry. "It was a long time ago."

"Let's do this," she said brightly, trying to take the focus off Gage, who seemed uncomfortable he had revealed something about himself.

They moved toward Willow's SUV. Gage took the backpack as they walked and opened Willow's door for her. Sloane reached for the door directly behind the driver's seat, but Gage opened it for her.

"Thank you," she said, thinking no man had ever opened a car door for her.

He and Tenley moved to the opposite side, and he opened Tenley's door, as well, before climbing into the back seat with Sloane, placing her backpack between them. The space had seemed large before, but his sheer size dwarfed it. She caught a subtle hint of sandalwood and knew it came from him.

"It'll take about an hour to reach the Cove," Willow informed her as she started the vehicle and drove from the tarmac to a gate.

Willow and Tenley began talking excitedly, mentioning all the places they wanted Sloane to see. Trails to hike. Beaches to see. People to meet. Shops to browse in. The more they talked, the more overwhelmed she became.

Then a swooshing ran through Sloane, like a tsunami slamming into her. Her hand, which rested atop her backpack, gripped it tightly. It seemed as if the walls of the car were closing in. Her heart began to race. Sweat broke out along her hairline. Nausea filled her.

Then Gage's large hand covered hers. The churning within her continued a moment and then slowly began to subside. She was able to take a breath. The sudden onset of fear began to subside.

As Tenley and Willow continued talking, he leaned close. "It was a panic attack," he said softly. "Have you ever had one before?"

She shook her head. "Never."

"When it happens again, I want you to breathe in slowly and deeply and count to four. Then hold for four seconds. Exhale through your mouth four seconds. Try it now."

"Okay."

She did as Gage had instructed, pushing air in and holding before deliberately easing it out, praying her friends wouldn't notice something was wrong with her.

"Better?" he asked.

She nodded. "I feel more relaxed. And more in control."

"It's called box breathing. It lowers your heart rate in a stressful situation. SEALS do it before they go into combat."

"How long, Sloane? Sloane?"

She blinked, trying to force herself to remain calm. "I'm sorry, Tenley. What?"

"I asked how long you plan on staying in the Cove? You know we're so glad you've come," her friend said. "It's going to be like old times."

Sloane looked at Gage as she answered. "As long as you want me around."

CHAPTER 7

They arrived in the Cove, and Willow drove them around the town square, pointing out Antiques and Mystiques, Rylie's store, and Buttercup Bakery, Ainsley's shop. She mentioned a few of the other places they would visit in the near future before turning off and heading toward Boo's.

Gage was paying close attention to Sloane. His hand still covered hers. From the look in her eyes, he could see she had calmed considerably from when the panic attack had hit her full force.

He knew what those were like. He suffered from PTSD, as many returning soldiers did. Once again, he vowed to help this woman get through her problems as she tried to return to a normal way of life. Though for Sloane, her way of life had been nomadic. She would need to figure out what her new normal would be, as well as if and when she could return to reporting in the field. And if she couldn't, she would need to consider what her next career move would entail.

They pulled into the long drive and up to Boo's house. He removed his hand from Sloane's, finding he missed touching her. She was an attractive woman, and he was quickly developing feelings for her. He needed to push those aside in order to focus on helping her as a person. Throwing his attraction— even sex—into the mix, would not be beneficial to either of them, especially Sloane's recovery.

As Willow cut the engine, Sloane said, "It's nice to finally see what Boo's house looks like in person. I'm so glad you and Dylan decided to move into it. Your grandmother was always so kind to me the few times we met over the years."

Willow smiled wistfully. "Boo was wonderful to everyone she met. I still feel her spirit in this house. I hope you will, too, Sloane."

They got out of the SUV, and Dylan appeared on the porch, coming down to greet them.

He smiled at Sloane and said, "I am so happy to finally meet you in person after all the stories I've heard. May I have a hug?"

Gage thought that was perceptive of Dylan to ask permission to touch Sloane and not immediately go in for a hug. He had been in the military for over a decade and would be in tune with what had happened to her.

She put a smile on her face and said, "A hug is just what the doctor ordered," and embraced him.

"Let's go inside," Dylan suggested. "Can I get your luggage?"

Sloane shrugged. "My backpack is all I have. The rebels burned the school and dormitory. My belongings were lost in the fire."

"I didn't even notice that you didn't have luggage," Tenley said apologetically. "You must be tired of living in what you have on. You're much shorter than Willow and me, but Rylie and Ainsley are close to your height.

Rylie's more curvy, but Ainsley is about your size and build. I'll text her now. I know she'll let you borrow a few things until we can shop for you. She'll have some sweaters. T-shirts. Maybe some leggings and sweatpants. I'll go over to her place and get them since she's already home from the bakery."

"You're sure she won't mind lending her clothes to a stranger?" Sloane asked.

Tenley hugged Sloane. "You won't be a stranger for long." She headed toward her car.

"Come inside and I'll show you your room," Willow said. "It overlooks the beach. It's the room I used growing up, and I think you'll really like it."

Willow wrapped her arm around Sloane's waist and guided her into the house and up the stairs. Gage fell into step with Dylan, and the two men entered the house.

Dylan paused in the foyer and watched, waiting until the two women disappeared before he turned his attention to Gage.

"How bad is she?" he asked.

"It's bad," Gage confirmed. "So far, Willow and Tenley have no idea." He paused, deciding he could trust Dylan with the information and added, "Sloane had a panic attack on our way back to the Cove. The other two were chatting happily about all the things they wanted to show Sloane and the people they wanted her to meet. They didn't notice what was happening in the back seat. I've also suffered from panic attacks," he admitted to his friend. "I helped Sloane to breathe and push through it."

"She's going to need help," Dylan said.

"I agree. We need to talk to Willow and Tenley about that. Our friends, as well. You know how tight our group is. They'll want to enfold Sloane into it. I don't want to betray any confidences, but at the same time, I want everyone to be aware of the situation. We don't want to exacerbate anything but we need to do what we can to assist her in pushing through this."

Gage looked up and saw Willow coming down the stairs, an odd look on her face.

She reached the bottom of the stairs and told them, "Sloane is going to shower and go to bed. She said she's exhausted. I gave her one of my flannel nightgowns to sleep in. It will swallow her, but at least it's clean."

Dylan asked, "Something wrong, Bear?"

"I can't quite put my finger on it," she said, clearly puzzled. "I thought Sloane would be so happy to be with Tenley and me. Instead, she seemed... a bit distant just now. Of course, she has flown more than halfway around the world the last couple of days. I know she's tired, and it will take her body time to adjust and reset to this time zone." She paused and then added, "I was going to heat up one of the casseroles Carter brought over earlier for our dinner, but Sloane said she would rather sleep than eat."

She looked to Gage. "Would you like to stay for dinner?"

"Yes, I would. I have some things I want to talk over with you and Tenley."

Willow retreated to the kitchen, telling the men to hang out until things were ready. Tenley returned with a suitcase and Carter in hand, and Willow asked them to stay for dinner, as well.

Twenty minutes later, they gathered around the large dining room table. Once everyone had their plates filled and had begun to eat, Gage said, "Dylan and I need to talk to you about Sloane."

Willow paused, her fork halfway to her mouth. "Is there something wrong?"

Dylan said, "Yes," and looked to Gage. "You have a better handle on this."

"We need to discuss with you—and the rest of our friends—what Sloane is going through. You know I don't speak about my days as a Navy SEAL. While I have years of good memories and the missions I was a part of and all the things we accomplished as a team, my last mission went very, very wrong."

He paused, the silence heavy. "Willow, you mentioned how Sloane might be going through a bit of a burn-out, based upon her career experiences of the last decade. Those experiences culminated with her brutal kidnapping, along with all those young girls from the school. She's been through something traumatic. An experience that very few can relate to, much less understand. Although she didn't spend long in captivity, we have no idea what went on in those hours she was with the gang."

Tenley gasped. "I hadn't even thought of that, Gage. We don't know what she saw—or what she went through. I feel awful not having thought of or acknowledged that. I was just so happy she'd been freed and was coming home to us."

"I'm just as guilty," Willow said quietly. "All I could think of was that we had our Sloane back."

"You do," Gage assured them. "But she isn't necessarily the Sloane of old. Certainly not the one from your carefree college days. I know you've gotten together periodically over the years and may have seen how her job has affected her as she's matured. Her kidnapping was horrific. We don't know what she experienced at the hand of the tribal lord or his men."

He looked around the table. "Sloane had a panic

attack in the car on our way home from the airport. I know—because I've experienced them, too. I was diagnosed with PTSD, and I'm sure if Sloane saw a professional, she would receive the same diagnosis."

"How did we miss that happening?" Willow asked, looking baffled.

"You were busy talking, telling her all about people and places in the Cove and your plans while she was staying here. My guess would be everything suddenly became overwhelming to her. It would be jarring having to face people she's never met when she hasn't even begun to process, much less heal from her recent experience. I noticed a few of the signs and quietly walked her through a SEAL breathing technique. She admitted to me earlier on the phone that she'd been through talk therapy and it didn't work for her. I mentioned that I practice yoga and how it calms and centers me. She seemed interested in learning it, and I would be happy to teach her. In fact, she admitted things had been rough and that she wouldn't share with the two of you what she had gone through."

"But we're like sisters," Tenley protested. "We want to help her through this time of crisis."

"Sloane knew I was a Navy SEAL, and I've told her that I'm here to listen to her. She said she didn't want what happened to her to touch her friendship with the two of you. I think with you, who've known her the longest, she wants to behave as if everything *is* normal. She will draw on your strength and that normality. That will be the base—the foundation—which she will use in rebuilding her life.

"On the other hand, I'm going to be her sounding board. The only one she shares with about the horrors she underwent. She may have buried the terror deeply within her, but it can surface at any moment. Your role will be to treat her as you always have. She needs that normality. That friendship. Your love. I'll be the one that she may relive those horrors with, in order to come out stronger on the other side."

"You don't think we should even ask her about the kidnapping?" Willow asked.

"No, because I guarantee that she would white-wash the entire experience. Just treat her as you always have and wrap her in love. I've told her how much the two of you love her and how we have a very special group of friends who've bonded together as family. She knows many of us don't have parents. How Carter's mom is really the only one left that serves as a parent for all of us. I told Sloane we are loyal to one another and because of that, we will be loyal to her. She will become one of us. The others will need to understand that she's been through a rough time and that they don't need to ask about it. They should simply offer her their friendship, the same as they have done to those of us seated around this table. Yes, you'll want to introduce her around, but it may take a while before she wants to do that. She may be shy—even wary—of strangers. Getting her outdoors will help. Physical exercise will help. There may be some days she'll push her body to the limits and beyond, seeking physical exhaustion as absolution. I'll do what I can to guide her through this experience since she doesn't seem to want to speak to a therapist."

"That's the last thing Sloane would do," Willow confirmed. "Her parents forced her into therapy for years. It did no good. I think since you share having gone through a terrible ordeal, Gage, that talking with you will help her more than anything. Yoga will also help. I know Ainsley and Rylie will also want to spend time with her. Ainsley will probably want to bake for her and with her, and I think it would be therapeutic. You know Rylie is our water sprite and may want to teach her to SUP as she did Nash."

"We'll let Sloane set the pace," Tenley confirmed. "And we won't pester you with how she's progressing, Gage. If you can help her, that will be enough for me."

"Dylan and I might also be able to help," Carter added. "Dylan has those years in the military, and I'm sure he also experienced things Sloane might be able to relate to. While I don't have that similar experience, I have lost fellow firefighters in the line of duty. Even my dad, who was my best friend. I know Tenley has mentioned how close Sloane was to her cameraman, and Ted's death had to be devastating. I'm happy to listen to her and talk with her about losing a loved one you work with, as well."

"Then we're all on the same page," Gage declared. "I'll leave it to Willow and Tenley to speak to Ainsley and Rylie about this. They can talk to Jackson and Nash. Together, we'll help Sloane put her life back together. I just wanted to warn you that she may seem different to you. She *is* a different woman from the woman you talked to in your last conversation with her before the kidnapping. We can't undo what she went through, but we can help her move forward."

They finished their meal, slightly subdued, and Gage said his goodbyes.

He arrived home and went through a few yoga poses before spending twenty minutes meditating, his usual bedtime ritual. He climbed into bed, his thoughts now cleared, and he hoped he would be able to sleep without worrying too much about Sloane Anderson.

His cell lit up with a notification since he silenced

it each night before bed. Curious, he picked it up and saw it was from Sloane. He opened the text.

If you're up, can we talk?

Gage figured she had spent some time alone and had acknowledged to herself she was ready to talk about what had happened to her in the car. He propped pillows behind him and leaned against them, texting that he was awake and ready to listen if she needed him.

Moments later, he saw her call coming in over FaceTime. Gage swallowed and touched the phone's screen.

"Hi, Sloane. I'm here for you."

CHAPTER 8

S loane sat on the bed, absently stroking Shadow. The dog had been waiting for her on the bed when Willow had brought Sloane to the guest room. Her friend had introduced the two of them, and Sloane felt an immediate bond with the Labrador/border collie mix. Though she had never owned a pet of her own—thanks to her parents thinking animals inside a house created a breeding ground for disease—Sloane hugged the dog, feeling the tension leaving her.

Willow said Shadow was often her shadow as she went around the house, and the dog even lay at her feet—sometimes on them—while she painted. She asked if Sloane would be comfortable having Shadow stay with her, once Sloane announced she wanted to go straight to bed. She had agreed having some warm company would be nice.

Though she secretly wished it were Gage Nelson who would be in her bed.

After Willow brought her a gown to sleep in and retreated from the room, Sloane had taken a long, hot shower, reveling in the ability to do so. Water in the bush could be scarce, and it was always treated as a precious commodity. To let the hot water sluice down her body as she lathered her hair and washed her limbs was a forgotten luxury. Willow had thoughtfully left all the amenities in the guest bathroom that Sloane might need. She shaved her legs and under her arms. Slathered her body in a lemon lotion, thankful that Willow remembered how she favored fresh, citrus scents.

She made use of the toothbrush, floss, and mouthwash and relished the cinnamon taste left in her mouth. She smoothed moisturizer on her face and neck and combed her hair before drying it. She used the nail clippers and emery board, lamenting at the pitiful condition her nails were in. Willow had even left hair ties and scrunchies in a drawer, along with hand lotion, artificial tears, and lip balm. Sloane applied everything and then pulled the flannel gown over her head.

Returning to her bedroom, Shadow raised his head, alert to her presence.

"It's just me, boy," she told him, running her hands along his body, his fur silky to the touch.

She had told Willow she wanted to sleep and saw her friend's disappointment. What Sloane really wanted was time alone. She sat in a chair in the corner of the room and gazed out the window. Darkness had fallen, but she could make out the waves rolling in and out and watched them for several minutes before turning her thoughts to what had happened to her in the car.

It had to have been a panic attack that hit her. She went to her phone, which was charging, and Googled it. What she read confirmed her suspicions. She had displayed several classic symptoms. Thankfully, the panic attack had not lasted the ten to thirty minutes cited in the articles she skimmed. Instead, it had abated almost instantly when Gage touched her. His simple gesture had brought not only warmth but comfort to her, as if having him there meant everything would be all right.

She now fought her attraction to him, knowing sex with the former Navy SEAL wouldn't be a permanent answer to her new problem, though she longed to have a go at him. Physically, he was as hot as a man came. Despite his intimidating size, he had displayed a sensitivity to her mood and knew exactly what to do to calm her. She didn't need to confuse gratitude for what he had done with the physical urges she was feeling for him. He was what she hoped would become a friend, one whom she might depend upon as she worked through the reaction to her kidnapping and feelings of loss and despair. Just because she was aching to kiss him didn't mean that was a good idea.

She had only had a few casual affairs in college and one intense one at the television station she had worked at upon graduating from UCLA. The weekend sports anchor had been sexy, confident, and possessed a massive ego. Their short time together had been intense. Then she had learned he had a live-in girlfriend, and Sloane had abruptly ended their affair. He had tried to blackball her at the station after that, spreading vicious rumors about her. Fortunately, she had been plucked from the affiliate station and went straight to New York three months later, jumpstarting her career as she was sent overseas.

Sloane supposed she didn't have the sexual maturity most women of thirty-one had. The last decade had been spent mostly celibate, with brief, one-night stands with other journalists to fight off the intense loneliness. Maybe that's why she was so strongly attracted to Gage Nelson. Not only was he devastatingly handsome and incredibly fit, but he lived in one place. Owned his own business. That idea of stability was enticing to her. But it wouldn't be fair to Gage, who really seemed to want to help her. Getting involved romantically would be a disaster. She needed a friend now, not a lover.

Sitting in the dark, staring out the window, she thought about Mwangi and the actions of his men. How she had felt so helpless. How she had worried what would become of her. Even though her time as a kidnap victim had been extremely limited compared to others abducted around the world, the experiences had colored her in ways she would see unfold in the days and weeks to come. She had been so busy up until now and knew she need to process the experience.

The solitude enveloped her. Even her thinking seemed loud to her, though it was all taking place in her head. She was right to keep this from Willow and Tenley. She needed her friends to treat her as they always had and would tell them so.

But with Gage?

Sloane was ready to let her guard down. The panic attack she suffered had scared the shit out of her. She needed to understand why it occurred and how to deal with it, if not outright eliminate it from happening again.

She returned to her phone and read three articles about panic attacks. It was helpful knowing the symptoms and what some of the triggers might be. Treatment was a mixed bag, however. Each article stressed to seek out the underlying cause of the panic attack, which she obviously knew was her kidnapping. Professional counseling or medications were recommended, along with training in breathing and muscle relaxation, which were also said to help. She hated learning that having panic attacks put her at a higher risk of suicide. While she had never experienced suicidal thoughts, she thought she might have if she hadn't been rescued by the SEAL team. The thought of the degradation she would have faced if repeatedly raped and subjected to torture caused her to shudder violently. Thank goodness she and most of the girls had been rescued.

Replacing her phone in the charger, she decided to try and sleep. Shadow curled up against her belly, his warmth a balm. Whatever she chose to do with the rest of her life, she decided that life would include a pet of some kind.

She awoke with a scream on her lips, muffling it in her pillow. Shadow nuzzled her, trying to comfort her. Sloane arose and went to the bathroom, splashing cold water on her face and drying it. She returned to the bed and saw she had only been asleep less than half an hour. Her heart still raced. She doubted sleep would come anytime soon.

Then she decided to see if Gage might still be awake. She picked up her phone and saw the time. It was close to nine. Willow had mentioned how early she and her friends went to bed because of their various jobs and workout routines. Still, she needed Gage's steadying hand. If not in person, then hopefully over the phone.

Quickly she texted to see if he was awake, waiting anxiously for him to respond. He replied immediately, saying he was awake and willing to talk. Sloane hesitated, not wanting to take advantage of him but desperate to talk to someone who understood what she was feeling. She propped pillows behind her and sat against them. Shadow moved to her side, placing his head on her thigh. As she stroked the dog's fur, she scrolled to Gage's name in her contacts and hit FaceTime.

Gage answered, his voice deep. "Hi, Sloane. I'm here for you."

"Thank you for agreeing to talk with me, Gage. I know it's late for you. Willow says everyone rises early and goes to sleep early in the Cove."

"I'm not sleepy," he told her.

She took a deep breath. "I don't know where to start."

His gray eyes held nothing but kindness. "Why don't we just talk? It doesn't have to be about this past week. In fact, I think it would be better if we avoid that topic for now." He held up a hand. "I *do* want to hear what happened to you. I'm not putting that off. But I think it's important that we build a little trust between us first. Do you agree?"

Sloane nodded her head. "I do. What should we talk about?"

"Anything. Everything. Nothing will be off-limits between us. Let's just discover things about one another. It could be things we've shared with others or things we've kept to ourselves." He paused. "I'll start."

"Okay," she agreed, stroking Shadow absently.

"I tested smart, but school bored the hell out of me. In fact, I quit at sixteen. I wasn't supposed to. My foster parents were supposed to make sure I went to school and was passing. But Stan Farthingale, my last foster dad, told me he was the same when he was my age. He owned his own auto body shop and let me start working there. The tradeoff was I had to get my GED in order to do so. That meant days were spent learning how to be a mechanic. I was on from six in the morning to three in the afternoon. Then I'd come home, help around the house, eat, and go to nightly GED classes."

"You sound very motivated for a teenager."

"I was. Stan said if I didn't work hard at the shop, he'd slap my ass back in school. I hated it. I didn't fit in with any of the social crowds. So I did what it took. Passed the GED. Worked for another year until I turned eighteen and aged out of the foster care system. Then I joined the navy."

"How did you get to be a SEAL? I know they're an elite group."

He smiled. "Funny you should ask. We had a career day in eighth grade. Parents came and talked about being everything from a lawyer to a dental hygienist. One guy, though, had been a Navy SEAL. He talked about the military in general, the different branches, and how it was a good way to get free training and an education and see the world. I stayed after and talked to him almost an hour. Told him I wanted to be a SEAL. He went into some of the nitty gritty, I think to try and deter me. Told me it was eighteen months of training and another eighteen of predeployment training."

She chuckled. "Most thirteen-year-old boys would've walked away after hearing that. Three years is a huge commitment."

"He told me about eighty percent wash out of the program. Instead of scaring me off, hearing that only made me more determined." Gage paused. "Give me something, Anderson. I'm spilling my guts here."

Sloane laughed. "I can be pretty determined myself. I'm only five-six, but I became a starter on my high school's basketball team. I can still sink free throws like there's no tomorrow. I've also trained in Krav Maga. Are you familiar with that?"

"Heard of it. I know it was developed in Israel, but that's about it. Tell me about it."

"When I went abroad, I was thrown into the thick of things. Rookies always get the worst assignments. For instance, new stateside reporters for the network always wind up covering the hurricanes. You seem them getting drenched, their hair in their eyes and mouth, holding onto something to keep from being blown away. The same is true with international reporters. Newbies get the worst assignments."

She paused, thinking back to those early years. "Some of the places I was sent to were terrifying. Actually, that never changed over the years. Networks tend to cover the bad at home—tornadoes, fires, murders. Abroad, we cover wars, military coups, drug wars. I'll admit I'm a bit of an adrenaline and news junkie."

"Oh, so you like jumping out of planes and ziplining?" he teased.

"Done both. And a lot more. I hope you can help me find a few exciting things to do in Oregon, beyond fishing. But back to my reporting. I had to meet with some sketchy people. I decided since network policy said I'm not supposed to be armed, I needed to know how to defend myself in situations if they got dicey."

"And that's where Krav Maga comes in."

"Exactly. It was developed for the IDF—Israel Defense Forces. It combines several techniques. Boxing. Judo. Wrestling. Karate. Aikido. It's known for concentrating on real-world situations. Reading the room and being efficient in your movements. It sprang from a guy named Imi Lichtenfeld, a wrestler and boxer who used both to defend the Jewish quarter from fascist groups in the old Czechoslovakia. He left there for

Palestine and did combat training. Krav Maga came from that training."

She stopped. "Sorry if I'm giving you a history lesson as an answer to your question."

He laughed. "I actually like history now. Hated it as a kid. But I appreciate it as I've gotten older."

"Anyway, I found a guy when I was reporting in the Middle East. He had trained in Krav Maga and agreed to give me lessons. I learned the basics from him since he was former IDF. Whenever I come back to New York between assignments, I also have a guy in Brooklyn I train with. I've built on those lessons." She grinned. "I can tell you now, Mr. Navy SEAL—you do *not* want to mess with me."

Gage burst out laughing. "Thanks for the warning, Anderson. Although I'm six-three and two-thirty, I think I'll stay on your good side. Just in case."

"You better, or I'll lay you flat on your back, Nelson," she retorted. "What else about you? Spill a little more."

He grew serious. "I've kept this on the down-low. I'm about to look into building a large work-out facility in the area, mostly likely between the Cove and Salty Point, the largest town in the area."

"Have you met with a loan officer? I'm sure that has to be expensive. Land doesn't come cheap, and erecting a large building would be astronomical."

"It will be. But I'm good for a large chunk of it. I've been investing quite a while now."

"Investing?"

"The stock market. I know—a guy with a GED playing the market? But I'm self-taught in business and investing. The downtime, when we weren't on missions, we would train for six to eight hours a day. The rest of the time, I studied. Hard. Took some online business courses. Learned a lot. The navy provided me with housing. Meals. Clothing. I banked almost my entire salary, though it wasn't large."

"SEALs don't get paid a lot?"

"Nope. All military elite special-ops groups, such as Navy SEALs, don't have a different pay scale from the regular navy. The only difference is we usually receive hazardous duty pay. That results in higher earnings than a sailor aboard a ship. But overall, military pay isn't generous. Still, I took almost all of it and poured it into the market while I was still in the navy. Once I left, I kept up with market trends and continued investing, half in risky ventures and half in steady-growth options. Since I've lived in the Cove, I've spent very little. I rent a small garage apartment from Liz Freeman, a tiny seventy-five-year-old widow. I take care of her yard, mowing and watering, and also do things around the house for her. In return, I pay very little in rent. She says she likes having a former military man on the property. Makes her feel safe."

Sloane shook her head. "You're telling me you have the cash to build a large workout facility."

"Mostly."

"How large are we talking?"

"I've completed work with an architect on the plans. It will have a weight room. Aerobics room. A general room with machines such as squat racks. Lat pulldowns. Ellipticals. Leg extension and curls. Indoor cycle bikes and treadmills. I teach classes now outdoors and also train individual clients outdoors. I'd like the place to have a couple of rooms for classes in things such as yoga and Pilates. And I'd love a spin room, too. It will also house an indoor pool and then locker rooms for both men and women."

She blew out a breath. "That sounds incredibly ambitious, Nelson. And incredibly expensive."

"I told you. I'm good for most of it. I've been meeting with Jackson. Jackson Martin. He's Ainsley's husband and Willow's brother."

"Yes, I've met Jackson. He was at UCLA, in law school, when I first became roommates with Willow and Tenley. He's advising you?"

"Yes, Jackson was a trial lawyer but came back to the Cove to take over a local guy's practice. Clancy Nelson. No relation to me. Jackson does everything from family law to financial planning. He's been really helpful. Jackson is the only person, other than the architect, who knows about my plans. I'm about to look at parcels of land, though, with Shayla Newton, our local realtor. We're meeting in the morning. Maybe you could come with me and help me choose a place where to build."

"I'd like that."

Sloane liked everything this man said. She liked *him*. She was still heavily attracted to him, but she also liked him as a person. She could tell Gage was a good guy. Capable. Loyal. Friendly. Disciplined.

"Then maybe we could drive around tomorrow after Shayla has shown me what's available. I have between three and five free to do so. How about you?"

She paused, pretending to think. "I suppose I can squeeze you in. Between doing nothing and doing a little bit more of nothing." She sighed. "Actually, I'm going to need to speak to Willow in the morning. I know she and Tenley have all kinds of plans for us, but I need some quiet time. Down time. Alone time. Walk on the beach and get my head on straight time. But I'm happy to ride around the area with you and look at potential spots for your facility."

"I'd appreciate your input, Anderson."

"And I appreciate you taking me under your wing, Nelson. I can do one-on-one for now. Maybe I can meet the group of friends in ones and twos before we all get together. I know you're famous for your Game Nights."

He chuckled. "Game Night would be overwhelming to anyone. The competition can be cutthroat, but it's a ton of fun. Especially when your side wins, and Ainsley bakes the dessert of your choice."

"Since I'm also a chocoholic, as I've heard you are, maybe we can team up and win us double fudge brownies or something else equally delicious." She yawned. "Sorry."

"You're on, Anderson. Now, I think it's time we both hit the sack. Feeling better?"

"Much. Thanks for the talk, Nelson. Even though we didn't discuss what I thought we might, I... feel good. About myself. About being in the Cove."

"At least you know enough to call it the Cove and not Maple Cove," he teased. "I'll text you tomorrow about exactly when I'll pick you up, but it'll be close to three."

"I'll be ready." Sloane smiled at his image. "Thanks for the talk. It hit the spot. Goodnight, Nelson."

"Goodnight, Anderson."

She ended the connection and placed her phone on the nightstand beside her. Shadow's head still rested in her lap, and she eased it off, slipping under the covers. Closing her eyes, Sloane breathed slowly in and out a few times and drifted off to sleep.

CHAPTER 9

Sloane awoke and stretched lazily. She couldn't remember the last time she had slept in such a comfortable bed. She went to the window and looked out over the ocean and knew she was ready to explore the beach below. She made up her bed, since she was a bit of a neat-freak, always thinking a room looked better for the bed having been made, unlike her teenage years when a maid had done it for her. Shaking off that thought, she went into the bathroom to get ready for the day. She had washed out her bra and underwear last night before bed. Thankfully, they were both dry. She put them on and slipped the night-gown back over her head, hoping Tenley had dropped off something for her to wear as she had promised. Wearing the same dirty clothes for four days running was getting old.

As she went to the door, she realized Shadow was no longer on the bed and supposed Willow must have come and let him out when she got up for her daily run. Sloane knew the dog sometimes accompanied her friend and husband on those runs.

Opening the door, she discovered two things waiting for her—Shadow and a suitcase.

She scratched Shadow between his ears, and a contented look appeared upon his face. He padded softly into the room as she brought the suitcase inside and placed it on the bed, opening it to see what it held. It contained three sports bras, which were stretchy enough to accommodate her. She found a few pairs of athletic pants and leggings. She tried on a pair of each and found they fit her perfectly, much better than anything her taller friends might have lent her.

She pulled out a couple of sweatshirts and sweaters that were tunic length and would go well with the leggings. Also inside were half a dozen pairs of socks in dark colors and half a dozen pairs of underwear, thankfully not thongs, which she despised. Sloane dressed in a pair of black leggings and socks and paired them with a dark-green, cowl-neck tunic sweater. She slipped her phone into the back pocket, grateful the leggings had one, and placed the rest of the borrowed clothes in the dresser drawers. She also found a pair of pajamas and added them to a drawer.

Glancing at the clock on the nightstand, she saw it was just after seven, which made it ten in New York. She had very little in the New York *pied-à-terre* she shared with a few other journalists and decided to contact one of them now. Cathy Stevens was home on a medical leave of absence. She had messaged Sloane a couple of weeks ago, telling her she had to have surgery on a ruptured Achilles tendon and would be in New York while she was recovering. Sloane called Cathy now, and her roommate answered on the second ring.

"Sloane, hi! I'm so glad to hear from you."

Being a journalist herself, Cathy was wise enough not to mention the kidnapping.

"How was your surgery? Better yet, how is recovery coming along?"

"Good to the surgery, better for rehab. I've already gone from cast to walking boot. The rehab has ramped up, and I should be able to lose the boot after another month, according to my doctor and physical therapist."

"When will you be able to go back to work?" Sloane asked.

Cathy sighed. "The doctor has said it would be four to six months after the surgery before I can return to normal activities. When I do, the network plans to send me to D.C. I'll vacate the apartment permanently then. Don't worry. I already have a friend coming from an Atlanta affiliate to work here in the city. She'll take my place in the apartment." Cathy paused. "Will I be seeing you anytime soon?"

"No, that's why I'm calling. I've taken a sabbatical from the network. Steve and I are negotiating its length, but it will be at least six months long. My two college roommates live on the Oregon coast, and I've decided to spend an extended amount of time with them."

"I think that's smart, Sloane. I'm sorry I'll miss seeing you."

"I have a big favor to ask of you, Cathy. I won't be needing a base in New York anymore and would appreciate if you could box up my clothes and ship them to me ASAP."

Sloane had done this before, finding it much cheaper to get a huge box or two and fill it with clothes, instead of packing suitcases and having those shipped.

"I don't have a lot," she continued. "Just my clothes and some shoes. A couple of coats and winter boots. You can toss everything into the FedEx box, and if you see anything else of mine, add it to the mix."

Years ago she had transferred all her pictures to digital, and so she had no photo albums. She'd never kept scrapbooks or diaries. She'd sold any books she had, preferring to download them on her Kindle phone app. She really couldn't think of anything else Cathy might find in the apartment.

"As far as kitchen stuff goes, leave it for whoever takes my place. They're welcome to any coffee mugs with the network logo on them. I'll pay my share of the rent for the next six months until the lease is up, so no one will have to worry about that."

"I'm happy to send you your things, Sloane, and I actually have someone who might be willing to take your spot in the apartment. She's new to the morning show. Came from Chicago. She's living in a hotel now and looking for a place she can afford."

"Would she want to be somewhere with so many people coming and going?"

"She'll be covering the entire East Coast, so she'll be traveling a lot. If you don't mind, I'll touch base with her and see if she wants to take your slot. If so, you can sublet to her and be off the hook for your rent."

"That would be great, Cathy. Just let me know what's decided. I'll call FedEx now and have a couple of boxes delivered and schedule the pickup."

"You don't have much, so once the boxes arrive, I'll toss everything in today. Schedule the pickup for to-morrow morning."

"You're a lifesaver, Cathy. Good luck with your re-habbing and the new job. I'll be watching for you."

"Same to you, Sloane. And you'll owe me a drink or two for this packing job. Whenever we're in the same city, I plan to claim that."

"You're on."

Sloane contacted FedEx and arranged for the boxes to be delivered to her New York address, as well as scheduling the pickup. She had express delivery done so that her clothes would reach her the day after tomorrow. It was still too early to call Elton Briggs, Ted's attorney, since he was based in San Francisco. She would do that later this morning.

Right now, she was starving and made her way downstairs to the kitchen, Shadow on her heels.

Willow sat at the breakfast table, her laptop open, sipping on a cup of coffee. Sloane entered the kitchen and immediately, her stomach gurgled loudly.

Willow laughed and said, "Sit. I'll get you coffee and something to eat."

"You don't need to wait on me. I don't want to be treated as a guest."

"You can take your time and nose around the kitchen later to see where everything's located. Let me spoil you for now, at least. You still like hazelnut coffee?"

"I would take *any* cup of coffee," she said fervently. "I haven't had a decent cup of coffee in a long time."

Willow went and turned on the coffeemaker, removing a single pod from the drawer beneath it. She brought a white bakery box to the table and opened it. A heavenly scent rose from it, yeasty and sugary.

"Dylan and I made sure we ran by the bakery this morning on our run. Ainsley put in a variety of things for you to try."

Sloane's eyes grew large looking at the contents. She saw a glazed and chocolate-glazed donut, along with a giant cinnamon roll, apple fritter, and huge croissant.

"I think I could eat everything in this box right now," she declared.

"It's all for you, whether you eat it today or over the next couple of days. I would recommend something to you, but everything Ainsley makes is wonderful."

"You said she went to a pastry school in Paris, right?"

Willow placed the pod into the coffeemaker and pressed Start. "Yes, l'Ecole Lenôtre. It's world-famous. People from around the globe apply to attend, some multiple times, trying to get in. Ainsley was accepted on her first try."

"I'm surprised with that level of training that she didn't remain in a large city and go to work at a Michelin star restaurant."

"She easily could have, but Ainsley was raised in the Cove. Her intention was always to come back here and open her own bakery."

"So, tiny Maple Cove has a world-class pastry chef, and I'm benefiting from it."

Willow placed a plate, fork, and napkin in front of Sloane, and she decided to be a purist and start with the glazed donut. Willow also poured her a tall glass of cold milk to go with her meal, another luxury. One bite into the donut and Sloane moaned.

"I told you," her friend said. "You should taste her cupcakes and eclairs. She also makes divine breads. Actually, Gus—her number two—has taken over most of the breadmaking."

"Keep me from eating too fast," she urged. "I want to savor each bite instead of gobbling it down."

Willow brought her the mug of coffee, and she

lifted it, inhaling deeply. "I could get drunk just off the smell of this coffee."

As they sat, Willow said, "I owe you an apology." She placed her hand over Sloane's, squeezing it. "Both Tenley and I realized we were pretty insensitive to your needs when we picked you up. We didn't acknowledge what you've been through, much less that you arrived with the clothes on your back. I'm sorry we let our excitement with you finally coming here cloud our judgment. I know you've been through a lot."

"Gage talked to you, didn't he?" she asked quietly.

"He brought it to our attention. We were so enthusiastic about having you here, but I realize this isn't just a vacation for you between assignments. If you want to talk about anything with Tenley or me, we're here and ready to listen. If you'd rather wait and process it on your own, we'll respect that, too."

"Thank you," she said earnestly. "When I was freed by the Navy SEAL team, all I could think of was coming here to the Cove and being with you and Tenley. I'll tell you now that I'm not merely on vacation. I'm not waiting for my next assignment to come in. I talked it over with my boss on the plane, and I am on sabbatical. Or a leave of absence. Whatever you want to call it."

"For how long?"

She shrugged. "Six months to a year. That will be up to me. I don't want to overstay my welcome, though."

"Boo's house is huge, Sloane. I'll give you a tour when you're through with breakfast, but it's large enough that you can stay the entire time and not bother Dylan or me. Of course, Tenley will be jealous and may want you to stay with her some, too. I know you've been through the ringer and need time to heal."

"Thank you for the open-ended offer, Willow. I will stay as long as you and Dylan will have me. I've given up my New York *pied-à-terre*, and I'm having one of my roommates there ship my clothes to me. For now, I'll be up front and tell you I need some time to myself. Yes, I want to go into town and see all the places you mentioned. I do want to get out and hike. Ride a bike. See some of the coast. But I have been through something painful. It's going to take me some time to wrap my head around it."

She paused, her gaze meeting Willow's. "I want everything to be like it always has been between us. When I'm ready to talk about what happened to me, Gage has offered to be my sounding board."

Willow nodded. "Gage would be perfect for that. He's one of the best men I've ever known. Don't forget, though, that Dylan served in the military for a dozen years. He would also be someone you could talk with."

"I appreciate that. Let's change topics. I do want to meet Ainsley and Riley and their husbands. I've enjoyed talking to your friends when I've called you and Tenley. I'm not ready for one of your Game Nights, though. Too many people and too much noise. For now, I want to savor the quiet. For me, that will mean long walks on that beach outside my window. I'll let you know when I'm ready to be more social."

"If you want to walk on the beach this morning, you'll need a heavier coat than that thin jacket you were wearing last night. Come on. Let me show you the house and where everything is."

Willow took Sloane on a tour, showing her everything, from how to operate the washer and dryer to which remotes operated the TV. She showed Sloane a sitting room on the first floor and said she rarely used it and thought it might make a good base for Sloane while she was here. It had a desk she could work from if she felt the urge to get anything down on paper, as well as chairs she could read in and a small TV.

"We've already talked about a few series over the phone that you wanted to binge on when you were stateside," Willow said. "I want you to think of this place as your retreat."

"I appreciate that more than I can convey."

Willow took her upstairs and showed her the various bedrooms, and then they went to the top floor, where Boo's art studio was located.

"The light in here is fantastic for painting," her friend told her. "It's as if I feel Boo's presence every time I pick up my brush."

"I think I'm ready for that long walk on the beach," she said.

"Just grab one of my coats hanging in the mudroom. In fact, let me walk out with you and show you the stairs leading down to the beach. Sometimes, they can be a little hard to find."

They bundled up and went across a wide expanse of lawn, where Willow pointed out the stairs her grandfather had built decades before, leading down to the water.

"Take your time. I'll be in my studio. You now know where everything is in the kitchen, so if you want to fix yourself a sandwich or salad, feel free to do so. Sometimes, I get so wrapped up in my painting that I don't break for lunch, so don't wait around for me."

"All right then. I'll see you later."

Sloane descended the stairs and set out to walk the beach, knowing she had much to think about.

CHAPTER 10

Sloane was anticipating Gage's text. When it came in, excitement filled her. She knew better than to pursue the attraction she felt for the former Navy SEAL, but she did want to take advantage of the friendship he offered her. Doing so would be a balancing act she wasn't sure she was up for, but she needed Gage's ear.

She texted back that she would be ready and then went to the mirror to check her appearance. Her hair was a bit windblown from her earlier walk along the beach, and so she ran a quick brush through it. She also went to her backpack and removed the lone tube of lipstick. Finding time to apply makeup wasn't practical when reporting from war zones and hurricanes, but the network consultant had always emphasized to her to apply a coat of lipstick before she went on the air. She did so now, knowing it brightened her skin and gave her a polished look.

Going down the stairs, Shadow by her side, she went to the front door and stopped before opening it, petting the dog and telling him he would have to stay behind with Willow. Shadow's intelligent eyes seemed to indicate he understood what she told him, and he reversed course, trotting back up the stairs. She assumed he would go to Willow's studio and sit on her feet while her friend painted.

Leaving the house, Sloane went and sat on the porch steps in order to save Gage from having to get out of the truck and coming to the door for her. Moments later, his truck appeared, coming down the long drive and stopping. She pushed to her feet, and Gage waved as he exited the vehicle.

"How has your first day in the Cove been?" he asked, following her to the other side of the truck and opening the door for her.

She knew the gesture wasn't a romantic one because he had done the same for Willow and Tenley at the airport. Still, it was thoughtful on his part.

He got into the truck and she replied, "I had a good night's sleep and a nice talk with Willow over breakfast this morning. She knows now to give me space. I told her I would let her know when I'm ready to start making the rounds and meeting people and going places. I'm sure she passed along that information to Tenley."

As Gage turned his truck and continued down the driveway, she added, "I also took a lengthy walk along the beach. It's so close that I definitely will take advantage of that each day. I found an actual cove—in the Cove—and explored it some, thanks to my phone's flashlight app. Maple Cove is a beautiful place. I can see why you decided to settle here."

"The entire Oregon coast has a lot going for it, but I just found a charm and warmth in the Cove that I didn't other places I stopped," Gage shared.

"I'm assuming you met with the realtor you mentioned, and we're going to look at properties you've already seen?"

"Yes, I went out with Shayla this morning between classes. She can be a bit of a gossip, but she's a lovely woman. I assume news will get out regarding my plans. Seeing the properties I did, though, I've decided to scale back on what I'm going to build."

"What would you eliminate from the facility?" she asked, curious.

"The biggest expense would be the heated pool. I decided my facility doesn't need one. There's a community center in Salty Point, which is the next town over. It has both an indoor and outdoor pool. I think I would rather get going on all my classes and trainings. If I change my mind down the road, I suppose I could seek additional financing and build the pool. This way, I have enough to cover purchasing the land and building the structure without having to take out a loan."

"Where do the bulk of your clients come from? The Cove?"

He grew thoughtful, and she admired his profile. "I hadn't really given that any thought. That should factor into my decision. I'd say sixty percent of my clients come from Salty Point. It might be wise to build closer to it."

"Where do you draw the other forty percent from?"

"Obviously, the Cove." He named a few other surrounding towns. "I've been able to have very little overhead because I hold all group classes outdoors and meet my individual clients outside, as well."

Sloane frowned. "What about rain? I thought this part of the country got quite a bit of it."

Gage laughed, deep from his belly, causing a shiver

to run through her. "Oregonians don't let a little rain get in the way of anything, because you're right—it is a constant in our lives. A lot of times, it's merely drizzle. That doesn't stop workout sessions. Most of my individual clients are dedicated enough to want to train, rain or shine. As far as the group classes go, there's a pavilion in a city park I use that's quite large. It has a bandstand and several picnics tables and it's covered. If the rain becomes heavy, we merely move underneath that. Because of meeting outside, I haven't had to pay rent anywhere. I have invested in numerous weights, which I carry around in the back of my truck."

"So, is it mostly aerobics and weight training you do?"

He nodded. "A lot of what in the old days was called calisthenics for the groups. We do a mixture of aerobics, along with some jogging and Pilates."

"I do Pilates when I'm on the road. I've always enjoyed it. I played basketball and was a softball pitcher in high school. I've always loved doing anything physical."

"I have seen you reporting from some pretty crazy places around the world. Pilates is easy to do on your own. Do you ever use weight-resistant bands?"

"Yes, I keep two in a compartment of my backpack. Thank goodness, my backpack survived the fire at the school. Two students saved it for me."

Gage pulled off the main road onto a smaller one, and then he turned into a bare lot and cut the engine.

He turned to her. "Loss of your personal items hurts. I know some people would say it's just clothing. Easy to replace. But sometimes losing that favorite shirt or lucky pair of socks is painful."

"You're right. I only had the clothes I wore that day

of the kidnapping. I actually threw them in the trash this morning. I'm now wearing borrowed clothes from Ainsley, whom I've never met. Tenley told me she was the closest to my size. Ainsley packed a few things for me. In fact, she's the first person I want to meet in the Cove in order to thank her."

"We can go by her place once we finish looking at three properties. The bakery will be closed by then, and she'll be home."

"All right. Let's get out and investigate this lot."

Sloane opened her own passenger door, not wanting Gage to have to come around and do it for her. They walked the parcel of land, and he told her more about what he and his architect had designed, showing her where various parts of the facility would be located. They discussed this specific piece of land, both its advantages and disadvantages.

"Let's go to the next one," he said.

They returned to the truck, and he told her that Shayla had shown him five prospective places to build on.

"But after what we just discussed in regard to Salty Point and the number of clients from there, I'm eliminating two of them. They're on the other side of the Cove, further from Salty Point. I don't think I would lose too many clients if I built on either spot, but I'm going to need a lot more business in order to be profitable. It makes sense to build between the Cove and Salty Point."

They arrived at the second lot and did the same as before, getting out and walking the property as he told her about it. They saw the last choice for sale, and both agreed it would be the ideal site for him to break ground. It had easy access off the Boxboro Highway and was slightly closer to Salty Point than the other properties they had seen, yet still convenient for residents of the Cove.

"I think I've made up my mind and can text Shayla. I'll also let Jackson know that I've decided to forego the pool and won't need any financing."

"It will be exciting even without the pool. You won't regret being in debt."

"Well, I've lived as a pauper all my life. To be able to spend over a million dollars on land and building the facility is almost a little surreal."

"You'll need to hire at least a couple of instructors," she pointed out, as he started the car and headed back toward the Cove. "You want to be able to use as much of the facility as possible. You will obviously gain more clients with such a large place to offer. You won't be able to teach every class and individually train others, as well as keep the books. Then there'll be making certain the equipment is working property. Plus, the entire facility will need to be cleaned daily, especially the locker rooms. In fact, those should probably be cleaned twice a day. You'll have too much on your plate to mop and swish toilets."

He looked at her sheepishly. "You know, I hate to say it, but I hadn't even thought that far ahead. I was focused more on finding the land and the actual building of the place. I've been going it on my own for so long that I never even thought I would need help. Do you have any more ideas for me, Anderson?"

"I might. Let me think on it a little."

She decided to mention her conversation with Elton Briggs to him. "After my walk today, I spoke with Ted's attorney. He's based in San Francisco, where Ted came from. Elton said he'll need me to sign some papers. I suppose I need to speak with Jackson, as well as

Ainsley. I'd like Jackson to read over the documents and give me his feedback."

By now, they had reached the square of Maple Cove, and Gage went partly around it, pointing out Jackson's law office and turning onto a side street. Half a block away, he said, "There's Jackson now, walking home from the office. Let's give him a ride."

Gage brought his truck to a halt and rolled down the window. "Hey, Jackson. We're headed to your place. Want a ride?"

Jackson said, "Sure," and climbed into the back of the cab.

Sloane saw the years had been kind to the attorney. She had first met Willow's brother when she arrived at UCLA and became Willow's roommate. Jackson was three years ahead of them and already in law school. Sloane had had a bit of a crush on her friend's brother, but Jackson had treated her and Tenley as additional little sisters.

He leaned up, his hand squeezing her shoulder. "It's great to see you, Sloane."

"You still look like the former athlete you were, Jackson. I think returning to the Cove has been good for you."

Jackson patted Gage's shoulder. "It's all thanks to this guy. I've got to give credit where credit's due. I still run daily, but Gage has me doing some weight and resistance training, as well."

"Gage and I were heading to your place so I could thank Ainsley for loaning me some of her clothes. I also need to hire you."

She watched shadow that crossed his face. "Is it in regard to your network?"

"No, the network and my boss have been terrific in the aftermath of what happened. I'm taking a leave of absence. My contract is up in three months, and I may not go back for another three to six after that. I'm in the Cove to take time for myself and weigh my options."

"I think that's wise, Sloane," Jackson said. "You've been through a tough time and need to think about what happened and what you want out of life."

As they slowed and then stopped in front of a beautiful house on a corner lot, she said, "My cameraman, Ted Castro, had asked me to be the executor of his estate. I contacted his attorney, Elton Briggs, earlier today. I also had Ted's body taken to a Portland mortuary. They are cremating him. I should receive a call from them tomorrow and collect his ashes. In the meantime, Elton had some paperwork he needed me to read over and sign. I also know I'll have decisions to make regarding Ted's estate. Would you be willing to represent me in all these matters?"

"I'm happy to do so, Sloane. I can also look over any contract the network sends you, if you decide to go back there." Jackson grinned. "One-stop shopping as far as legal advice goes. That's what you get in the Cove."

They got out of the car and she remarked upon how pretty the house and lot were.

"The place belonged to Clancy Nelson, a mentor to me and lawyer who served the residents of the Cove and beyond for decades. I took over his law practice when he retired and moved to Houston with his new wife. I have my office where he did, and Ainsley and I were fortunate to buy Clancy's house, as well. Rylie helped decorate it, and we also had a local contractor, Pete Pulaski, update the inside of the house for us. We are really pleased with the property. It definitely feels like home."

Jackson unlocked the door and led them inside, calling, "Ainsley, we've got company! Sloane and Gage are here."

Ainsley Martin appeared, her rounded belly an obvious giveaway that she was pregnant. She came straight to Sloane and took her hands.

"I'm delighted to finally meet you in person, Sloane. I'm sorry for what you went through in Africa, and I hope you'll be able to spend some time decompressing here in the Cove."

Sloane squeezed Ainsley's hands and said, "Thank you so much for letting me borrow some of your clothes. I lost everything in the fire the rebels set."

Ainsley released Sloane's hands and patted her belly. "As you can see, I'm not able to get into any of them at the moment. I just threw some things together for you, but you're welcome to raid my closet and borrow anything else you like."

"I actually contacted my roommate in New York, and she's shipping my clothes to me. I really do appreciate, though, what you sent over, and I'll be sure to return it soon."

"Keep it as long as you like," Ainsley said. "I won't be needing it for several more months."

"When is your due date?" Sloane asked.

"April fifteenth. Tax day." She smiled. "It's a boy. We're negotiating names now. Would you two like to stay for dinner? It's a crockpot roast, so we have plenty."

Sloane looked to Gage, who said, "I'm game if you are."

"Let me text Willow and let her know I won't be home for dinner."

She did so as the others moved to the kitchen. Her friend immediately responded.

Glad you've met Ainsley and become reacquainted with Jackson. See you later.

Sloane pocketed her phone and moved to join the others. "Can I help with anything?"

"Not a thing," Ainsley assured her. "Jackson is getting drinks. Hope iced tea is okay with you. Gage is always a water drinker."

"Unless it's Game Night," he said. "Then it's beer and water."

"I've heard about the famous—or should I say infamous—Game Nights," Sloane said. "And that you provide the prize to the winners."

Ainsley lifted the roast from the crockpot and placed it on a plate, then scooped out carrots and potatoes, placing them alongside the roast.

"I don't mind. It's an easy reward. The winner or winners choose the dessert, but we all profit by getting to eat it. I hope you'll come to our next Game Night, Sloane."

The thought of a full room of loud people took her aback. "We'll see," she said, putting Ainsley off.

"Here, let me carry that in for you," Jackson said, taking the platter from his wife and heading from the kitchen into the dining room.

Sloane started to follow, but Ainsley touched her arm.

"I cannot imagine what you went through. I doubt you want to talk about it and relive it. But I know it had to be stressful. I have something that might help you, though." Ainsley hesitated. "Don't laugh. Baking bread."

"What?"

"The making, actually," Ainsley corrected. "You really have to work some doughs. I've always found the kneading to be soothing. If you're game and don't mind getting up early one morning, I'm happy to have you come to Buttercup Bakery and give it a whirl."

"Willow has said her circle rises pretty early. What time are we talking?"

Ainsley chuckled. "I get there at three. But you could come about five. I'd have enough out of the way to spend some time with you. Also, Gus would like to spend time with you. He religiously watches the news and knows my friends are friends with you. He's my Number Two and does a good deal of the baking."

Sloane didn't hesitate. "I would really enjoy trying it. During my time in the Cove, I want to do things new to me. Would you mind if I did show up at three? I'd like to watch you at work if it wouldn't bother you."

"Not a bit," Ainsley said. "You can sit silently and take it all in, or I could tell you about each step as I do it."

"Maybe a little of both. Would tomorrow be okay?" she asked.

Ainsley smiled. "I would love to have you come by."

Jackson leaned around the corner. "Are you two coming?"

"We are," his wife said, slipping her hand through Sloane's arm and leading her into the dining room.

As they ate, Sloane wasn't overwhelmed by being around three people. She relaxed and enjoyed the food and their conversation. When it came time to leave, she was comfortable enough to hug Ainsley.

"I'm glad I made a new friend tonight," she said.

Ainsley smiled brightly. "I feel the same. See you tomorrow."

"How does your schedule look, Sloane?" Jackson asked, walking her and Gage out to the truck.

"Well, I'm getting up extremely early and going to

Ainsley's bakery to knead bread tomorrow. I am supposed to hear from the funeral home in Portland and will need to claim Ted's ashes. Why?"

"How about when you finish at the bakery you snag us a couple of pastries and head to my office? We can go over the documents Elton Briggs sent to you and discuss any questions you have."

"That sounds good, Jackson. I'll e-mail them to you when I get home." She hugged him and then got into the truck, Gage holding the door for her.

"Back to Boo's?" he asked.

"I suppose so. I'm meeting Ainsley at three, so I'll need to go to bed pretty soon."

"Since you don't have a car, would you like me to drive you into Portland after you hear from Mr. Pinkerton?"

She hesitated. "I don't want to take up too much of your time, Nelson."

His grin was downright wicked. "If you become too much of a pest, I'll let you know, Anderson."

They drove the short way to Boo's in an easy silence. Gage hopped quickly from his seat and came around to help her from the truck. He walked up the porch steps with her.

"Thank you for your input regarding the properties," he told her. "And I was serious. If you have any other ideas, let me know. Put them in writing. You seem to think out of the box. I could use that point of view."

"Happy to do so. You've really helped me. I appreciate how long we talked last night. It was just the thing I needed to quiet my mind and help me sleep. And I appreciate you taking me to visit with Ainsley and Jackson. So far, no more panic attacks." She paused. "Though the idea of a loud, rowdy Game Night had me freaking out a bit."

"You'll know when you're ready for something like that," he assured her.

"Thanks for your time and your ear," she said, leaning in to hug him as she had Jackson.

But everything about Gage was different. The feel of him. His scent. Her racing pulse. Her dry mouth. Sloane pulled back and gazed up at him, shocked when she saw the heat in his eyes.

Then he lowered his mouth to hers—and the fireworks exploded.

CHAPTER 11

G age surprised himself when he kissed Sloane.
His self-discipline had been legendary
among his fellow SEALs. He was always in control,
thinking five steps ahead. Others turned to him in a
time of crisis because he kept a cool head.

But his body burned for this woman.

And he wasn't willing to deny himself a taste
of her.

The moment their lips met, it was as if it had been
declared the Fourth of July and fireworks blazed
across the night sky. The spark between them was instant. He grabbed her by the waist, yanking her to
him, a sizzling heat rippling through his limbs.
Though he had dreamed of slowly exploring her tight,
compact body, all he could think of now was tasting
her.

She opened to him with no resistance. His tongue
plunged into the sweet depths of her mouth, sweeping
along, wanting to discover everything within. One
hand left her waist, slipping to the small of her back,
pressing her body against his. The other went to her
nape, holding her firmly as his assault continued on

her mouth. Gage had never tasted any woman who moved him with such speed. Desire flooded him.

Then his mind finally put on the brakes that his body had refused to listen to. He broke the kiss and released Sloane, who swayed slightly. Her eyes opened, confusion in them. He clasped her elbows to steady her, only to see the heat in her eyes. The want. The need.

Sloane grabbed him by his coat and yanked him back down to her, their lips colliding. For a long moment, Gage yielded, allowing her to take the lead, her tongue to stroke his, her sighs and his low groan revealing the growing need within both of them.

But it wasn't right for him to be kissing her.

Once again, Gage broke the kiss, his hands still clasping Sloane's elbows, holding her at arm's length. Her erratic breathing made him aware of his own.

"Why did you stop?" she managed to ask.

"Because," he said stubbornly, trying to think how to voice the rational thoughts in his head when all he wanted to do was kiss her into next year.

She scowled at him. "That's not an answer. I demand you give me a reason. And it better be a damn good one because I was enjoying myself."

He backed up several steps, to where a porch swing hung. Releasing her, he sat and indicated for her to do the same. Anger still sparked in her green eyes, but she did take a seat next to him. Her lemony scent filled the air surrounding them.

"You have been through a harrowing experience, Sloane," he began. "I understand that. I've been in situations when I didn't know if I would make it out alive. You underwent the same. You teetered on the edge of life and death—and you won. You beat death. That makes you want to reaffirm how alive you are.

You may be having a delayed reaction to your experience. Sex is a powerful thing. You want to have sex now to show how alive you are. That you cheated death. It's an adrenaline rush."

Her eyes narrowed. "If I'd wanted to celebrate escaping Mwangi's hands, I would have had sex with the hot Navy SEAL who rescued me. Hell, I might have had sex with the entire SEAL team. Yes, they saved me. They saved those girls. And I did believe I was going to die. First, a slow death. One of repeated rape and degradation, breaking my body, my mind, my spirit. Then a physical death, when they had tired of me or used me up. I get what you're saying. You think me wanting to have sex with you is an extension of gaining my freedom."

"Yes."

Fire lit her eyes. "Well, it isn't. I have been attracted to you ever since you answered Willow's phone and your image lit up my screen. No, I'll take that back. I think the attraction began when Tenley and Willow first told me about you. How quiet and selfless you are. How you're always there when someone needs something. In every picture, you're in the background. You don't call attention to yourself. That piqued my interest, along with your rugged looks.

"But after we spoke, I couldn't get you out of my head. I still can't, Gage. Every time I shut my eyes, you're there. From the moment I wake up, my thoughts turn to you. So don't give me some line about the only reason I want you is to affirm I'm alive. Hell, yes, I'm alive. And, yes, I want to celebrate being alive and out of that war zone and in a place where I'm safe."

Gage took her hand. "But see, that's the problem. I've taken on a role as your friend. Your sounding

board. Something to help you through the darkness—
and it will continue to creep up, Sloane. I guarantee
that. I feel we have a connection. That we're building
trust between us. Beginning a physical relationship
could really screw that up. I don't want to be your
fuck-buddy. I have too much respect for you to become that. What I do want is to help you to heal. If we
become physical, the dynamics between us change.
The relationship changes. You don't need that kind of
complication in your life right now."

He squeezed her hand. "I'm sorry I'm the one who
crossed the line. I know how fragile you are right now,
even if everyone else around you doesn't see it. If you'd
been in a car wreck and broken your leg and wound
up in traction at the hospital, people could see how
hurt you are. Instead, you look the same to them.
You're mostly acting the same. But you have been
through a huge shock. You're emotionally and spiritu-
ally injured. Wounded. You're suffering. No one can
see that damage. Maybe not even you. You need to
admit to yourself that while you are strong, you need
help. You've told me talk therapy didn't do it for you
previously. It might now."

She began shaking her head violently.

"If you still don't want to go that route, then you've
got me. Talk to me. Tell me what's hurt. What your
greatest fears are. The things hiding deep within your
soul. What you can't share with anyone else because
they simply wouldn't understand in a million years.
But I do. I'm here for you. To listen. Not to get physical.
If you really want my help, Sloane, then a line in the
sand has to be drawn—and we both have to abide
by it."

Tears glistened in her eyes. "I get what you're
saying."

"I'm the monkey who threw the wrench into things when I took the initiative and kissed you first. Yes, I am attracted to you. More than I have been to any other woman. But I know we can't start a relationship when you're hurting the way you are. We've got to table sex."

A single tear cascaded down her cheek. "For good?"

"Maybe. Maybe not. I'm not sure. I only know if we come to a point where you're as close to being back to yourself as you can be, and we still want to pursue a relationship, then that's when we'll do it. I like you and respect you too much for it merely to be sex between us, Sloane. If we go that way—invest in each other— then I'll be all in. Not for a night or two. Not for a week or a month."

She swallowed. "You mean... forever, don't you?"

Gage nodded slowly. "I'm thinking that. Hell, I've never had a relationship that lasted a month, much less forever." He touched her cheek with his fingers. "But you are something special, Anderson. Really special. I've always been a lone wolf. Ironically, the fact of the matter is, wolves actually mate for life. So when a lone wolf finally discovers his mate, it's forever."

He released her hand allowed his fingers to caress her cheek a moment longer. She closed her eyes, leaning into his touch. In that moment, Gage knew he had fallen in love with Sloane.

And would love her for all time.

His fingers fell away, and she gazed up at him.

"You have work to do. We won't rush anything. You need to be completely open with me. Hide nothing. Share everything. You'll know in your heart when you've regained your equilibrium. Only then should we consider giving things a go. Agree?"

He looked down at her, wanting her with a fierceness that transcended any emotions which had previously come. In this moment, Gage knew his life would always be divided into Before Sloane and After Sloane.

He only hoped the After would include Sloane in his life and not her leaving him to move on. That was a huge possibility, though. Instinctively, he figured her identity was wrapped up in her career as a journalist. Traveling and meeting others. Reporting on what she saw. Making sense of it to her audience back home. If she left reporting behind, she might not know who she was.

Or who she could be.

Or if she could be someone different. With him.

"I agree," she said softly, wiping away her tears. "I do trust you, Gage. I promise I will be honest with you. Open. No secrets. When I came to the Cove, I knew I had some soul-searching to do. I don't even know if I want to continue as a news correspondent, or even be a journalist in print or on local TV. I thought that was what I would decide when I arrived. Now, though, I understand that I can't make that decision until I've dealt with what happened to me. Seeing Ted murdered. Watching the terror of the girls, knowing some of them were abused. I need to work through what I witnessed and learn to push through it. I did survive. I need to be stronger. Become whole."

Sloane smiled ruefully. "I don't plan on having sex with anyone else to get through this. Even a hot ex-Navy SEAL. It would only be a Band-Aid on a bullet wound. I see that now. It might fill a quick need, but it would be like eating cotton candy—no substance. Nothing lasting."

She captured one of his hands with both of hers, bringing it to her lips and kissing it reverently. "I will become who I am meant to be. And when I do, I hope we can see if we have a future together or not."

Gage nodded. He brushed his lips against her cheek and then pulled Sloane to her feet.

"It's cold outside. You need to get some sleep, Anderson. Bakery hours are awfully early."

Gazing up at him, she smiled. "Thank you for being my friend, Nelson," as they both reverted back to a playful address. "I couldn't ask for a better one. Good night."

He watched her go inside Boo's house and retreated from the porch, returning to his truck. His body still ached, wanting to make love with this remarkable woman. He would do his best to invest in their friendship and her recovery.

And hope they might one day have a future to share.

~

SLOANE QUIETLY ENTERED Boo's house and heard laughter coming from the den. She moved toward it and found Willow and Dylan sitting on the couch, a bowl of popcorn in Dylan's lap.

He spotted her in the doorway and paused the program they were watching. "Hey, Sloane. Did you enjoy dinner with Jackson and Ainsley?"

"It was great finally meeting Ainsley in person. She is glowing."

"Ainsley has always been a nurturer," Willow said. "She'll make for a wonderful mom."

"I also was happy to see Jackson again. I haven't since we graduated from college and he took the three of us out to celebrate."

Willow shook her head. "That was such a long

time ago. I'd forgotten about that. I remember feeling so grown up. A degree in one hand and a flute of champagne in the other. Our lives ahead of us."

Dylan kissed his wife's brow. "And who knew you'd wind up back in the Cove with your high school boyfriend all these years later."

Willow's eyes shone with love. "I couldn't be happier."

A rush of envy filled Sloane, seeing how happy they were together, wanting that for herself.

"Ainsley asked me to come to her bakery tomorrow. She's going to teach me how to bake bread."

Willow turned from Dylan. "She's always said kneading bread helps her get out her frustrations. What time do you need to be there?"

"Three. When she gets there."

"Whoa! Even *we* don't get up that early," Dylan said. "Bear, why don't you give Sloane your key card? That way she can drive herself into town."

"Good idea. Be right back."

Willow returned and handed Sloane the card. "This is the extra. Just keep it. I work most days, so it can be at your disposal. If I happen to need transportation, I can always drop Dylan in town and use his."

"I hate to leave you stranded like that," she protested. "I should have thought about renting something when I landed."

"You had way too much on your mind," Willow chided gently. "Really, take my SUV whenever you want. No need to rent anything."

"Okay. For now," she told her friend, thinking it might be wise not only to rent a car but a small place to stay while she was here. She didn't want to impose on either Willow or Tenley. Both women had been married a short length of time, and they had shared how they were each ready to start a family. Sloane decided to talk it over with Gage and see if he knew of any place she could rent during her stay in the Cove.

"Thanks. Good night. See you tomorrow."

As she headed up the stairs, Shadow, who had been curled up in a chair, jumped from it and followed her. Sloane petted the dog's head as she entered her bedroom and Shadow jumped onto the bed. She sat next to him, running her fingers through his coat, wondering how long she would stay in Maple Cove.

Or if she might want to leave.

Her conversation with Gage had been enlightening. She was glad the attraction hadn't only been on her part, and that he, too, was drawn to her. While she understood why he didn't want them to have sex at this point, she didn't think it would be a substitute. Or that he would be a substitute.

No, the more she was around Gage Nelson, the more she wanted to remain in his orbit. The saying *still waters run deep* ran through her mind, and she thought it fit Gage to a T. He was quiet and thoughtful. She longed to hear more about his past, then decided she wouldn't bring it up, simply because she didn't want to talk about hers. At least not now. She had other pressing matters on her plate to deal with. Thatcher and Tish had brought enough pain and havoc into her life. Sloane had learned to push them on a far back burner.

Her recent trauma, though, was definitely something she needed to deal with. Once she did, she might have a better idea of what her purpose would be. If she were to stay in the Cove, she couldn't be a network correspondent. Just the thought of reporting from far-off places left a sour taste in her mouth.

Where once news had been like a lifeline to her, a part of her, suddenly it didn't seem so important. Discovering what was—and how she wanted to live the rest of her life—would be up to her.

Slone only hoped in some way, Gage Nelson would be a big part of it.

CHAPTER 12

Sloane's eyes flew open. Terror seized her, paralyzing her. She couldn't move. Couldn't breathe. Coherent thought was impossible. Her heart raced so fast, she believed she was having a heart attack. She tried to cry out for help, but her vocal cords froze. Her chest seemed in a vise, hurting more than she dreamed possible. Nausea flooded her.

She trembled so much the bed shook. Squeezing her eyes closed, she prayed for death to take her. She couldn't stand the pressure. The fear. The pain.

Yet somewhere deep within her, Sloane rebelled at the thought of truly letting go. She mentally pushed through the abyss threatening to drag her back down into nothingness. Fighting her fear, fighting the pain, she pictured herself as if trapped in deep water. She kicked furiously, pushing her legs and arms against the water.

And then she broke through to the surface.

Her eyes flew open. She was at Boo's. In Willow's old bedroom. Safe. She was safe. She reached for Shadow, who was warm against her leg, combing her fingers through the dog's fur.

Slowly, her heart quit galloping. She began to breathe again. The tension filling her body subsided, leaving her drenched in sweat. Sloane tried to sit up and felt weak when she did so. She forced herself to remain upright, though, pushing aside the covers and swinging her legs over the side of the bed. She concentrated on her breathing, as Gage had taught her when the first panic attack had hit her on their way home from the airport.

Finally, her breathing stabilized. Calm descended upon her. She could think again. The feeling of impending death had fled, causing her to feel silly at having thought she might die. But she had read up on panic attacks and knew this was what she suffered from. The articles she had scoured mentioned how significant personal loss, life transitions, and life changes could all trigger these attacks. Witnessing a close friend murdered and being kidnapped by international rebels whom you thought would also torture you to death certainly qualified, shooting her to the head of the line for those who suffered panic attacks.

Yet realistically, she knew her story had a happy ending. How many soldiers had she interviewed who had later died or been physically incapacitated by their war injuries? How many people had she spoken with over the years who had suffered loss through acts of God or drug lords? She had seen places demolished by a barrage of shells during war or a tsunami. Viewed mass graves of victims of genocide. Walked beside dying parents who had no work and no hope as they watched their starving children succumb to agony and death.

Yes, she was one of the lucky ones. Her suffering and terror had been short-lived. Her government's military had helped free her before any physical harm could come to her.

That didn't mean her fears weren't real, though. She acknowledged that she had been through a tough experience. The psychological horror might be with her for some time. But Sloane had choices, something most of the people she had reported on didn't have. She had money in the bank to live on for quite a while. A college education that would allow her to move into another professional job if she chose not to go back to field reporting.

She breathed in and out, clearing her mind, listening to her breath. After several minutes, she rose and saw her alarm was about to go off, and so she silenced it. Heading for the shower, she washed away the fear-induced sweat, dressing again in borrowed clothes from Ainsley Martin. Hopefully, she would receive her own clothing sometime today, as well as hear about picking up Ted's remains. She left Shadow still snoozing on the bed but kept the door open in case he wanted to leave the room.

Hoping that Ainsley would be able to give her a cup of coffee, Sloane tiptoed down the stairs, backpack slung over her shoulder. She brought it for her meeting afterward with Jackson, having forwarded the e-mail Elton Briggs sent her so that Jackson would have access to the various documents the lawyer had sent to her. She would pull up Briggs' e-mail, along with the docs, hoping Jackson could cut through the legalese and walk her through what she needed to do for Ted's estate.

She started Willow's car, adjusting the seat and mirrors before putting it into gear. The trip into the Cove at this time of the morning was quiet. She didn't pass a single car from Boo's until she reached the town square. Not wanting to take up parking directly in front of Buttercup Bakery, she parked across from it, facing a gazebo. This must be where Nash Edwards had played his impromptu concert that she had heard about. Sloane didn't listen to music often, but she was eager to download some of the country singer's tunes, especially now that he and Rylie were married and Rylie had become not only a muse for Nash, but his occasional songwriting partner.

The lights in the bakery were on, but Sloane found the door locked. She knocked on the glass and moments later, Ainsley appeared. Most women looked bloated when pregnant, but Ainsley Martin was blooming with good health.

Unlocking the door, Ainsley said, "Come on in. It's chilly this morning." She relocked the door. "I'm always aware how I'm here alone at this time and take precautions. I have given my employees keys, though, so if I'm in the middle of something and can't stop, they can let themselves in. Gus will be here soon. Would you like some coffee?"

"Definitely. Black is fine," Sloane said.

Ainsley went to the coffeemaker and poured Sloan some, attaching a lid to the tall Styrofoam cup and handing it over.

"Here you go. I've already had my half-caf, half-decaf cup. The doctor said as long as I kept it to the one a day, I'd be good."

"Has it been an easy or hard pregnancy?" Sloane took a sip of her coffee as she followed Ainsley to the back of the store.

"I think average," Ainsley said, slipping into an apron and tying it, then bringing one to Sloane, who put it on. "I was fairly sick in the early months, but once I hit the second tri? Smooth sailing and I was full of energy. Jackson and I took a delayed honeymoon back in October. We went to Paris, where I had trained as a pastry chef. It was a blast showing him the city."

While she spoke, Ainsley was getting out equipment and ingredients, her movements precise and organized. Sloane asked a few questions, including what typical items Ainsley made in a day and how many customers they served off-season versus when tourists hit the Oregon coast. Ainsley also told her about her employees, mentioning how much she relied on Gus.

"He had trouble finding a job since he had been incarcerated for several years. But Gus is a moral man, dependable and hardworking. I'm able to turn over quite a few things to him. I'm also teaching Gloria and Sheila how to bake certain items. Sheila really picks up things quickly."

"I'll be quiet now," Sloane promised. "I simply wanted to watch you at work."

Gus arrived a few minutes later. Ainsley introduced them. Sloane wondered why Gus had been in prison. He seemed a bit gruff but gave her a friendly smile, telling her how much he enjoyed her stories on TV.

She thanked him and said, "I hope you don't mind if I watch you and Ainsley at work."

"Nope," he said. "Watch away."

She did, thinking he had a magic way with his hands and dough.

Watching Ainsley and Gus at work proved to be interesting. Once the first donuts came out of the fryer, Sloane was able to sample one.

"Light as air," she proclaimed.

She also met the two women who worked the counter during the morning rush. Ainsley had explained once it was over, Gloria and Sheila alternated days. One would remain in front to wait on customers, while the other would come to the back and bake.

Around five-thirty, the door chimed and a nonstop crowd came and went. Sloane was glad she was sitting in the back and didn't have to see the number of people circulating through. Crowds—especially strangers—still gave her pause. It would be something to talk over with Gage. She had avoided thinking about him this morning and told herself to keep doing so.

Around nine, things slowed down. Ainsley told Sloane to watch as she dumped what she termed active dry yeast into a bowl with warm water, telling her this would wake up the yeast and get it ready for them to use to bake bread. Gus took a break. Ainsley did, as well, sitting with Sloane as she ate a cake donut and drank a small carton of milk.

They discussed the various items Ainsley had made that morning, which had included the usual morning goodies, from donuts to cinnamon buns to muffins.

"I like how you had more than the typical blueberry muffins," Sloane pointed out.

"They are popular, so I always have those on hand, but I do different specialty muffins each morning. Today's was quinoa-banana, which also had honey and cinnamon in them."

"I noticed you started on non-breakfast items around seven-thirty."

"I do. By then, Gus has taken over a good portion of the morning crowd's goodies, so I begin other things. The tiny tarts and cookie sandwiches. Cannolis and macarons. After I teach you about bread, I'll also bake cupcakes and two birthday cakes today."

Sloane laughed. "I'm all about cupcakes. Small

and tasty. I can easily buy half a dozen and eat them in two days."

"What's your favorite? I'll make some for you today."

"You don't have to do that."

Ainsley frowned. "I want to, Sloane. I know Carter baked some fabulous meals for you. I'll send you home with some desserts. I remember you're meeting with Jackson after you leave here. While you're kneading, I'll put some different cupcakes on to bake. For the bakery as well as you. Then when your meeting is over, just stop by and I'll give you a variety box. Believe me, you won't be allowed to eat every one of them. Dylan is cupcake crazy. He'll sniff them out the moment he walks in the door tonight. So, what kinds do you like?"

"The basics. Vanilla and chocolate. Anything beyond that would be a bonus."

"Okay. Let me consult today's list." Ainsley reached for a clipboard and lifted a page, skimming it. "I was doing carrot cake, red velvet, caramel, and hazelnut today. That's on top of vanilla, strawberry, and chocolate."

"My mouth is watering just hearing those flavors," Sloane said. "One of each—and then I'll fight Dylan. Maybe I'll save time and simply cut them all in two."

"Good plan. Break's over," Ainsley announced, as she downed the last of her milk. "Ready to learn about bread?"

By now, Gus had returned to his work table. He had been working on various breads, in addition to other items, so Sloane hoped she had picked up a few tips from watching him earlier.

Ainsley explained the basic ingredients of bread

and then had Sloane lightly dust the wooden work surface.

"Just a quick, sideways flick of your wrist gives your work area a light coat. If you have a heavy hand with the flour, it can make your bread turn out dry."

Ainsley brought over the large bowl where the yeast had been percolating, adding sugar and letting it stand until bubbles popped up on the surface. Then she had Sloane whisk in flour, salt, and a bit of honey. Once blended, Ainsley poured in oil and had Sloane beat it until it was smooth.

"You can cover it with Saran wrap, but I usually just drape a clean towel over it. It will need to rest now. Come help me start some of the cupcakes."

They worked together on the cupcakes until half an hour passed and then returned to the bread.

"Here's where it gets a little tricky. As you knead the bread, you'll add in a bit of extra flour. If you knead in the remaining flour instead of attempting to mix it in at the beginning, it keeps the bread from becoming too dense. I'll guide you on how much to add and when."

Sloane took over, flouring her hands at Ainsley's suggestion, and then scooping the dough from the bowl and putting it on the wooden table. She sprinkled a touch of flour on top, per Ainsley's advice.

"Now, you'll knead." Ainsley joined her and side-by-side, they began working the dough. "Use the heels of your hands and press it away from you. Good. Like that. Then you turn it ninety degrees. Uh-huh. Fold it over—like this—and press down again with your heels. You'll keep doing this for about eight minutes. No more than ten. Don't push so hard that you tear the dough. Nice and gentle is the way to go. You want it soft and supple.

Just keep repeating the process. Add a little more flour if the dough feels wet or sticky, but it will also soak up the flour you sprinkled onto the table as you go."

She did and found the moves soothing. The dough became elastic and smooth, just as Ainsley had said it would.

"It needs time to rise now," Ainsley said, returning to the work space.

She had Sloane put a thin layer of flour into a bowl and work the dough into a ball. After placing it in the bowl, again she was told to sprinkle a bit of flour on top before covering it.

"Now, we wait. Thirty. Forty. Maybe even forty-five minutes," Ainsley explained. "Eyeballing it until it doubles in size."

"Why such a big time swing?" she asked.

"It can take longer in colder weather."

They returned to the cupcakes. By now, Sheila had joined them. Ainsley explained what cookies needed to be baked today, and Sheila began working on them. Sloane continued to help Ainsley with the cupcakes as the first rise finished.

Ainsley grinned. "This is the fun part, punching the dough."

"Punch? Like throwing a punch in a fight?"

"Exactly." Ainsley demonstrated. "If you have any pent-up anger, take it out on your bread."

Sloane punched the hell out of her loaf. A rage she hadn't known existed within her took over, and the bread received the brunt of that rage.

They placed the dough into a greased baking pan, forming it into a flat, loaf shape. Ainsley had them do a second rising, having Sloane check until the dough crept over the edge of the loaf pan.

"All that's left is baking and then cooling on wire racks. Voilà! You have made bread."

She beamed. "That was fantastic. I did find the kneading to be relaxing."

"You have good muscles in your forearms. That helped," Ainsley told her. "You must work out a lot."

"I practice something called Krav Maga. It's a mixture of several defense methods. Of course, when I was punching the bread, I had someone in mind."

Mwangi...

"I think your first loaf will turn out nicely. Why don't you go meet with Jackson now? I'll keep an eye on your loaf and remove and cool it. When you stop by for your cupcakes, you can also take your bread home."

Sloane hugged Ainsley. "Thank you. This was exactly what I needed. I made a new friend. I learned something easy and practical. And I know I could repeat this in Willow's kitchen. Kneading was incredibly relaxing. And punching was plain fun! I appreciate you taking the time to walk me through all of this, Ainsley."

"I'm happy to do so. I've heard so many stories about you from Willow and Tenley, and I always watch you on the evening news while I'm cooking dinner. It was nice to connect in person."

"I would like to spend time with you outside the bakery," she said. "I know you work long hours here and want to reserve time to be with Jackson, but I hope our friendship can grow."

Ainsley hugged her. "I know it will. See you soon."

Removing her apron, Sloane washed her hands and reclaimed her coat and backpack. She told Gus and Sheila and also Gloria goodbye as she left the bakery and walked the short distance to Jackson's law office.

Entering it, she saw a waiting room but no receptionist at the desk. She hesitated, wondering if she should call out and see if Jackson was busy or not.

Before she could, he appeared in the doorway. "Make yourself at home, Sloane. I'm finishing up in here. There's coffee. Soft drinks and waters in the fridge."

"Thank you."

She opened the refrigerator and removed a bottle of water, finding she was hot after spending so many hours near the ovens, which had been in constant use. Ainsley had to be incredibly organized to keep track of everything that needed to be baked and what was in which oven. Plus, it was the off-season. Sloane couldn't imagine how much busier the bakery might be when tourists invaded the Oregon coast.

Quickly downing the water, she placed the empty bottle in the bin marked for recycling. She checked her phone and saw she still had no message from Mr. Pinkerton, wondering if she should contact the funeral home director.

She glanced up and saw Jackson stepping from what must be his office.

And Gage was with him.

"Thanks for the good advice, Jackson," Gage said, offering his hand. "Shayla will be drawing up the papers. We'll close on the property on Monday." He looked up, spotting her. "Hey, Anderson. I can tell you've been baking."

Gage stepped toward her and brushed his thumb across her cheek, causing Sloane's heart to beat violently against her ribs.

"You had a little flour on your face," he explained.

"Ainsley always checks in the mirror before she heads for home," Jackson said. "I thought you might be here sooner."

"Bread takes a lot longer to bake than I imagined," she explained. "Oh! I forgot. I was supposed to bring you something to eat."

Jackson chuckled. "Don't worry. I get plenty of my wife's treats at home."

Gage cleared his throat. "I need to push off. Have a client to meet. Sloane, have you heard from Mr. Pinkerton yet?"

"No, I haven't," she said worriedly. "I'm going to call him if I haven't heard from him by the time Jackson and I finish."

"If you need a ride into Portland to pick up Ted's ashes, I'd be happy to give you one," he said, his gaze intense.

She had Willow's car. She could easily go by herself.

But Sloane didn't want to. She wanted Gage's company.

"I'll text you when I hear from him. I appreciate the ride."

Gage nodded. "Talk to you soon."

Jackson ushered her into his office, and Sloane said, "Let me pull up the e-mail so I can see what documents this attorney sent."

"No need to. I printed out hard copies for both of us." Jackson paused, studying her carefully. "Sloane, have you read over what Elton Briggs sent to you?"

"Nope. I thought I'd let you decipher everything and tell me in plain English what my obligations are, since I'm the executor of Ted's estate."

"You're more than that, Sloane," Jackson told her. "You are Ted's only heir."

"Ted left me money? Really?"

"After distributing the bequeathals mentioned in his will and paying the inheritance taxes, you'll have a hefty amount coming to you." Jackson paused. "I've calculated it at approximately a million and a half dollars."

CHAPTER 13

"What? Ted wasn't wealthy," Sloane declared. "He came from lower middle-class roots. Put himself through two years of community college and worked fulltime while he did so. Then he began working for a local TV station and worked his way up the ladder."

Jackson shrugged. "Your friend may have handled his finances well. All I can tell you is from what I've reviewed, you have a nice chunk of change coming your way, once you handle any debts of the estate. Elton Briggs couldn't find any, but we'll need to give it a bit of time to see if anyone steps forward. You will need to close out Ted's bank accounts. See to his furniture in his apartment and end the lease. That kind of thing."

He handed her a notebook. "I've made tabs for your various duties, and you'll find the related paperwork behind each one. Why don't you take some time to read over this, and we can meet again when you're familiar with everything?"

Overwhelmed, Sloane nodded. "That sounds like

good advice. I need to wrap my head around what you just told me."

"It's Friday." He flipped his desk calendar. "Would you like to come in Monday and discuss things?"

"Sure. Let me know what time."

"Ten that morning okay?"

Sloane nodded. "I'll be here." She stood. "Thanks, Jackson. I'm glad I'll have you to walk me through everything."

"Elton Briggs would have done the same. I did speak to him and let him know I'm representing you. He'll copy me on anything else he sends to you." He rose. "If you have any questions between now and Monday, just text me."

Jackson gave Sloane his cell number. In a daze, she returned to the bakery.

Sheila greeted her. "Hi, Sloane. I have your cupcakes and bread. Ainsley is tied up with a bride right now. They're working on the design for her wedding cake."

She accepted the bakery box and wrapped loaf of bread and returned to Willow's SUV, sitting in thought for several minutes.

How did Ted get so much money?

Then she realized he had probably followed the same plan Gage had. Ted's apartment was miniscule, about four hundred square feet. Thanks to the short length of his marriage, the judge in his divorce settlement had ruled Ted would only pay alimony for a year, which had been almost three decades ago. He had spent a majority of his time on the road, joking about banking the bulk of his salary and using his per diems wisely. If Ted had invested as Gage had, it made sense he would have as much as he did after working his entire adult life. She was only sorry he hadn't lived to enjoy retirement, which he had recently begun talking about.

Opening the notebook Jackson had given her, she skimmed through the contents, knowing she would read carefully through it later. Ted had asked for money to be awarded to some of the charities near and dear to him. The SPCA. Greenpeace. The San Francisco Ronald McDonald House. Even after dispersing those funds, however, Jackson had been right.

Sloane would pocket a huge amount of money.

She hated that it had come at the expense of her friend's death and was sad to read in the paperwork that Ted had no living relatives. He had mentioned once that his parents had been killed in a car accident not long after he graduated from community college. Sloane knew he had been an only child. He had been her friend—but treated her as a daughter. She had always looked upon him as the father she wished she had.

It would take time for her to decide what to do with the money she had inherited, and she would make it part of the journey she was now on as she learned more about herself.

Her phone rang. She saw it was the funeral home and answered it. Mr. Pinkerton informed her that she could claim Ted's ashes. She asked what their hours were today and tomorrow, deciding she did want to have Gage go with her into Portland to pick up the urn.

Texting Gage, she asked if he had time this afternoon or tomorrow to help her with this errand.

Today is better. Have one more client & could pick you up at 3. Good for you?

She told him yes, and they arranged for him to come to Boo's. Sloane drove there and entered the house. Shadow came bounding down the stairs, and she bent to love on him.

"You're a good boy," she told the dog. "I may have to think about getting a pet myself."

If she did get a dog, it would mean she couldn't go back on the road as she had. It would be unfair to an animal to board it for weeks at a time. Suddenly, the idea of staying home and playing with her dog after she got home from work sounded far more appealing than traipsing around the world in the heat, rain, and cold, dealing with crooked politicians and drug lords.

Sloane wanted a home. A place to call her own. Where she slept in her own bed each night and her refrigerator could be stocked with fresh fruit and vegetables. Where she could have decorative pillows and curl up with a throw and binge the latest Netflix series everyone was talking about.

More importantly, she wanted to share that home —and her life—with a partner. One who was kind and passionate and interesting and fun.

She wanted with all her heart for it to be Gage Nelson.

But Gage was off-limits. At least for now. She understood why he had thrown up the barrier between them. If she was going to put in the work needed to save her sanity, they couldn't be involved intimately. After she had healed, though?

She remembered he had said they could give things a try between them. That he would be all in.

Forever...

How could he think that? Or even believe that?

But she understood that, too. They had already forged a powerful connection. She wanted to spend all her time with him, which was ridiculous. He had a business to run. On top of that, he had just purchased the land to build his fitness center. Gage would be crazy busy in the next several months, seeing to that, as well as staying on top of his business.

Sloane smiled to herself.

She had an idea where some of Ted's money might go to.

~

GAGE ACTUALLY CANCELED his final client of the day once he heard from Sloane. He did not want her going by herself to collect her cameraman's ashes. She was a tough woman, both physically and mentally, but she was emotionally fragile now. The more support he could give to her, especially with anything regarding Ted Castro, the better.

He turned into Boo's drive and went the length of it. Before he could get out, Sloane opened the door and hurried down the porch steps and to his truck.

She climbed into the pickup. "Hey, Nelson. Thanks for the ride into Portland."

"Not a problem, Anderson."

They didn't speak until they had passed through and then left the Cove, on the highway that would take them into Portland.

"Ted wanted his ashes scattered over the water. I don't know if I'd told you that. Willow told me Boo had wanted the same. She offered to talk to Walt, the guy who has a boat and took her and Jackson out after Boo's death."

"Yeah, Walt Willingham was the former sheriff in the Cove. He handpicked Dylan to run in his stead."

"That's why his name sounded familiar," Sloane said. "Anyway, Walt agreed to ferry me out tomorrow so I can scatter Ted's ashes. I had thought about sunrise at first and then decided to go with sunset instead." She hesitated. "Do you think you could make it? Walt said we would leave his dock around five. Sunset is a few minutes past five-thirty this time of year."

Gage would have to cut his last class short by a few minutes, but he wanted to be there for Sloane at such an important time.

"Sure. I can make it. I'll have to meet you at Walt's, though. Anyone else coming?"

"I talked to Tenley. She and Carter will come. So will Willow and Dylan. The girls have met Ted before. I'm glad they'll be there."

"Are you planning any kind of memorial service for him?"

He listened as Sloane told him her reasons against doing so, and he agreed that it would be fine if she said a few words tomorrow before she emptied the urn into the Pacific.

"Just speak from your heart," he advised. "I wouldn't prepare anything in advance. I think Ted will be there with you—in spirit—and he'll guide you on what you need to say."

They drove in silence a few minutes before she said, "I had a second panic attack."

He glanced at her and then back at the road. "When?"

"As I woke up this morning. It was way worse than the previous one."

"Tell me about it," he urged.

"I think I must have been dreaming. About Mwangi and being at his camp." She hesitated. "For a few minutes, I thought I might die. I was literally paralyzed by fear. I felt Shadow against my side, but I couldn't move a hand to pet him. My heart raced so fast, I thought my chest would explode. It was as if something sat on my chest, keeping me from breathing, pinning me down. For a moment, I really wanted to die. I thought all the pain and terror would be over.

"Even though my thoughts were jumbled, I remembered what you had me do. I started concentrating on my breathing, blocking everything else out. The in and out. Deep, calming breaths. Holding it. Exhaling slowly and evenly. Eventually, I calmed down and realized I wasn't paralyzed. But it was the most frightening thing I've been through." Sloane chuckled. "And I've been in two hurricanes, in the midst of several civil wars, and a tsunami."

"Your memories of what happened the day of the kidnapping are clear?"

"Crystal clear. I have a terrific memory to begin with, but the events of that day are ingrained in me."

"You've probably dreamed of it before. Your subconscious can be pretty active when you're asleep."

"You know what helped?" she asked. "Making bread with Ainsley. I had to knead the dough for several minutes. Elongated it. Fold it. Turn it. I found all those motions very relaxing. A calm descended over me."

"Physically activity can help with PTSD and panic attacks."

She snickered. "And after kneading? I got to pound. I'm talking about punching the hell out of that dough. I pictured Mwangi's face. It was exhilarating."

"I'm glad you discovered an outlet for your anger."

"Gage, I didn't even know I was angry until I took it out on that poor dough. Scared? Yes. Anxious? That, too. But I didn't know rage had built within me."

He removed a hand from the wheel and covered hers. "That's natural, Sloane. You were in a situation you couldn't control. Others were in danger, as well as yourself. You felt helpless. That had to make you angry, knowing a rebel lord had all the power and he was using it for evil."

"He ordered the school I'd been reporting from burned to the ground," she said, her voice quiet. She placed her free hand atop his. "I was unconscious, but he allowed several of his men to rape the school's teacher in front of the students. Salana Owusa and I had grown close. When I came to, a few of the girls told me about it. They were so frightened. They didn't know if Salana was alive or dead."

"And that was on top of seeing your close friend killed in front of you. No wonder you have unresolved anger still inside you." Gage glanced to her. "Did your friend survive?"

Sloane nodded. "She was still unconscious when I left Africa. I gave a nurse my cell number and asked her to call when Salana awoke. I haven't heard from her yet."

"I'm sorry, Anderson. That's rough. As much as your friends in the Cove love you, they won't ever understand the rage and hurt and pain inside you."

"But you do."

"I do," he agreed.

"Can you tell me why you get me? What happened to me?" She paused. "If you'd rather not talk about it, I understand."

"No, I think you should know. I've never talked about that day after my debriefing. No one in the Cove knows much about my career. I've only talked in generalities."

As he drove, Gage told her about that final mission. Who went on it. He described each of his friends. The purpose of being where they were. The man they were to bring back for questioning. The threat he posed to their nation.

And how it turned into a giant shit show.

"I got out," he concluded. "I was the only one who did. I relived it in nightmares again and again, waking up drenched in sweat, screaming. I had survivor's guilt and wished I would've been killed along with my buddies. My chosen family. I showed up at the stupid counseling sessions but wouldn't talk to the therapist about anything that happened once we touched the ground. I couldn't. My throat would freeze up. My body would grow cold. My tongue so thick I couldn't speak."

Gage sighed. "I have the scars from the bullets that day. They remind me of who I lost. Your scars are on the inside, as I've told you, but they're just as real."

"How long did it take for you to get over it?"

He pondered her question. "I don't think I'll ever truly be over it. Have the nightmares subsided? Yes. They only come now and again. I do yoga and meditate to keep my mind clear. Every day, I look at my scars. Touch them. They'll always be a part of me, the same as the friends and brothers I lost that day. But time does help in the healing. The more distance, the less my pain. I can actually think of Sawyer or Jessop and the rest of the guys with me that day with fondness now. Sure, there's a little hurt thrown into the mix, but I recall more of our good times now than that one, awful, miserable day."

Gage squeezed her hand and then brought his back to the wheel. "You'll get there. You already are. Talking to me about it will help. Scattering Ted's ashes will, too. Don't rush things, Anderson."

"Even if I want to?"

He saw in her eyes exactly what she meant. That

when she had gotten over the worst of things, she was ready to see if they had a future together.

"Even if you want to," he said with determination.

They arrived at the mortuary, and Mr. Pinkerton met them.

"I have Mr. Castro ready for you," the mortician said solemnly, leading them to a room with dim lighting. Soft music played in the background.

He collected a small metal urn of blue, decorated with silver filigree at its base and head. Handing it to Sloane, he said, "I am terribly sorry for your loss, Miss Anderson."

"Thank you, Mr. Pinkerton," she said softly. "Ted would have liked this urn. Blue was his favorite color."

"I'm glad you are pleased. I know this can be a touchy subject, but I do have a bill to present to you."

"I'm Mr. Castro's executor. I'll handle payment as soon as I sign off on the paperwork with Ted's lawyer. That should be sometime on Monday. Thank you for taking care of my friend."

Gage walked Sloane back to his truck and helped her inside. She cradled the urn in her lap.

"I thought it would be larger," she mused. "Not that I've ever dealt with cremated remains before."

"I think some urns can be large," he said. "Ones meant to be displayed on a mantel, for instance."

"This is very pretty." She fingered the filagree. "I don't want to dump it in the ocean. Do you think Ted would mind if I kept it as a reminder of him?"

"Once you have a desk—and a permanent home— that would be a great idea."

"Speaking of that," she said. "I want to talk to you about something. I didn't know it, but I was Ted's beneficiary. He did have some requests to donate funds to a few charities he supported, but he left me a decent amount of money since he had no family."

"I'm sure he considered you family."

She blinked away the tears that began to form. "We did think of each other that way. We spent all that time on the road together. Christmases. Birthdays. Through hell and high water. But more than anything, Ted loved children. They were drawn to him. He had a way about him that just sucked them in."

Sloane cleared her throat. "I have a suggestion. Take it or leave it. I won't get my feelings hurt if you say no."

Gage eyed her from the corner of his eye. "Say no to what?"

"I'd like you to go ahead and build that pool as a part of your fitness center. And name it after Ted. You didn't want to go into debt on the project. Now, you don't have to. You can build the pool and make it a part of your facility. I know you didn't know Ted, but you would have loved him, Gage, I know you would have. Ted loved the water. Being in it. On it. Around it. I'll donate the money you need to add the indoor pool, so that you won't have to take out a loan. Just put Ted's name on the natatorium in return."

He blew out a long breath. "That's a lot of money. Are you sure you want to hand it over to me? It's not as if you're investing in the center. You wouldn't see any kind of return."

"But the residents of the Cove and others who use your facilities would see Ted's name every time they came. To take swimming and diving lessons. To swim laps. Do water aerobics. Ted would live on that way. He would have been thrilled to be associated with something like this."

Gage didn't hesitate. "I would be honored to have

Ted Castro's name on the natatorium. Deeply honored. We can even have a bust commissioned of him and have a plaque that accompanies it so everyone who comes to the center will know exactly who Ted was."

He pulled onto the shoulder of the road, cutting the engine and turning on his flashers.

"This will really make my center be everything I dreamed it could be. Thank you, Sloane."

Moved by her generosity, Gage wanted to show his appreciation and embrace her. Instead, his palm cupped her nape, pulling her close for a kiss.

CHAPTER 14

G age poured everything he felt for this woman into the kiss. All the pent-up emotions he had tried to hold back flooded him, and the kiss took on a life of its own. Need for Sloane rushed through him, both physical and emotional.

She responded in kind, clinging to him, devouring him as much as he did her, a desperation taking over, filling them both, like a car zooming at ninety miles an hour, the brakes gone, the thrill of the speed and rush overtaking everything.

He didn't know how long they kissed, only that when he broke it, they both panted, out of breath, their foreheads leaning against each other's, bracing them.

"Gage?" Sloane asked, lifting her brow, her green eyes intense.

He cradled her cheek. "I'm sorry. I thought I could keep my distance from you. My team used to talk about how composed I was, how no situation ruffled me. How I was clear-eyed and thought fast on my feet and was indifferent to danger."

Gage's thumb stroked her cheek. "That all flew out

the window the minute you came into my life. I can't think of anything but you, Sloane. I know I said we shouldn't become involved. I still think it might be a mistake at this point." He hesitated. "But I'm willing to try—if you are."

In reply, she jerked on his shirt, pulling his mouth to hers, for an endless, blissful kiss.

When she broke the kiss, her eyes danced with mischief. "Is that answer enough?"

"Plenty." He kissed her again, swift, hard, wanting to possess her. A feeling he had never held with any woman.

"I'm not whole yet," she admitted. "I think when the pieces are put back together, they'll fit differently than before. But whomever I become, I want to become her with you in my life. Not just as my friend or confidant. But my lover. I need you in so many ways, Gage."

He smoothed her raven hair. "I'll help in any way I can. Listen to you. Advise you. But it may not be enough, especially with our relationship changing and becoming more personal in nature. You might need to find someone else to talk to."

"We'll cross that bridge if we need to," she told him. "For now, I need *you*. I've had a hole inside for a long time, Gage. Maybe forever. I'll tell you now that I've never felt loved. My parents, Thatcher and Tish, are both narcissists and can't stand me. They are the biggest snobs on the planet. Everything I did embarrassed them, especially playing sports and having the audacity to have a career and be seen on television."

"That embarrassed them?" he asked, looking puzzled.

"I should have found a rich husband in college and dedicated my time to the Junior League and spent vacations in Paris and summered in the Hamptons. They view TV as pedestrian, and a woman working—especially in journalism—as an affront to their position in society. My sister is ten years my senior and got out as soon as she could. She lives on a goat farm in Canada, like some modern-day hippie. I haven't spoken to or heard from her in over twenty years."

Sloane took a deep breath and expelled it. "Willow and Tenley were the first close friends I had. They became my sisters. My chosen family. I've been involved with a handful of men over the years, but it's my job I've been married to ever since I became an adult. I'm good at it—but it's not enough. I want more in life. Out of life.

"I... want you."

She buried her face against his chest, and Gage wrapped his arms around her, kissing her hair.

"I want you, too, Sloane. I'm laying all my cards on the table. I told you before that I wanted to be all in when the time was right. Well, there may never be a right time. I can't put it off. I don't want to put it off. I want to be with you in every way possible."

She raised her tear-stained face. "Tonight. Promise me we'll be together tonight."

He kissed her tenderly. "Yes. I want it as much as you do. We'll go from there."

He reached into the console and handed her a napkin to dry her tears. "Best I can offer."

She dabbed at her eyes. "I usually use my shirt in the field. Tissues are a luxury. I've had too many things make me cry as I did my job. I'm ready for less angst and more joy in my life." She smiled. "And sex with a hot ex-SEAL. Lots and lots of sex."

Gage laughed. "I will do my best to keep up with you, Anderson." He glanced into the rearview mirror.

"Oh, boy. We've got company. It's Nash and Rylie. Give me your phone and follow my lead."

She handed him her cell, which he promptly shoved under her seat, then rolled down his window as he watched Nash and Rylie approach.

"Hey, Gage, everything okay?" his friend asked. "We recognized your truck and saw the flashing lights. Thought you might've had car trouble."

"Hey, guys," he said. "This is Sloane Anderson. Sloane, Nash and Rylie Edwards."

"Hi. It's so nice to meet you in person," Sloane said easily. "I heard you've been on a buying trip for Antiques and Mystiques."

Rylie smiled and leaned in. "Ainsley told me you'd made it to the Cove. She said you baked bread together."

"Kneading bread is relaxing," Sloane said. "Ainsley may find me haunting her bakery and begging to do more. In fact, I may ask to hire on as part-time help," she joked.

Rylie walked around to the passenger side, and Gage lowered Sloane's window. Rylie leaned in and hugged Sloane.

"I know you've been through a terrible time." Rylie indicated the urn still in Sloane's lap. "Is this your friend?"

"Yes. Ted. Ted Castro. We worked together for many years. He was like a father and best friend all rolled into one," Sloane shared. "Gage took me into Portland to retrieve his ashes. We're going to scatter them tomorrow at sunset. Ted loved the water, and that's where he'll always be."

"I know we've only talked over the phone, but I feel like I know you," Rylie shared. "Would you like to have breakfast with me tomorrow? I'm sure Nash will be up before the crack of dawn, running with his friends. Maybe that could give us some time to visit."

"I'd like that," Sloane said, taking Rylie hand and squeezing it. "Thank you."

"Back to where we started," Nash said. "Is your truck giving you trouble?"

"Nope. We stopped because Sloane dropped her phone and she was expecting a call. I pulled off so we could look for it. She didn't want to spill any of Ted's ashes."

"Here, let me look," Rylie said helpfully, opening Sloane's door and feeling under her seat. "Here it is. Got it!" She handed the phone to Sloane.

"Thank you, Rylie," Sloane said. "I couldn't reach it while balancing the urn."

"Not a problem. Hey, do you do yoga? I'm usually in the water mornings, except during winter, when I focus on yoga."

"I don't, but I've wanted to learn."

Rylie grinned. "Well, I love it and was going to get in a session before breakfast tomorrow. Why don't you come over and I'll teach you a few poses, then we can gab and eat?"

"I would love that," Sloane said. "I'll stop at the bakery before I come over and pick up something for us to munch on."

The women arranged a time and Nash asked, "Running tomorrow?"

"Meet you at the gazebo," Gage promised.

Rylie and Nash retreated to their car, and Gage started his engine.

"I guess I looked like a raccoon," Sloane said. "I always do when I've been crying."

"But we'd just picked up Ted's ashes, so you had a reason to be crying," he pointed out, turning his blinker on and then easing behind the trailer Nash pulled. "I don't think they thought a thing about it."

"Rylie and Ainsley favor one another. Same eye color. Some of the same gestures," she said. "I really believe I'm going to grow close to both of them. I love Tenley and Willow to pieces, but it will be nice to make new friends while I'm in the Cove."

Her words put a damper on Gage's feelings. He was ready to explore not only her body but a future with her. Yes, Sloane was here now.

But how long would she remain?

SLOANE ATE DINNER WITH WILLOW, one of the meals Carter Clark had prepared and brought over. Dylan had gone to testify in a case and had made plans to have dinner with the prosecuting attorney, so it was just the two of them and Shadow, who wasn't allowed table scraps, but sat nearby in case anything might spill.

"I can't believe how talented Carter is," Sloane said. "Ever since he began vlogging, I've watched him and learned a lot. I've never been a cook, but he makes me want to try."

"Maybe you'll have time to try it while you're here in the Cove," Willow suggested.

"Well, I know I could bake you a loaf of bread. Ainsley was a great teacher."

"We should do a baking party soon," her friend suggested. "It could be all kinds of breads. Or cookies. Just something we could do to hang out together and have fun. Maybe on Sunday?"

"I would love that," she said enthusiastically. "I

haven't gotten to really see Tenley much. And I just met Rylie today."

"She's back? Where did you see her?"

Sloane stuck with the fictitious story of losing her phone and Gage pulling over so she could find it, explaining how Rylie and Nash saw them and stopped to see if they could help.

"Rylie asked me to come practice yoga with her tomorrow and have breakfast."

"You'll like Rylie as much as you do Ainsley," Willow predicted. "She's bright and friendly."

"I told Gage that I believe I will become good friends with both Ainsley and Rylie. Thank you for sharing them with me."

Willow studied her a moment. "You're becoming close with Gage. I think that's a good thing."

Deciding to come clean, she said, "When dinner is over, I'm seeing Gage tonight."

She let the statement hang in the air a moment. Willow immediately picked up on what that meant and nodded sagely.

"I think you and Gage have a lot in common. You both are smart. Talented. Loyal. And loners."

"We've talked about that," Sloane admitted. "We are independent and keep to ourselves. But when I'm with him, Willow, I feel like sharing everything. Nothing seems to be off-limits. I've never found a man I could talk with so easily. From everything you and Tenley have said, Gage is fairly quiet, but he and I... we just click."

Willow placed a hand over Sloane's. "That's a good thing. Be careful, though. You both have a lot of baggage from your past. Don't let it clutter your present— or future."

"I think I may stay in the Cove, Willow," Sloane

said, surprising herself as she spoke the words that had been in her heart. "It's a decision I don't want to make in haste. But I have an affinity for this place." She smiled at her friend. "Knowing you and Tenley have roots here is a part of it. I just need to figure out what I could bring to this place. I want that sense of community."

"You'll figure it out, and you've got plenty of time to do so," Willow encouraged. "No rush. You said your boss is being supportive. With work not breathing down your neck, you've got time and space to really figure out what you want out of life." She paused. "I have something to share with you. I'm pregnant."

"Oh, Willow, that's fantastic!" Sloane exclaimed. "When are you due?"

"Late September. It's very early. I'm going to tell the others on Sunday when we get together, but I want to keep it within our circle. But that's what important to me now, Sloane. Being in the Cove. Starting a family with Dylan. Finding fulfillment through my painting and being a part of this community. I want the same for you."

"I hope to find everything I'm looking for soon," she said. "I really hope Gage will be a part of my future."

"Let me clean up the dishes. Your clothes arrived today. I just now remembered. The boxes are waiting in your room. You can wear something of your own to see Gage tonight." Willow paused, grinning. "And if you don't come home, I won't mention it to Dylan."

She felt the hot blush stain her cheeks. "Yes, let's keep things between us for now. Okay, I think I'll freshen up."

Going upstairs, Sloane opened both boxes, finding her one nice set of bra and panties, both black and

fairly new. She took a quick shower and then slipped
into them. Most everything else was wrinkled, though,
so she put on one of Ainsley's sweaters, a deep purple,
and paired it with her own tight-fitting jeans. She
brushed her hair and then applied lipstick, thinking
she might want to pick up a few more colors for
variety.

When she came downstairs, she gave Willow
a hug.

"You look fantastic," her friend praised. "Enjoy
tonight."

When she reached Willow's SUV, Sloane realized
she had no idea where Gage lived. Instead of texting
him, she called.

"Hi," he said, his deep, rumbling voice sending
chills through her.

"I thought I better find out your address. Forgot
about that little detail until I got behind the wheel just
now."

"I'll talk you here. Back out of Boo's driveway, and
head toward town."

She followed his directions, which had nothing to
do with the names of streets. Instead, he gave her the
landmarks to turn at until she pulled into the driveway of the large white Colonial.

"Keep coming down the drive," Gage said.

She did as instructed, seeing a detached garage
and a tall, sexy, ex-Navy SEAL leaning against a
handrail. He strode toward her, ending the connection
and sliding his phone into his pocket.

Before she could even unfasten her seatbelt, he
opened her door and unbuckled the belt, pulling her
from the driver's seat and into his arms for a searing
kiss. Sloane's knees went weak and she wrapped her
arms around him for support.

Gage kissed her thoroughly before breaking the kiss.

"Should I move the car in case your landlord needs to get out?" she asked.

"Liz left today to go to Seattle to see her daughter. She won't be home until next weekend." His eyes lit with desire. "Which means we can be as loud as we want."

With that, Gage scooped her into his arms and carried her up the stairs to his apartment.

Sloane's knee... ...

CHAPTER 15

Sloane's heart beat rapidly as she got a whiff of Gage's cologne, a subtle sandalwood. She had linked her fingers behind his nape but now placed her palm against his face, smooth to the touch.

"You shaved," she said.

He opened the door and stepped inside, kicking it closed with his foot, before striding across the room and placing her on her feet.

"You smell divine," he said, his arms pulling her close as he nuzzled her neck. "Always smelling like fresh lemons."

She chuckled. "You can thank Willow for that. I don't use any scent when I'm out on the road, but I've always loved how bright and captivating citrus is. Willow remembered and stocked soap and lotion for me."

"Willow is a genius," he said, nipping at her throat, causing a rush of desire to run through her.

Gage suddenly stopped, his gaze meeting hers. "I want to gobble you up," he admitted, his voice husky. "But I'm going to take it slow. I want to explore every inch of your perfect, compact body."

"Compact?" she asked.

"Your Krav Maga practice has toned your muscles in all the right places. You're a tight, compact package, but you've still got some womanly curves that need investigating." His slow grin turned wicked. "I'm talking a *thorough* investigation."

She placed a hand against his heart, noticing it beat quickly, as hers did. "What's good for the goose is good for the gander. I believe I'll be doing a little probing and researching myself." Sloane's fingers spread wide, feeling his pecs. "Maybe a lot of research."

Gage's growl sounded low in his throat as he encompassed her, his muscular arms binding her to him, his mouth hot on hers, his tongue delving deeply into her mouth, searching, teasing, tempting. They kissed until her limbs grew lethargic, her blood molten, their bodies entwined with no space in between.

He broke the kiss. "I'm on fire. I need to get out of these clothes. I need my skin against yours. My mouth on your body."

His words fanned the flames rising within her. "Let's do this."

She started to remove her sweater, but he caught her hands. "No, that's my job. Part of my pleasure is seeing these removed."

She kissed him. "I'll keep out of your way. Have at me, Nelson."

"With pleasure, Anderson."

He took the hem of the sweater she wore and lifted it. Sloane brought her arms up straight beside her ears to help him. But Gage only raised it a bit, revealing her belly. He pressed hot kisses to it, causing her to shudder with desire. He turned her slightly, kissing his way from her front to her side to the small of her back. She trembled like never before.

His hands went up and found hers, his fingers entwining with hers, bringing them back to her sides. He kissed her nape, his erection now pressing against her, his hands releasing hers, moving under her sweater, pinning her to him. He cupped her breasts, his large hands kneading them as she had kneaded the dough on the work table. Sloane grew hot at his touch, beginning to moan.

Gage's fingers returned to the sweater's hem, and this time he lifted it up and over her head, tossing it aside before they returned to her. One hand held her back against his chest, while the other slipped beneath her bra, teasing her nipple.

"Take it off," she commanded hoarsely. "I need skin against skin."

He eased her away and unfastened the bra, sliding it from her. It fell to the ground and she leaned against him as he cupped both breasts now, massaging them, his lips against her throat, trailing to her shoulder. Sloane's heart banged against her ribs. Her breath caught as Gage lightly bit her shoulder, soothing it with his tongue.

"You are beautiful," he murmured, his arm going about her waist, holding her to him as his hand went lower, stroking her between her legs.

She gasped.

"You like that?" he murmured into her ear, nibbling her lobe, causing desire to sizzle through her.

Sloane merely nodded because she was incapable of words.

His hands went to the button on her jeans, undoing it, then sliding down the zipper. His fingers slid inside and tugged, then a deep chuckle sounded.

"These are tight, Anderson. Really tight."

She spun in his arms, linking her fingers behind his neck and kissing him hard. "You've had tougher missions than getting off a pair of jeans, Nelson. I think you're up to the task. All that SEAL training, you know. I'm sure it prepared you for just about everything."

His gaze pinned hers. "Nothing could have prepared me for you," he said, his voice raw.

His lips found hers, his kisses drugging, even as she felt him work her jeans over her hips. He broke the kiss to bring them to her ankles and bent, pulling off her shoes and helping her step from the jeans.

Glancing up at her, his gaze was scorching. It left her eyes and slid down the length of her body.

"Black. You look good in black, Anderson. But I'll bet you look better out of it. Let's find out for sure."

He remained kneeling, his fingers slipping into the lacy black panties she wore, and they glided down her legs. He lifted her foot and slipped them off, then did the same for the other foot. His tongue raked her belly, climbing higher as he rose, until it met her mouth. Another searing kiss occurred. Sloane now reverberated with heat and energy and desire.

"You're not ready to play," she said. "You have everything still on."

"I'll bet you have a solution."

She tore his shirt open, buttons flying through the air. Parting it fully, her lips brushed his muscular chest, as did her hands. She felt the muscles quiver as she kissed her way across it, her hands kneading him as they had the bread she'd worked. Her mouth found his nipple, and she let her tongue tease it.

Gage let out an expletive and clasped her elbows, bringing her up. "That's the fun *I* want to have." He walked her backward to the bed and nudged her until she fell onto it. He followed, his mouth on her breast, sucking, nipping, laving, driving her mindless for the next several minutes. She writhed on the bed, her hands pushing into his hair, tightening in it.

He released her breasts, smiling up at her. "I want to make you come. I want to hear you scream my name. *My* name. No one else's."

Pushing from the bed, he quickly removed the rest of his clothes. Sloane's eyes widened.

He was magnificent.

Sculpted muscles. An eight-pack of incredible abs. Thighs and calves that she could write poetry about. He was also nicked up. Scars here and there. But they only made him who he was.

"You are beautiful," she said, the awe in her voice obvious.

His smile turned bashful, and he knelt, pulling her legs toward him, spreading them.

"And you are all mine, Sloane Anderson," he said, his voice low and rough, sending a chill up her spine.

His hands held her hips as he went to work, tongue and teeth and lips worshipping her core. She felt the orgasm building, tight and spiraling, then spilling from her.

"Gage!" she cried out.

"Again," he ordered.

"Gage, Gage, Gage!" she shouted, waves emanating from her, the orgasm sweet, breaking out as rays of sunshine spreading and then erupting, over and over.

"Gage," she said weakly, coming back to earth.

Coming back to him. To the man she wanted. The man she needed.

The man she had fallen in love with, long before this moment.

"Gage," she whispered as his body covered hers, his cock pushing inside her, filling her.

He made love to her tenderly at first, then as their bodies heated with passion, he moved faster and faster. Sloane clung to him, her arms holding tightly to him, her legs wrapped about his waist, as they danced the dance of love.

Then her orgasm rippled through her and she cried out, hearing him doing the same. He collapsed atop her, and she clung to him, never wanting to let go.

After several minutes, their breathing slowed. Gage rolled to his side, his mouth finding hers for sweet, long kisses.

Resting his brow against hers, he sighed in contentment. Then he gazed deeply into her eyes. In them, Sloane saw love. A vulnerability she had never seen on his face. Her fingers touched his cheek.

"Gage," she said, the one word covering a multitude of feelings.

The vulnerability faded, replaced by a teasing light in his eyes. "Not bad for a first time, Anderson. You might get better with practice—but you'll need a lot of it."

Sloane laughed as she never had before, a carefree laugh full of joy and light. Gage joined in, his laughter rich.

"I'm content, Sloane. Really happy," he said. "I've never been able to say that in thirty-four years."

"Same," she told him, happiness bubbling through her. "I've felt fulfilled. Happy when I nailed a story. But this? It's... different."

Gage kissed her. "It's a feeling of satisfaction. Warmth. Gratification. Contentment. All rolled into one."

She met his gaze. "I'm feeling it, too, Gage. It's as if I found a piece of me I never knew was missing—and suddenly I'm whole."

He brought her to his chest. Sloane's ear rested against his beating heart. Her hand stroked his chest.

This is love...

THEY TALKED FOR SEVERAL HOURS, Sloane lying in his arms. No topic was off-limits. She started with the small things, telling him she liked watching reruns of *Friends* and eating ice cream.

"Or gelato. Or frozen yogurt. Anything I can find that is cold and sweet."

"Have you had Tillamook ice cream?" he asked. "I know they carry it in different areas of the country, but it's from these parts. The Oregon coast."

"No, I've never had it."

"They have a factory. You can take a tour. And stop for ice cream at the end." He grinned. "Or skip the tour and head straight for the double dip cones."

She laughed. "I like that you skip ahead and have dessert first. I think everyone should do that once in a while."

He outlined the shape of her mouth with his tongue. "You're dessert enough for me. Then again, you aren't Waffle Cone Swirl or Coffee Almond Fudge. Those are my favorite Tillamook flavors."

Sloane stacked her hands on his chest and rested her chin on them. "I thought you were a clean eater. That you only cheated on Game Nights when Ainsley brings dessert."

Gage twisted a pretend mustache. "Oh, what my friends don't truly know about me."

They laughed and kissed some more, the shared intimacy bringing them closer.

"Well, I'll have to try some of their ice cream soon. And just so you know, my favorite flavors are sea salt caramel and chocolate mint."

"Duly noted," he said, lacing his fingers through hers and kissing them. "Why do you like *Friends* so much?"

She laughed softly. "Because it's on some station no matter what country I'm in. If there's a TV, it's playing an old episode of *Friends*. I've been in hotels in Scandinavia. The Far East. The Middle East. Even Africa, in big cities. I swear, I can always find an episode. And I've seen so many of the shows so many times, I know the plotlines, despite Ross whining in Danish or Korean. I see them—those six friends—and it's almost like a piece of home has come on the road with me. Those six are family. They love one another. They drive each other crazy at times. They'd do anything for each other."

He stroked her hair idly. "That's like what we have in the Cove. Dylan and Carter were tight since high school. I showed up in town and met Dylan, who introduced me to Carter. Then Willow came back from Europe. Tenley moved from New York. Ainsley was already here, and Rylie followed soon, with both of them opening their own places. We all just folded together and became a group. Then Jackson came home from L.A. Nash found his way here. And we're... family."

Gage paused. "I have something serious to tell you. It might change things between us."

"What?" she asked, afraid what he might say, biting her lip.

With a solemn look, he said, "I have never seen a single episode of *Friends*."

"Aagghh!" she cried, grabbing a pillow and smacking him with it. "That's un-American."

They wrestled playfully, with play turning to love-making—swift, passionate, and hot. Naked, entwined limbs again, they caught their breaths.

"That will be my mission. To make sure you see every episode of *Friends*," Sloane told him.

"Didn't it run like a gazillion years?" Gage asked.

"Pretty much. So, you'll have to keep me around for at least that long."

They settled in again, sharing things they enjoyed. Sports. Foods. Places.

Then Gage said, "To understand me—to really know me—you have to know something about my past."

"I know you wanted to be a SEAL from the eighth grade. And that you're super-smart and invested well. That you bore easily."

"Before all that," he said quietly.

Sloane stroked his forearm. "You can tell my anything, Gage. You know that."

"I went into foster care right after I turned two."

He paused but she kept quiet. The reporter in her wanted to pepper him with questions, but she knew he would tell his story in his own time.

"My mom was a drug addict. She OD'd. She and I and were living with her mom, a chain smoker with a bad heart. Apparently, her health was shot, and I was a pretty rambunctious toddler. My grandmother relinquished me to the state, and I stayed in foster care until I aged out at eighteen and joined the navy."

She couldn't help it. "What about your dad? He wasn't in the picture?"

Gage shrugged. "I don't know even know if my mom knew who he was. If she did, she never said. My birth certificate has *Unknown* listed where my father's name should have gone."

She continued stroking his arm. "That must have been rough."

"It made me tough as hell, I'll tell you that. Boys are harder to place than girls. The older you get, the harder a placement becomes. And when you're a little on the wild side and you find there are no takers, you develop a bad attitude. I became a smart ass. Then no one wanted me for sure."

"It was a defense mechanism," she said.

"Yeah. You're right. It was. I could make a joke. Or say the joke was on me, before anyone else could. But it hurt. God, Sloane, it hurt a lot. Not to be wanted. Not to have anyone who cared." He paused. "At least I learned a lot from Stan Farthingale at his auto repair shop. Not just about fixing cars. I became like a Mac-Gyver type, who could do anything. I could fix stuff. Good with my hands. Even did a little woodworking. Nash does some woodworking, too. We're going to make a dining room set—table and chairs—for the home he and Rylie are building now."

"That's wonderful, Gage. I wouldn't have guessed that about you. Being a SEAL, I think of you as being high tech. Not someone who would help a friend make a table. It's very cool."

"It is," he agreed, grinning at her. "Whenever I sit and eat at that table, I'll know its history. Hopefully, it'll be passed down to their kids and their kids after that. So, it's like a piece of me will live on." He frowned. "So much of what I did as a SEAL was classified. Government missions that could never be spoken about, even now. I loved what I did and the guys on my team, but it was like I was a ghost all those years. I guess that's why I get a kick out of helping people now. Seeing their progress. Cheering them on for doing those two extra chin-ups or running one more lap. Losing that last five pounds. Seeing the pride they have in themselves when they reach a goal."

Sloane reached up and took his face in her hands. "You'll see even more of that when you open your fitness center, Gage. You'll see all the different ages and genders coming in. You'll create the schedules. Oversee the classes. Continue to work with clients but have a better, bigger picture. You will make a difference in this community."

"I hope so."

"I *know* so," she said fervently.

She initiated the kiss, a slow, long, delicious one that had her memorizing everything about him.

"I am lucky to have you as a friend and a lover," she told him. "But I think I need to go home now. We need to keep some boundaries for now."

"I agree."

They both rose from the bed and dressed. She glanced around as she did. "Boy, you weren't kidding. This is a small place."

"I sleep and eat here. I'm gone most of the time. I don't need a lot of room or stuff."

"You sound like me when I'm on the road. But it's nice to be in one place now."

He escorted her to Willow's SUV, opening the door for her.

"I like that you do that," she told him, as she climbed into the driver's seat. "You're always such a gentleman."

Before she got in, he gave her a lingering kiss. "I've

got a full day tomorrow, but I'll meet you at Walt's dock," he promised.

"Okay," she said softly, pulling him down for one, last kiss.

Sloane drove herself back to Boo's and crept up the stairs.

The lamp on the nightstand was on. Shadow lay on the bed, lazily lifting his head and then lowering it. Sloane kissed the dog's head and quickly changed into her pajamas before crawling into bed. As her head touched the pillow, she could still smell Gage on herself.

She couldn't tell him yet that she was in love with him. If she did, it might frighten him away. No, she would take her time and let them get to know each other and grow on one another. She hoped he would come to love her. Maybe it would be best to wait and see if he told her that he loved her. With him being so quiet, though, Sloane wasn't sure if he ever would.

She fell asleep, thinking of what she might do for a living.

Because she was staying in the Cove forever.

CHAPTER 16

When Sloane's phone alarm went off, she quickly silenced it. For a moment, she had to think why she had set it, and then she remembered her breakfast date with Rylie Edwards. She hadn't put away the clothes which had arrived from New York and went to the drawers where she had stored the borrowed clothes from Ainsley, choosing a long-sleeved T-shirt and pair of yoga pants. She actually wore yoga pants for their comfort but had never attempted to practice the ancient art. She was looking forward to what Rylie could teach her today.

Going downstairs with Shadow following her, she saw a light in the kitchen and headed that way. She found Dylan downing a tall glass of water, getting ready for his daily run.

He set the empty glass on the counter and said, "Good morning, Sloane."

"How was your trial?"

"I think my testimony will help put away one very bad guy," he told her. "How are you doing? Willow told me about going out on Walt's boat later today. Are you sure you want me there?"

"I would like you to come if you don't mind. I know you didn't know Ted."

"Willow has told me about him," Dylan said. "I'm sorry the world lost such a good man in a horrible way." He paused. "I've lost friends, too," he said quietly. "It happens too frequently in the military, and I never got used to it. If you need to talk about Ted—or what happened to you—I'm here for you, Sloane."

His words caused her eyes to mist with tears. "I appreciate that, Dylan. More than you know. I also am grateful for you and Willow giving me a place to stay, but I think I may want to rent something on my own. You two need your privacy, and I also need mine."

Dylan smiled. "It wouldn't have anything to do with a tall, former SEAL, would it?"

Sloane felt the hot blush spill across her cheeks. "It just might," she said saucily, and he laughed.

"I know everyone has told you what a great guy Gage is, but you're pretty great yourself. I think you would be a dynamic duo."

Willow entered the kitchen, dressed for her run. "Good morning. You headed to Rylie's?"

"I am. See you both later."

She left the house and went to Willow's SUV, reaching for her phone to tap in the directions when a text popped up from Rylie.

Skip going to the bakery. Nash will run the errand for us and bring breakfast home after his run. See you in a few!

Sloane texted a thumbs up and put Rylie's address into her phone. She headed toward the center of town since Rylie lived only a few blocks from the square. When she reached it, she spotted Gage's truck and caught sight of him and Jackson stretching by the gazebo. A warm glow filled her. Though she hadn't gotten much sleep, she felt energized this morning. Sex with Gage had been phenomenal. The best of her life. It would only grow better as they got to know one another's bodies and how to please each other.

She arrived at Rylie's house and saw Nash coming out the front door.

"Morning, Sloane. Any requests for breakfast?"

"Whatever Ainsley gives us will be fine with me. Thanks for stopping to pick it up."

"Not a problem. Enjoy your girl-time with Rylie."

She knocked at the door, and Rylie answered right away. "Come on in, Sloane. I was just setting up mats for our session."

Looking around, she saw the mix of antiques and contemporary furnishings. "This is so cozy."

Rylie chuckled. "*Cozy* is a real estate term for small. At least that's what Nash would tell you. Ever since he moved in with me, we've both anxiously awaiting the day our new place is finished and we have some elbow room."

"I'll have to hear about it at breakfast," she said.

She slipped from her jacket and tossed it onto a chair. Rylie suggested she also take off her socks and shoes.

"Barefoot is better when it comes to yoga. Have you had any experience with it?"

"I'm a neophyte. Putty in your hands."

"Then let's sit on our mats in a cross-legged position. We'll focus on breathing first. Breathing is key in yoga. Awareness of your breath is the most important aspect of your practice."

They settled onto their mats, and Rylie walked Sloane through several minutes of breathing exercises. They reminded her of the breathing technique she had done with Gage, but Rylie emphasized awareness of the breath more than he had. After five minutes of deep, even breathing, Rylie said they were ready to begin.

"We'll go through ten to twelve poses today to get you familiar with the practice. There are actually dozens, and you'll come to learn which ones you enjoying doing the most. Which ones your body really responds to. We'll do a variety of standing, balancing, sitting, and resting poses. You look as if you're in terrific shape."

"I practice Krav Maga."

Rylie nodded enthusiastically. "I'm familiar with that. One of my friends from college, a car salesman in Portland, practices it. I'll have to put you in touch with him."

"That would be terrific, because I'll also need a car. I can't borrow Willow's forever."

"Okay, let's start with Sun Salutation."

Rylie was an excellent instructor, giving short, clear instructions. She helped adjust Sloane's posture and position on a few of the poses. They did two different kinds of Warrior, Mountain, Triangle, Tree, Cow's Head, and Downward Dog before moving to a seated position, where they tried Cobra, Bridge, and Cobbler.

They moved to Child's pose and ended in Corpse position. Rylie walked her through how to let go of tension in every part from head to toe, and they spent several minutes breathing in and out in this position to end their session.

"I think that's it for today," Rylie said brightly, sitting up.

Sloane also sat up. "I can't quite describe how my

body feels. It's a mixture of energy flowing through me, and yet I am as relaxed as a rag doll."

"Then you've discovered the essence of yoga," her new friend said. "Practicing yoga helps clear your mind and makes you at one with your body. You will feel more energetic throughout the day, and if something stressful occurs? It won't affect you as much as it usually does. I do a few yoga poses before I go to bed and sleep like a baby. Let's go have some warm lemon water."

Rylie heated two cups of water in the microwave, squeezing fresh lemon juice into both. "We can go sit and veg on the sofa. Nash should be home soon."

"Why lemon water?"

"Multiple reasons," Rylie explained. "It boosts your immune system and is heart-healthy. It helps maintain your body's fluid balance and is good for your brain. It aids digestion and freshens your breath. It even clears up my skin. I start every day with a cup. When I do yoga, I have a second cup."

As Sloane sipped, she said, "It's almost as if I don't need coffee. That's surprising."

"You may not, but I have a variety of pods if you do. Nash loves his morning coffee."

"Tell me about this house you two are building."

"When I came to the Cove to start Antiques and Mystiques, I wanted to buy something of my own to come home to. That's how I wound up with this place. Real estate is usually a good investment, and though I was a bit strapped doing so, I went ahead and committed to purchasing this house. Then Nash arrived— and my world turned upside down—in a good way, of course. He rented a place between Willow's and Tenley's. Once we married, he gave up the lease and moved in here. We knew we would need much more room, though, both now and in the future. One of the things we are building on a considerable parcel of land in back of the house is a separate recording studio."

"He won't have to record in Nashville then."

"Exactly For his last album, he went and met his bandmates in Portland. He used two different studios. Both were great, but there is the hour or more commute on both ends of every session. He has the money, and we found a place big enough for our house and the studio."

"Will his band mind coming to the Cove to record?"

"His drummer is actually from Salty Point, which is why Nash wound up in this area to begin with. Billy lives there when they're not recording or touring. Wills, his keyboardist, has places in Nashville and L.A. He's fine with coming up, and we are also building a small, two-bedroom cabin next to the studio for anyone who comes in to record. Dart, his guitarist, has decided to leave the band. Nash will be looking for a replacement soon, but I don't think that will be a problem."

"I've heard a few of the songs off his latest CD. Tenley told me you actually wrote the lyrics to one of them."

"Yes, *The Love in Your Eyes.* As you can guess, that was a pretty personal one. I wrote poetry a long time ago. That's all song lyrics are, poetry set to music. Nash and I have been doing a little writing together, and he also has a songwriting partner from Salty Point. Enough about me. Tell me what's going on with you. How long can you stay in the Cove before the network is screaming for your return? And how are *you* doing? We were all very worried about you when you were taken."

"I'll be upfront. I've had a couple of panic attacks since the kidnapping. Gage has been through something similar and has worked with me on some techniques on how to calm myself. After my yoga session today, I definitely plan to practice yoga. I think it will clear my mind and calm my soul."

"I've got a couple of apps that you should download if you're serious about committing to yoga. I'll text them to you."

Rylie sent the names of the apps for Sloane to download.

"I think you'll find them helpful. They go through and explain each pose, similar to how I did with you. You can load sessions of different lengths and types of poses to create a personalized experience."

"I have a similar app I use with Pilates. I practice it on the road, too."

"Oh! I would love to do a Pi-Yo class, where both are mixed."

"You have such an easy, natural way of teaching. You should be teaching yoga."

Rylie smiled. "I taught Nash how to SUP. Stand up paddleboarding. And Gage took a class that combines SUP and yoga."

"Wait. You mean yoga on a paddleboard in the water? I find that concept fascinating."

"After his class, Gage used Nash and me as guinea pigs and taught us poses on our boards. If you're still around when spring comes and I get back on the water, I can teach you, too."

The door opened, and Nash came in with a box from Buttercup Bakery.

"It's croissants today," he told them. "They're fresh and smell heavenly."

"Would you like a cup of coffee with yours, Sloane?" Rylie asked.

"I really would. Croissants and coffee just go hand in hand."

"I'll handle the coffee, babe. You two keep talking. How do you take your coffee, Sloane?"

"Black. It's not always easy to get coffee when I'm traveling abroad, and I learned to drink it without any frills."

"Be back in a few." Nash disappeared.

Sloane decided to talk over her plans with Rylie. "I am seriously considering remaining in the Cove. I haven't told Willow or Tenley yet. I've been staying at Boo's, but I think I would like to have a little place of my own to rent for a bit and see if the Cove is right for me."

"You know what? I'll bet the two-bedroom Nash rented is available. It's February and we don't get many tourists this time of year. If you'd like, I can call Shayla Newton and see if it's available. As I mentioned, it's right between Tenley and Willow, so you'd be close to them both." Rylie paused. "I know you have had upheaval in your life and that we've only talked on the phone a few times, but I am here for you, Sloane. An ear if you need someone to listen. A willing body if you want to practice yoga together." She smiled. "Or someone to toss back a few margaritas with and have a good time."

"That means the world to mean, Rylie. Ainsley has also extended friendship to me. I can't think of two women I want to become friends with more than you and your cousin."

Nash appeared with a tray containing mugs and plates of croissants.

"They're already buttery, but I included a crock of strawberry jam in case either of you wanted some. I'm going to hit the shower and then head over to Jarrod's to do some writing. It's good to have you in the Cove, Sloane. I'm hoping you'll cross the male/female divide at Game Night and join our team. We could use someone with a global view."

She laughed. "I've heard about the famous Game Nights. I have to say thanks for the invitation, Nash, but I've got to stick with my home girls."

He shrugged, smiling. "It was worth a try. See you soon."

Rylie said, "I hear that we're supposed to get together tomorrow, just the girls. Willow sent out a text that we're baking. Tenley offered her place since they have that ginormous island."

"I've seen it in in Carter's cooking vlogs. I look forward to being with everyone tomorrow."

They talked about a few things to do in the Cove, including kayaking, hiking, fly fishing, and disc golf.

"I enjoy hiking," Sloane said. "We'll have to set a date for that soon."

"I also want you to come by and see Antiques and Mystiques. Nash and I got some fabulous items on our buying trip this week. That reminds me that I also need to get ready and head to the store and start inventory."

Sloane stood and hugged Rylie tightly. "Thanks for introducing me to yoga. I think it's something I will continue to do for a lifetime."

"I'll contact Shayla and see if the cottage is available," Rylie promised, giving Sloane a yoga mat to take home for her own use.

She returned to Boo's, taking a shower and dressing in her own jeans and a sweater. She took time to sort her clothes from New York and retrieved Willow's iron and ironing board from the laundry room. As she ironed, she thought about what she would say as she scattered Ted's ashes later today.

CHAPTER 17

Sloane had dressed in black pants and a dark sweater. The weather all day had been cold, and it had rained for a brief period between noon and three. Now, though, the sun had come out. She was glad the weather had cleared up and hoped the sunset would be a nice one for Ted's send-off.

Her phone rang and she picked it up, not recognizing the number. Something told her to answer the call, though.

"Hello?"

"Miss Sloane? Miss Sloane, can you hear me? It is Tapiwa. From the hospital," the lilting voice said.

Immediately, the image of the nurse calling came to mind. "Yes, Tapiwa, this is Sloane. Do you have news about Salana?"

"I do, Miss Sloane. Miss Owusa has regained consciousness. She had surgery two days ago. To... repair some of the damage."

She didn't know what damage the nurse referred to, but the woman's hushed tone led Sloane to believe it was done to repair injuries from the gang rape Salana suffered.

"How is Salana? May I speak with her?"

"She is eager to talk with you. I told her I would call you and bring the phone to her. Miss Sloane, she has trouble putting words together. The doctors say Miss Owusa will improve with time, but please. Speak slowly. Be patient with her."

"Of course, Tapiwa. Thank you for calling me."

"One moment, miss."

Sloane swallowed, preparing herself. She had interviewed soldiers who had been victims of roadside bombs. Men who had suffered everything from concussions to traumatic brain injuries. From what Kumani and Akachi had shared, Salana had been not only raped but repeatedly kicked in the head and body. While Tapiwa said Salana's doctors said she would improve, that might not be the case.

"Hello?"

Just hearing her friend's voice caused Sloane's throat to grow thick with tears. She flipped her journalist switch, going into reporter mode and tamping down her feelings.

"Salana, it's Sloane. I am so happy to hear your voice."

"I... am happy, too. Sloane. Happy."

Remembering to slow her speech, she said, "I am sorry I am not there with you. I miss you."

"I miss... you. Very much."

"Are you eating?"

"Yes. Good food. Very food. Good."

"Do you have anyone staying with you, Salana?"

A long pause. "Yes. My... sister." Another pause. "What... who..."

In the background, she heard a voice say, "Let me talk to your friend, Salana. That's good. Thank you. Close your eyes. Get some rest."

Footsteps sounded and then a voice said, "Miss Anderson, this is Johari Owusa. I am Salana's sister."

"Yes, Johari, of course. Salana mentioned you to me. Please, be frank. How is she? And call me Sloane."

"Salana suffered greatly at the rebels' hands, Sloane. The doctors have used the term TBI. You are familiar with this?"

"Yes, traumatic brain injury. Did they say whether it is closed or penetrating?" she asked.

"They have used both terms. Those animals. They kicked her in the head. The doctors say there was bruising and tearing of brain tissue. The trauma was great."

"I noticed her speech is slower and hesitant. What else have the doctors shared with you? What have you observed?"

Johari sighed. "When my sister came out of the coma, she did not remember what happened to her or the girls. The doctors say she may never recall those events, which I think is a blessing. She is confused about some memories. She can only do one thing at a time. If I said to her to smile and wave, she can only do one. She cannot remember the other. Her vision is blurred some. She is quieter. Not the Salana who was once filled with joy."

"She may never be that Salana again, Johari. But she is alive."

"Yes, she is. She will undergo physical and speech therapy. She tells me she will teach again." Another sigh. "Only time will tell. But she recalled you and wanted to speak to you."

"I will call her every day if that is convenient."

"Let me think on it," Johari said, not sounding keen on the idea of daily contact. "I believe now my sister needs to work on gaining her strength and getting better. She has had surgery for her broken leg and... female parts." Johari paused. "She will never be able to have children."

"I am very sorry to hear that. I hope one day Salana can return to her classroom. She treated her students as her own children. Perhaps teaching might bring her comfort." Sloane cleared her throat. "I will let you contact me when you think it would be good for Salana to chat with a friend. And if there is anything I can do financially, Johari, I may be in a position to help."

"Thank you. I will keep that in mind. You are very lucky, Sloane. You are home and whole."

"I am fortunate. Please give Salana a hug for me."

"I will do so. Goodbye."

Sloane's knees shook. She sat on the bed, her heart pounding. She ached for her friend and what had been done to her. A sudden rage filled her, and she wanted to scream.

Instead, she moved to the ground, sitting cross-legged. She began breathing in the same manner she and Rylie had done this morning, her focus on her breath. Sloane pushed everything from her mind. Only her breath remained. In. Out. In. Out. She continued the slow, deep breathing, feeling her anger dissolve. After several more minutes, she opened her eyes, feeling in control.

She hoped she would hear from Johari again. She would pray for Salana's continued recovery. Even with the money she was donating to Gage in Ted's name, there would still be some left. It would remain earmarked for Salana's therapy until she heard otherwise.

A knock sounded on her door. Springing to her feet, Sloane answered and found Willow there.

"It's about time to leave for Walt's. The wind isn't

bad, but you'll still need a coat. Take your all-weather one. We may get a bit wet out on the water."

"I'll be right down."

"You okay?" Willow asked, concern in her tone.

"Yes. I just talked briefly to Salana. She's out of her coma, but she has a long way to go. She had some physical injuries and TBI."

Her friend winced. "That's rough."

"I spoke longer with her sister. Johari will keep me posted. They'll know more in the next few weeks about her recovery."

Willow embraced her. "Are you sure you want to do this now?"

"Yes," Sloane said, determined to give Ted's ashes a place to rest. "Be down in a minute."

She went to the bathroom and tied back her hair so it wouldn't constantly whip across her face. Then she collected the beautiful urn from the dresser and went downstairs.

Tenley and Carter were already there, and her friend came and enveloped her in a hug.

"I heard Salana woke up. That's good news," Tenley said.

Nodding, Sloane said, "She'll be doing some rehab now. I wish I could bring her here to do it, but I doubt her sister would go for it. She's about fifteen years older than Salana and was more a mother to her than a sister. She's with her at the hospital now."

"Hopefully, you'll be able to stay in touch and hear about her progress." Tenley gave her a tentative smile. "You ready to tell Ted goodbye?"

"Yes."

They rode together to Walt Willingham's ranch house, which sat less than thirty yards from the water. Dylan introduced Sloane to the former sheriff.

"I can't thank you enough for agreeing to take us out today, Sheriff Willingham."

"Walt. And I'm happy to help out, Sloane. I follow you on the news." A shadow crossed his face. "I'm sorry about what the rebels did to that girls' school. Your reports featuring those young ladies really brightened my day."

"Thank you. They were an amazing, resilient group of young women. It was a privilege to cover their stories."

Walt turned to the group. "Let's start boarding."

Sloane looked around anxiously, not seeing Gage. She hated to leave him behind, but Walt was doing her a favor by taking her and her friends out to sea.

As they began moving toward the water, Walt fell into step with her. "Gage texted me about five minutes ago. He's on his way."

She breathed a sigh of relief. "That's good to know."

"He's a fine young man, Sloane. Did his service to this country. Cares about the people of the Cove and beyond." Walt paused. "Told me he thinks a lot of you."

For Gage to have said anything of that nature surprised her, especially to this man she didn't even know.

"Why don't you wait for him here? I'll get everyone settled and get the motors going. I can take your friend if you'd like." Walt indicated the urn she held. "That's really pretty. As pretty as the one Boo had."

"You were friends with Boo?"

He smiled, his weathered face looking content. "Boo Martin was a friend to everyone in the Cove. We miss her every day. Glad to have Willow and Jackson back with us, though. I'm betting Boo's sitting on a cloud looking down, pleased as punch."

Walt ambled off with the urn containing Ted's ashes. Sloane walked back toward the road. Moments later, Gage's truck turned the corner. She felt her body relax.

He bounded out and came to her, bending for a quick kiss. "You doing okay?"

"I am now," she said.

Lacing his fingers through hers, he said, "Let's go down to the dock."

She stopped in her tracks, pulling him back. "Are you sure about... this?" She held up their joined hands.

"Absolutely. And I'll tell you now, no explanations will be needed. I think just about everybody has figured out how I feel about you, Sloane."

His words warmed her as the sun would on a summer's day. She squeezed his fingers. "Let's do this."

They headed toward the dock. Walt offered her his hand and as she boarded, he said, "A slight wind from the south. Just keep that in mind as you disperse the ashes. You want them to go with the wind and not against it."

Sloane nodded. Tenley motioned her over. "Carter would like to talk to you," she said quietly. "Could you come over a few minutes early tomorrow before the Great Bake-Off begins?"

"Of course." She frowned. "Is there anything I should know?"

"Carter just wants to share a few things with you. Help you as you try to muster through things."

"Okay." She glanced up and caught Gage's eye. He came and sat next to her.

Walt took them a few miles from shore and said,

"Sunset will be in about ten minutes. Are you ready, Sloane?"

She rose and accepted the urn from him. "Thank you. Thank you to everyone who came today. I know none of you men met Ted before, but Willow and Tenley did a few times over the years. I'm grateful for their support—and you supporting them. I'm also thankful to Walt for taking us out on the water, a place Ted loved."

She moved so that she stood in front of all of them.

"Ted Castro was a true friend. A dedicated journalist. Happy-go-lucky and helpful to anyone in need. He was an only child who lost his parents when he was barely out of his teens. His one marriage only lasted a short while. But anyone who knew Ted Castro understood he was full of love."

She gazed across the water as she continued to speak. "Ted was someone everyone turned to in a crisis. He had a kind ear and dispensed good advice. He was the consummate cameraman. Always early. Always wanting to get that one, last, great shot. Ted was not only my best friend, but he was more of a father to me than my own father. I turned to Ted in good times and bad. In happy times and sad.

"The one place Ted was happiest was on or in the water. He swam and dived. Surfed. Skied. Fished. His idea of a happy retirement was to live on a houseboat so he'd be on his beloved water."

She swallowed, blinking back tears. "The Pacific is the largest of all the oceans. It covers a third of the planet. It reaches from the north to the south and touches five continents. Its depth runs thirty-six thousand feet. I figure by placing Ted's ashes in this ocean, he'll continue to travel the world in death as he did in life."

Sloane paused a moment. "Ted's favorite author was Ernest Hemingway, another man known for his love of the water. Hemingway said, *'Every man's life ends the same way. It is only the details of how he lived and how he died that distinguish one man from another.'*"

She gazed at those gathered. "Would you join me in a moment of silence, remembering Ted Castro?"

The group rose as one and Willow and Tenley joined hands, taking their husbands' hands, as well. Gage clasped Dylan's, while Walt took Carter's. Everyone bowed their heads.

"Thank you," she said quietly, after a minute passed. "I'm going to return Ted now to the place he loved best. I'll never see the Pacific without thinking of him."

Moving to starboard, where Walt motioned her to go, she said, "I'm going to recite a poem I found by Captain Chad Theesfeld. I couldn't find his nationality, but I like what he wrote. His poem is entitled *Alone I Will Not Be.*"

Sloane began reciting the short poem. With each line, she sprinkled some of Ted's ashes across the water.

Alone I will not be
My comfort will come from the sea.
The stillness of calm waves will gently drift by,
I will be as one with the sea.
When the sun sets on the ocean blue,
Remember me as I will always remember you.
As the sun rises... go live life as full as can be
Apart... you and me... but at peace for I am free.

Distributing the final bit, Sloane gazed across the water. "Now, Ted is one with the water."

She returned to her seat. Gage came and put an

arm about her. "That was beautiful. You did Ted justice, Sloane. He would have been so proud."

Tears blurred her vision. She leaned into Gage and absorbed strength from him.

"Take me home with you," she asked. "I don't want to be alone tonight."

CHAPTER 18

Gage let Sloane say her goodbyes to Walt, Willow, and Tenley. He told Dylan he was taking Sloane home with him.

"She did a wonderful job honoring Ted," Dylan said. "But I can see she's pretty fragile right now." He squeezed Gage's shoulder. "She'll be in good hands with you."

"And she's getting together at our house tomorrow with all the girls," Carter added. "Those bonds of friendship will carry her a long way in this process."

Sloane returned to his side. "Ready if you are."

He took her hand. "Let's go."

In the truck, she asked, "Is Walt ill? He seemed fine but a little too thin."

"He has cancer," Gage told her. "It's a slow-moving kind. It's the reason he wanted to vacate his office and have Dylan take over in his place. He's probably got another year or two, but he wanted all his ducks in a row—and that included making sure Maple Cove's residents were taken care of."

"I'm glad Dylan won the election. It must be a re-lief to Walt."

"He knows when his time comes, things are in good hands with Dylan." Knowing she wouldn't want to eat anywhere in town since he knew she had yet to go into stores or restaurants, he said, "Do you mind if I stop at Eats 'n Treats and pick up takeout for us? We'll need to eat, and I haven't shopped in a few days."

"Whatever you want." She gave him a rueful smile. "I suppose it'll be something healthy and not a cheeseburger."

Grinning, he said, "My order will be clean and mean, but you can have whatever you'd like. Pull up the menu and order online for us. I'll take the grilled chicken salad."

Sloane tapped on her phone. "What's in it? That actually sounds good to me."

"Besides the chicken, which the café seasons perfectly? Feta, sundried tomatoes, celery, some onion. Red peppers and fresh dill. Cucumbers and avocado. They also have a version that adds some spiral pasta."

"No, it sounds good just as you described it. I'll order two of those. Anything else?"

"I think soup would be good. It was pretty chilly on the water. They have good clam chowder and tomato bisque. Lobster bisque, too."

"I'll want the tomato bisque."

"Make it two," he told her. "Put it under my name."

"Done," she said.

They reached the square a few minutes later. Gage went in to pick up their order.

"Two tonight?" Billie said as she placed the brown paper bag on the counter. "You must be getting for tonight and tomorrow."

He handed over his credit card. "Actually, Billie, it's for me and a date."

Her eyes widened and she gave him a grin. "Good for you, Gage. Anyone I know?"

"Sloane Anderson. The TV reporter."

The gray-haired clerk handed him his card and slip to sign. "I love her. She goes everywhere and never looks ruffled. Always gets the story. And she's a looker."

"She certainly is," he agreed, returning her grin. "See you, Billie."

"Have fun," she called, as he left the café.

In the truck, he handed the sack to Sloane. "Well, the news is out. Or will be out within the next five to ten minutes."

Her brow furrowed. "What are you talking about?"

"When I paid for dinner just now, I told Billie that I had a date with Sloane Anderson. She knew exactly who you were. Likes your work, by the way."

"And you think she's texting like mad now, letting the Cove know?"

"Since I haven't had a date in months? Yes, Billie will find that newsworthy. The fact that she knows who you are will only add gas to the flames."

"Are you all right with that?" Sloane asked quietly.

He took her hand and raised it to his lips, kissing it. "I'm more than fine with it. It's not enough for our friends to know. I want everyone in the Cove to know you're off-limits."

She sighed dramatically. "And here I was hoping Gus at Buttercup Bakery might finally make his move on me."

Gage roared with laughter.

"Hey, Gus kneads a mean dough," Sloane told him. "Those forearms were pretty darn sexy if you ask me." She reached and squeezed his forearm. "Then again, you rock forearms yourself. And pecs. Abs. Calves."

"Keep flattering me, Anderson. If you're lucky, I'll let you touch all of those. And more."

Her fingers danced lightly along his arm. "Strong jaw. Chiseled cheeks. Strong hands. Broad shoulders. Sexy gray eyes."

He couldn't help but smile. "Let's go tit for tat. Sleek raven hair. Mesmerizing green eyes. Megawatt smile. Body with all the right curves. Flat belly. Firm breasts. And a mouth made for sinning."

Now, it was Sloane's turn to laugh. As Gage turned into Liz Freeman's driveway, she said, "I already feel better."

"Laughing cures the blues. Food will help give you the energy for what comes after."

"After?" she asked, her tone teasing.

"Yeah. After dinner comes dessert."

"But I didn't order dessert."

Gage cut the engine. "*You* are dessert tonight. And my sweet tooth needs filling."

"Bring it on, Nelson," she challenged.

They climbed the stairs to his apartment, and Gage suddenly wanted her to stay. Not just tonight. But every night.

Still, they hadn't known each other long. She was at a vulnerable time in her life. He couldn't ask her to move in and have her regret it later. Besides, he didn't know how long she would remain in the Cove. She was at the top of her game, a world-class journalist. It wouldn't be fair to ask her to give that up to stay with him. He also knew once she returned to covering world affairs, she would be on the road ninety percent of the time.

He didn't want ninety percent of her. Or a leftover ten percent. He wanted all. Even a hundred percent of Sloane would never be enough.

Gage told himself to quit borrowing trouble. Sloane couldn't stay forever. He had her now, though, and he would make the most of it.

And when she left, she would take his heart with her. Gage knew it would never belong to anyone else but her.

~

SLOANE DABBED her lips with a napkin. "That hit the spot. I'm glad you suggested the tomato bisque. It's one of the best bowls of it I've ever eaten. And that salad? It was a meal in itself. I'm sorry I couldn't finish it."

Gage rose. "I'll put it in a container. That way you can take it home with you."

"No, you keep it. We still have loads of stuff Carter made to plow through. It can be a snack for you. Or breakfast. Are you one of those people who eat weird things for breakfast?"

"Not really. I stick to oatmeal and berries or an omelet with veggies. I usually alternate days."

"Hah. Creature of habit," she accused. "I eat anything for breakfast. Cold leftover pizza. Cookies. Yogurt. A peanut butter sandwich. Or peanut butter smeared on Granny Smith apples. Now *that's* a big favorite."

"What about when you're traveling?" he asked.

She sighed. "Depends upon what continent and which country I'm in. I eat a lot of street food or pick up things at the local market. African breakfasts are some of my favorites. In Ethiopia, I like fatira. It's a big, crispy, wheat flour pancake. They also have genfo, a porridge. It's fun to watch a street vendor add the boiling water to the dry-roasted barley flour. He'll stir until it's smooth and thick, then he'll make a hole in the center with a finjal, an Ethiopian coffee cup, and fill the well with spiced butter and berbere spices. Sometimes, if you're lucky, you'll get a scoop of yogurt on top."

"Sounds good. What else?"

"Morocco means bessara, basically pureed beans, either fava or split peas. It can be thin as a soup or thicker, like a porridge. They season it with olive oil, garlic, and lemon juice, and you dip crusty Moroccan bread into it, sprinkled with paprika and cumin. Egypt has their own version of an omelet—eggah— but eggs aren't the star of the dish. They're used to bind the filling, which can be chicken, lamb, spinach, or leeks and lots of fresh herbs. It's shaped like a pan- cake, but they cut it into wedges, almost like pizza slices. Probably my favorite is attiéké, an Ivory Coast couscous with cassava roots, onions, tomatoes, and grilled fish or chicken. They eat it for any meal during the day."

Sloane paused. "All of those are in the bigger cities or even large villages. It's great when I report from those places. It's harder when I move deeper into the interior of a country, though. Food—any kind of food —can be scarce. Too often, foreign aid is confiscated by the gangs, leaving a huge chunk of the population starving. I feel guilty putting anything in my mouth. Ted and I would always try not to eat anything around others in those situations. We wouldn't even buy food for ourselves because that meant taking it away from others. We would stuff our backpacks and pockets with granola bars, trail mix, and dried fruit. I learned to understand food scarcity and savor each bite I took."

She leaned her back against the sofa. His arm went

around her shoulders. "Enough about food and traveling. I want to enjoy being here. With you."

She rested her cheek against his chest, bringing her feet up and curling them under her. They sat in companionable silence for several minutes. Sloane liked that they could do so. Around others, there always seemed to be a need to talk. To fill those silent spaces. With Gage, though, the quiet felt right. Natural. Real.

"I watched an episode of *Friends*," he told her. "I came home between classes this morning. Mixed up a protein shake. Scrolled through e-mails. Then for some reason, I turned on the TV. I came in about ten minutes after the episode started, but it was easy to catch on."

"Which one?" she asked. "I guarantee I'll know it."

"Ross wore leather pants on a date." He chuckled, the rumble against her ear. "I may never look at baby powder the same way again."

"Oh, *The One With All the Resolutions*. It's about New Year's resolutions. Chandler resolves not to crack jokes about everyone. And fails miserably, I might add. But Ross in those pants? Classic comedy."

He rubbed her back absently. "Yeah, it really was. I don't know how it was written, but the actor did a helluva job with no dialogue. His movements. His face. I can see why you like the show."

"Watching it wherever I was in the world always seemed like a little bit of home," she told him. "That those people would actually be fun friends to have." She leaned up and nipped his throat. "But I can think of a few other fun things to do now. I believe you mentioned dessert, Nelson."

He glanced down at her. "I thought you said you

were full," he said, his eyes sweeping up and down her.

"My dessert compartment always has room."

Suddenly, he was on his feet and had swept her into his arms. In a few strides, he had reached the bed and placed her on it.

"Then let's top off our meal, Anderson. With a lengthy, time-consuming dessert."

His words brought a shiver through her.

They slowly undressed one another, knowing there was no rush. That they had the entire night together. Sloane allowed Gage to touch and kiss every inch of her, lying there and enjoying the feel of his big, callused hands moving on her. He flipped her onto her stomach and began rubbing her shoulders.

"You're tense. It's all the stress from today."

"I guess."

She allowed his magic fingers to work on the tight muscles in her neck. Shoulders. Back. Hips.

"If this trainer thing doesn't work out, you should get your massage therapist license," she said, her words slurring sleepily.

Gage lay next to her, turning her to her side and pulling her back against his chest. His arm around her made her feel safe. Everything about him made her relax and want a different kind of live than the one she had led up until now.

"Sleep," he urged. "Dessert can be in divided segments."

"Okay," she agreed, her eyes closing, warmth surrounding her.

She awoke, not knowing how much time had passed. The light was still on next to the sofa. Gage was still covering her like a blanket. Fierce need rolled through her, and she stroked the arm against her belly.

"Hungry?" he asked, his lips touching her ear, sending a rush of molten desire through her.

"For you. Only you."

They began touching one another, learning what pleased the other. Long, deep kisses and searching hands. Whimpers and sighs of contentment. Then a burning need to have him inside her. She stroked his cock, feeling it swell, brushing its head, urging it toward her.

Suddenly, they flipped. Sloane found herself on top. Gage captured her waist and raised her above him, then slowly lowered her onto his shaft. He went deeper, deeper, until she was seated and filled with him.

"You set the tempo," he said, his voice raw, full of need. "You're in control."

Doing as he asked, Sloane moved against him, a delicious ripple of pleasure racing through her. She moved again, hearing his groan, delighting in it. Soon, she rode him hard, fast, their bodies slick with sweat, their cries in unison.

Then she exploded, a wave of pleasure rocking her body to its core. Gage called out her name and they held tightly to one another, moving until they were both spent.

She collapsed onto him, her mouth seizing his, kissing him as if it might be the last kiss she ever experienced. He held her to him, delving deeper with his tongue, finding everything about her he needed to know.

Breathless, she broke the kiss, gasping for air. Her head fell beside his, his breath hot against her ear. He murmured something, but she couldn't hear it since it was her damaged ear. She started to ask him to repeat it, but she was exhausted and closed her eyes, sleep swallowing her up.

When Sloane awoke the next time, the bed was empty. She reached and still felt the warmth of where Gage had been a short while ago. It was dark now. He must have gotten up at some point and turned off the light. She gazed across the small space and found his outline on the floor. Heard the deep, even breaths.

He was doing yoga.

She thought he had mentioned that he did a few poses each morning. Maybe when he had told her he would teach her. As her eyes adjusted to the darkness, she could see his silhouette, thanks to the glow of the bedside clock.

Gage stood, naked, and she watched him run through a few of the poses Rylie had taught her, admiring his muscular physique. She thought of the bullet wounds she had found on his body last night, scars from different missions. Things he could never reveal to her, his actions still classified by their government.

It didn't matter. Gage had shown her the man he was in other ways. He was smart, resourceful, loyal, and loving. He might not love her yet, but their bodies were in tune with one another. She would keep coming back to the well of Gage Nelson, drinking her fill.

And hope he also found what he needed in her.

CHAPTER 19

Sloane kissed Gage and hopped out of the truck. It was a quarter until six, and he had his first class of the day in a few minutes. He had told her weekends were his busiest time since so many people worked long hours during the week and tried to get a majority of their exercise in on the weekends. He had a full slate of classes today, along with a few individual training sessions with clients.

As she let herself into the house, she went up to her bedroom, eager to try another session of yoga. She had heated a cup of water and squeezed a splash of lemon into it before Gage brought her home, and she was ready now to see if yoga on her own would energize her as much as it had when she'd practiced with Rylie.

Changing into a T-shirt and yoga pants, she grabbed her mat and went down to the room Willow had urged her to use because it had an open space that would be ideal. She hadn't seen Shadow and supposed Willow and Dylan might have taken the dog on their run this morning.

Instead of trying one of the apps she had downloaded, Sloane replicated yesterday's session from memory, moving from one pose to the next and hearing Rylie in her head as she held each pose. She focused on her breathing and really stretched into each movement, finding them easy to do. She held each one a bit longer than yesterday, wanting to challenge herself with the workout.

By the time she ended in Corpse pose, she felt the energy flowing through her. She enjoyed relaxing her body one section at a time, amazed at how tranquil she now felt. When she finished, she rolled up her mat and placed it in the corner, planning to make yoga a part of her daily routine. Going to the kitchen, she found she really didn't crave a cup of coffee and warmed a mug of water in the microwave, slicing a lemon and squeezing a generous portion into the water.

"Good morning," Willow called as she and Dylan came in, her long hair damp and hanging loosely about her, Shadow dogging her footsteps.

Dylan waved. "Gotta shower. See you two later."

"How are you today?" Willow asked, retrieving a large container of yogurt from the refrigerator and a bag of blueberries.

"Good. I just did a little yoga. It really surprises me how it pumps me up."

"Want some yogurt and berries?"

"Please."

Willow spooned yogurt into two bowls and sprinkled a handful of fruit atop it. She turned on the coffeemaker and then brought the bowls to the table.

"I think you did a fabulous job yesterday," her friend praised. "It was a perfect sendoff for Ted."

"I felt good about it."

"I really liked the poem you recited. Did Ted request it?"

"No. I found it online. It just seemed to fit him perfectly."

"I'll make coffee for you first. What flavor?"

Sloane chuckled. "Actually, I'm going to stick with lemon water."

"Oh, Rylie's got her claws into you," Willow teased.

"You haven't asked about Gage," she said.

Her friend's brows arched. "Do I need to? Actually, I was doing my best to avoid the topic. I don't want to pry."

"It's not prying. You know I always tell you and Tenley everything."

"Then give me the scoop."

"I'm in love with Gage," she blurted out.

"Oh, honey. That's incredible." Willow came and wrapped her arms around Sloane. "Have you told him?"

"No." She shook her head. "I'm afraid to."

"Why? I think you should. I've seen how he looks at you, Sloane. I'm sure Gage feels the same way."

"I will. When I'm ready. Or I think he's ready to hear it."

Willow frowned. "You think it might scare him?"

"Yes. And I don't want to lose him."

"You won't," Willow said with certainty.

They talked about getting together with their friends and wondered what Ainsley would have them bake.

"Would you mind if we went half an hour early?" Sloane asked. "Tenley said Carter wanted to talk to me about something privately."

"Sure. We're supposed to be there at one-thirty.

Let's arrive at one. I can help Tenley set up while you and Carter chat."

Once Sloane finished eating, she said, "I'm going to go for a walk on the beach. Want to come?"

"I think I'll pass. I saw this great tree on our run this morning." Willow pulled up a picture on her cell and showed it to Sloane. "I liked its shape. How unusual its growth pattern was. I'm going to try and capture it on canvas. Enjoy your walk, though. I'll rinse the dishes. You go on."

Once she put on socks and shoes and her jacket and hat, Sloane went down the stairs to the beach. She thought about how busy Gage was and how he had so many things to consider in building his new facility and equipping and staffing it. Mentally, she made a list in her head and after she came home went to the sitting room and wrote down all the things she had thought about which he needed to do. Several things she could help with, and she planned to volunteer to do so when she presented him with the list.

She showered and went to the kitchen, where Dylan was making sandwiches. They had a quick lunch, and then she and Willow left for the Clarks' house, Dylan urging them to bring home whatever they made.

Tenley greeted her warmly. "Carter's in his study, prepping for tomorrow's shoot."

"What are you talking about?" she asked.

"He begins filming his new show with the Food Network."

"The last you told me was that he had shot a pilot, and they wanted him to tweak it some."

Tenley said, "He tried again. This time, he had Nash with him. He pitched a show where he teaches others how to cook. They fell in love with it and thought he and Nash had great chemistry. Carter will be teaching both well-known and ordinary people how to cook. They'll use the Nash show as one of the episodes. Tomorrow, Nash is bringing Pops, his grandfather. They'll film together." She laughed. "Pops is a real pistol."

"Should we even be here baking, Tens?" Willow asked. "I'm sure Carter doesn't want his kitchen a wreck the day before he begins filming his new show."

"He's fine with it," Tenley assured. "After we finish, he'll obsess for hours, getting everything just right. Let me show you where his office is, Sloane."

She followed Tenley down a corridor. The door was open. Carter was at his desk, notecards spread everywhere.

"Sloane's here," Tenley said.

Carter looked up and smiled. "Thanks for coming. Have a seat."

She took one and Carter turned his desk chair around to face her as Tenley closed the door.

"First, I want to make sure you don't feel awkward about this," he said. "I know we're not friends—at least not yet—but you are family to Tenley. That means you're family to me."

She relaxed. "I appreciate that, Carter. I know how happy Tenley is. You've made that happen, so you're already one of my favorite people."

He grinned. "Well, you've inherited me, Dylan, and Jackson as brothers. The tribe has spoken." Then he grew serious. "But I wanted to talk to you about Ted. You did a wonderful job honoring him yesterday."

"I think he would have liked it."

"I lost someone close to me," he said softly, his eyes misting with tears.

Sloane knew with Carter being a former fire-fighter, he certainly would have lost comrades on the job. "It must have been hard losing people you worked with every day."

He shook his head. "No, I'm talking about how you and I have had someone we love die in our arms."

Her throat tightened with his words.

"You see, my wife—my first wife—died in my arms."

"What?" Sloane had known Carter had been married before, to his high school sweetheart. Tenley had told her his first wife had died, but Sloane didn't know any of the details. "I didn't know, Carter. I'm so sorry."

"Emily and I were out of town. In Seattle for a foot-ball game. We were at a park we liked to visit on our annual trip there. It happened so fast. One minute, we were talking and laughing. The next, she had a blinding headache and collapsed. It was a brain an-eurysm. I frantically called 911. Did CPR. But Em died in my arms."

He looked at her steadily, his eyes bright with tears. "She was ten weeks pregnant."

Sloane shook her head, speechless.

"So, I lost my wife and my child in the blink of an eye. I know how you're hurting with Ted's death. How you held him as he died. I understand more than most what it's like to lose someone you care for out of the blue."

He leaned out and clasped her hands in his. "I know it gutted you. It did me. I had survivor's guilt. You might, too. But you described Ted as I would've described Em. Full of life. Em would have wanted me to go on living. Not just living, but happy in my life. Ted had a zest for life, as well. He wouldn't want you moping. Yes, there's a time to grieve—and a time to set aside that grief and pick up again. It takes time and distance. It did for me. I was a hermit for a long time. But when I decided to make the most of the life I had, that's when Tenley came into it.

"I still love Em. Tenley gets that. But Tenley is my life now. My reason for living. She brings me joy." He paused, a slow smile spreading across his face. "She'll tell you and the others today, but I want to share now. We're pregnant. Life does go on. I'm happy now, Sloane. I hope you will be, too. And I want you to know that I am here for you. If you need to talk. Exercise helped me. Running. But do whatever you have to do. Cry. Scream. Shout. Whatever it takes to move through it."

Sloane burst into tears. Carter stood, pulling her to her feet, wrapping her in a bear hug.

"Cry it out," he said gently.

She did, sobbing in a way that left Carter's shirt wet and her exhausted. But she did feel better once the tears subsided.

"Rylie taught me some yoga poses," she shared. "I also walked on the beach today. Both of those helped."

"That's good," he encouraged. "Do what you have to do. And I know Gage will also help you through this. Gage is the gold standard. You won't find a greater guy around."

He handed her a tissue and she blew her nose. "Sorry about your shirt."

"Not a problem." He went to the small fridge beside his desk and withdrew a bottle of water. "Drink this. It'll help."

She did, feeling calmer and more centered than she had before. "Thank you, Carter. I needed this."

"I'm glad. Being with your friends will also help."

"I hear you're filming tomorrow."

"Yes, Nash and his grandfather, who raised him, will be here. I'm trying for a mix of the famous and unknown." He chuckled. "Some of those unknowns are my friends. Nash has reached out to some of his buddies in the music industry. I've got a few commitments from them. Jackson represented an actor a few years ago and put me in touch with him. He's suggested a few of his friends, so I'm slowly building the guest list for this first season. I'm looking for people at different levels in their cooking experience. From those who don't know how to boil water to people who do a little bit of cooking."

"I really like your videos. I'm not much of a cook, but you make things look doable."

"Thank you. I appreciate that. We'll shoot two dozen shows, and then the network will arrange the order they'll be shown in. They'll use the first one I shot as a pilot with Nash. I'm sure they'll schedule several more between it and the one I film with him and Pops tomorrow."

Sloane thought a moment. "You said you're using friends. I'm happy to volunteer. I'm comfortable on camera even if I don't cook."

His face lit up. "Would you really be willing to tape a spot with me?"

"I'd be happy to."

"Are you sure you feel like doing this?"

Nodding firmly, she said, "I do. I don't want what happened to me to keep me from living my life."

"I understand that. Whether you return to broadcasting in some capacity or find something else to do, it's important to find what brings you—and others—joy."

Sloane thought that was the wisest advice anyone had given her. She did want to find her purpose. Her gut was telling her it was no longer in journalism. At least not in the form she had experience in.

"Think about what you might be interested in learning how to make," Carter said. "Maybe you'd like to come watch us film tomorrow to get an idea about the format. We're starting at one."

"I'll be here," she promised. "I'm seeing Jackson in the morning regarding Ted's legal affairs, so I'll be finished in plenty of time to watch."

A knock sounded on the door, and Tenley opened it. "Hey, you ready? Everyone's here."

Sloane said, "I'm more than ready." Turning to Carter, she said, "Thank you. For everything."

As they left Carter's office, she told her friend, "You married quite a guy."

CHAPTER 20

Sloane followed Tenley into the large kitchen and saw the other three women had arrived. Ainsley was distributing aprons to everyone, and the group put them on.

"Flour can be messy," Ainsley said. "It gets everywhere. Even wearing an apron, I've still found it in my hair and even in my ears. So, I'm warning you now."

She took the lids from five bowls and said, "Sloane will vouch for me. Bread is easy to make but time-consuming. I went ahead and saved us some time since I know how long this process is. I mixed the ingredients for a basic white bread, and then I let it rest for an hour in these greased bowls."

"What are some of the things in it?" Willow asked as they moved to stand in front of their separate bowls which Ainsley spaced out along the massive island.

"Water, active dry yeast, flour, milk, butter, honey, and salt. That's it," Ainsley said. She looked to Sloane. "What's next?"

Feeling confident, she said, "We need to lightly sprinkle our work surface with flour so the dough doesn't stick."

Sloane demonstrated at the spot in front of her, and the others mimicked her. Then they turned back to Ainsley.

"Now, comes the fun part. Punching. You do this with any yeast bread. When the dough rises, little air pockets form inside it. You punch to reduce and remove those gasses and unite the dough so it's one, cohesive form. Make a fist and push it gently but firmly into the center of your dough"

They did so, watching the puffy dough deflate. Ainsley had them fold the edges into the center, working it until the dough formed a ball.

"Remove it from the bowl now and work it at your floured space," Ainsley instructed. "We'll knead it for four minutes. Watch Sloane or me."

She felt proud to be able to show off her limited skills, showing Rylie how to use the heels of her hands in the process.

Ainsley next had them divide their dough into three equal pieces.

"We're going to make long ropes now," she told the group. "Flatten the first portion and then start rolling between your hands."

They watched her flatten and fold the sides, sealing the seam with her fingertips before she began rolling the rope. Ainsley explained folding and rolling helped give shape and structure to each rope.

"Aim for a foot to fifteen inches," Ainsley continued as they all started with their first piece, moving to the second and third until everyone had three equal ropes before them.

"If you can braid hair, you can braid this dough. The only difference is you'll start braiding loosely from the center to the end."

She demonstrated as they watched, capping off the end with pinching and then tucking the end under.

"These loaves will be plain. You can add different things to your loaves so they are sweet or savory. Cardamom and honey. Cinnamon and sugar. Garlic and herbs. Even cheese. You would do that when you mix up the original dough and let it rise for an hour, which is what I did before I arrived. If you'd like, you can sprinkle sesame or poppy seeds or even sunflower kernels on top of your braids for some variety now."

Sloane and Tenley opted for sesame seeds. Tenley tried poppy seeds, and Willow added sunflower kernels to hers.

Ainsley supervised how much to sprinkle onto the completed braids. They set their loaves on greased baking sheets and covered them with cloths, learning the bread would need to rise again for another forty-five minutes before baking it.

"Look at your loaf now. In three-quarters of an hour, it will have doubled in size. Let's wash our hands and catch up while it's rising."

"Anyone want some iced tea?" Tenley asked. "It's herbal. A ginger and turmeric combo that's decaf and tasty."

Everyone agreed to a glass, and they took their drinks to the large den, which was open to the kitchen.

Sloane spoke up. "I have some news that I want to share with all of you." She looked to Willow. "I'm going to be leaving Boo's soon. You've been a great hostess, but I am going to rent a small place for a few weeks." She grinned. "You all know that I'm seeing Gage, and I want to spend as much time with him as possible as I'm making my final decision."

"Which is?" Tenley asked, a hopeful look on her face.

"I want to join you in the Cove. Permanently."

Loud squeals sounded. Everyone leaped up, taking turns hugging Sloane.

When things had settled down, she said, "I think I was lucky to have been able to travel the world and report on so many fascinating stories over the years. Professionally, I was very fulfilled. Personally, I've had no life. What happened with Mwangi in Africa was a wakeup call to me. I decided I don't want to be fifty years old and have only a body of work to show for my life. I hold each of you dear and want to build on those friendships. I also find that I need to put down roots. I want to have a family of my own someday. I can't think of a better place than the Cove to make my home and raise those kids. I can't say if it will be with Gage, but I'm hoping so."

"Do you love him?" Ainsley asked her.

"I do. but I know neither of us need to rush into anything. By staying here, I'm giving us a chance. To see if love can take root and grow."

"I spoke with Shayla Newton," Rylie said. "She said the house Nash rented is available if you want to see it. I told her we would give her a call this afternoon. She's happy to show it to you, and if it doesn't suit you, she has a couple of other places in mind you might like."

"I'll definitely look at it today," she said.

"Do you think it will be hard for you to settle in one place after traveling so much for so long?" Willow asked.

"I loved everything about my job, but it was beginning to wear on me. News, for the most part, focuses on sadness. Tragedies. Conflicts. All of that seeped into my soul. I'm ready for happiness and light to replace it. Yes, I will still want to travel in the future, but only for pleasure. What I have to do now, though, is discover what I'm meant to do here in the Cove."

"Is journalism totally out?" Tenley asked. "Would you consider writing for a newspaper or even working for a station in Portland?"

"The days when I get my adrenaline fix with news are over," Sloane said firmly. "I might follow you, Tenley, and write. At least one book about my experiences in the world of news. I also realize that I don't have to choose one career and stick with it. I've been a journalist for ten years. I'm ready to flex my muscles and explore a new field. It may be the literary world. I may think of some business venture. I know, however, that I don't have to do the same thing for the next four decades. Whatever I choose to do, I want to be able to have time to be a good mom."

"It wasn't hard for me to switch gears," Tenley commented. "The world of public relations is dog eat dog, and you constantly have to pitch new ideas. I like being a writer. It uses some of the same skills as I did in PR, but what I really enjoy is being my own boss and using my imagination. I've been lucky the sales of this first book are good and the reviews are glowing. Readers are looking forward to the other two books in the trilogy. I'm excited for you, Sloane. I think we can all help you think of ideas of things to pursue in the Cove."

"Fortunately, I'm not worried about money," she told them. "I made an excellent salary for a decade and banked most of it. Ted also left me money, which I'm investing part of in Gage's new workout facility."

Sloane briefly told them about the fitness center

and how the money she was contributing would build a natatorium named in Ted's honor.

She concluded with, "This will be a living tribute to Ted. Gage suggested we create a bust of him and have a plaque at the entrance to the natatorium so people will know exactly who Ted was."

"I may be able to help you on that front," Willow said. "I don't have Boo's sculpting skills, but I do have a few artist friends who are sculptors."

"That would be terrific," she said. "I've gone through and pulled a few pictures of Ted that an artist might be able to work from. Contact your friends and see if any of them are available to meet with me. We can Zoom. I can send them the photographs, and they can see if they would be interested."

"I'll set it up," Willow promised. "And as long as we're sharing, I have some very big news." She paused. "Dylan and I are expecting. The baby should be here in late September."

Another round of hugs and congratulations followed and then Tenley said, "You won't believe this, but Carter and I are also due near the end of September, too. What if we give birth on the same day? Wouldn't that be crazy?"

More congratulations followed and Tenley added, "I will be watching Ainsley very closely. I need your guidance on everything from changing diapers to bathing a baby. I know nothing!" she exclaimed.

A timer went off, and Ainsley said, "I'll be happy to share with you and Willow. Now, we need to go back to our loaves of bread."

They returned to the kitchen and slid their bread into the preheated ovens.

Ainsley set the timer for thirty minutes. "Each oven bakes at a different rate. Some are slow and some are fast. This loaf calls for thirty-five to forty minutes of baking. I like to check after half an hour and eyeball it. We'll be looking for a golden-brown color."

"Do you want to call Shayla while we're waiting?" Rylie asked.

"Definitely. Put her on speaker phone," Sloane said.

Rylie dialed the realtor's number and told her she had Sloane with her, along with Ainsley, Tenley, and Willow.

"We've been baking bread," Rylie informed Shayla. "And talking about Sloane renting a place in the Cove while she's deciding if she wants to move here permanently."

"Sloane, what are you looking for in a rental?" Shalya asked.

"I want to be in or as close to the Cove as possible. I would prefer a two-bedroom so that one might be able to be used as an office. I'm not much of a cook, although Ainsley is trying to turn me into a baker, so kitchen size doesn't really matter to me."

Shayla chucked. "I think the cottage Nash rented would be ideal. Would you like to see it now? I can meet you there. I just finished showing a client a property and am about two minutes away."

She looked to Ainsley, who said, "You and Rylie go ahead. We can remove your loaves and let them cool. You can stop by and pick them up after you've seen the house."

"Then we can meet you now," Sloane told the realtor. "See you soon."

She and Rylie thanked Ainsley for the baking lesson and went to Rylie's SUV.

"I'd like you to put me in touch with your friend in

Portland who sells cars. I'll need one of my own. I don't know if I want to lease or buy."

"Tom Presley will be able to help you make that decision. He's not pushy as most salesmen are. He'll listen to your needs and advise you accordingly."

"Carter invited me to watch the taping of his show tomorrow with Nash and his grandfather."

"Nash is at the airport now to pick up Pops," Rylie told her. "You'll love Pops. He lives on Nash's farm just outside of Nashville. It's really a peaceful place."

Tenley turned into a drive, and Sloane said, "You weren't kidding. This is between my two roommates' houses—and close to the beach. I love that."

As they went up to the house, the door opened. Shayla greeted them.

"It's so nice to meet you in person, Sloane. I feel as if I know you since I've seen you on TV so often."

She shook the realtor's hand. "I get that a lot. People watch for years in their homes, and they come to think of you as a friend." She glanced at the house. "I like the outside and the fact that it's so close to two of my friends and the beach. Let's see the rest of it."

Shayla walked them through the furnished house, pointing out various features. The kitchen was small but had been updated the previous year. It also had plates, pots and pans, and cutlery. The bathrooms were stocked with linens. The house was wired for cable and Internet. Both bedrooms were about the same size.

"I think I could be happy here," Sloane told Shayla.

"It has been rented consistently starting the first week in June. You could have it up until then if that suits you. I would need a day or two before June first so I could have it cleaned and readied for the next tenant."

"Then I'll lease it through the end of May," she said. "Maybe by then, you and I will have worked together and found something for me to buy."

The thought of a home sale lit Shayla's eyes. "Then I'll also want to sit down with you in the near future and see what you would like in a house."

"I'll need to think about that," she admitted. "I've never owned a home. I've kept a small *pied-à-terre* in New York for years as a stopping point when I come home from overseas. Home ownership would be an entirely new ball game for me. I'll pick Rylie's brain and get advice from a few other friends before I meet with you."

"I'm happy to help out," Rylie told her. "I know you won't want something as large as what Nash and I are building, but we could run out to the property this week so you can see it and get some ideas."

"It's a date," Sloane said. Turning to Shayla, she asked, "What do I need to do regarding this rental?"

Shayla walked her through the highlights of the agreement, promising to e-mail her a copy and telling her she could sign it at the leasing office tomorrow and move in.

"I'll also need a deposit from you, as well as the first month's rent."

"I'll pay for all three-plus months when I see you tomorrow. I've got a meeting with Jackson Martin in the morning at nine and could stop by your office afterward, if it's convenient with you."

"I look forward to seeing you then." Shayla gave Sloane her card. "My contact info is all there. Text me if you have any questions before tomorrow."

Since it hadn't taken long to view the rental, Rylie

drove them back to Tenley's house, where Ainsley had just removed the five loaves of bread they had created.

Ainsley slipped off her oven mitts. "These need to cool a few minutes, and then you can take them home."

Carter entered the kitchen and inhaled deeply. "There are some pretty wonderful smells here. I'd like to sample some of each of these loaves."

"That's a good idea," Ainsley said. "In a few minutes, we can slice them and everyone can take home some of each loaf."

Willow went and gave Carter a big hug. "Hey, Daddy. We heard your news." She touched her belly. "Dylan and I are in the same boat."

A smile lit Carter's face. "That's fantastic, Willow." He glanced to Rylie and winked. "You and Nash need to get busy and catch up."

"It's not for a lack of trying," Rylie informed him pertly.

Sloane was happy for her friends, with three of them now carrying children and Rylie trying for one. It did make her feel left out, though. But all four had husbands, while she had just started seeing Gage. She might already be in love—but Gage Nelson had a lot on his plate.

She promised herself not to rush things. To take one day at a time. And prayed that Gage would fall in love with her.

CHAPTER 21

Gage finished with his class, encouraging everyone to keep up with their food and exercise diaries, and then placed the equipment they had used in the back of his truck. He climbed inside, knowing he needed to head to Jackson's office.

Where Sloane would be.

He had given her an excuse when she called him after her baking lesson with her friends, telling her he was scheduled to have dinner with the owner of a fitness center in Portland in order to pick his brain. Guilt flooded him when Sloane had responded with enthusiasm, telling Gage it was a great idea, and she couldn't wait to hear more about what they talked about. She told him she'd also composed a list of things to discuss about the facility with him. He told her he would see her at Jackson's office.

Sloane would arrive before him to handle business regarding Ted Castro's will. Jackson had arranged for the two of them to speak with Ted's attorney. Sloane had mentioned they would work on how to disperse the funds for a few charities Ted had left money to, as well as see if Elton Briggs had anything else for her to do regarding the estate.

He was coming to discuss the funds Sloane would be turning over to him from Ted's estate. More guilt filled him, and Gage thought maybe he shouldn't accept such a huge handout from her. Still, it would allow him to build the natatorium he thought would be a huge draw to the facility, and it would be a way to honor Ted Castro's memory, as well as keep him out of debt.

Gage parked in front of Jackson's office and entered, the bell tinkling as he did.

Jackson appeared in his office door. "Come on back. Sloane and I are just finishing up."

He walked down the corridor and entered the office. Sloane sat in one of the two chairs in front of Jackson's desk. She was dressed in a turquoise sweater and slim black pants. Her hair was pulled back in a low ponytail. She radiated beauty.

And she didn't love him.

He had finally worked up his courage to tell her that he loved her Saturday night. They had made love again, and she was nestled in his arms. He thought it was still too soon to declare such deep feelings for her, but he had whispered in her ear that he loved her. That he would forever.

She hadn't responded.

Her silence spoke volumes to him.

He realized he had made a terrible mistake in voicing how he felt. But with her continued silence, he knew she didn't feel as he did—or she would have echoed the same sentiment. Instead, she said nothing. After all, what could she say when she didn't feel the same way toward him?

Sloane had fallen asleep after that, exhausted by

their lovemaking. But Gage had remained awake. Upset. Worried. Fearful that she would tell him it was too much, too soon. That she wanted out. The more he fixated on it, the more sleep refused to come.

Finally, he had gotten up and turned to yoga, something that had always helped.

It didn't.

She had awakened and dressed. He dropped her at Boo's. She deliberately kept away from the subject, blithely talking about other things, and he took his cue from her. Gage knew he would not bring it up again. His wariness had kept him away from her last night. Lying to Sloane was the last thing he thought he would have done. But he didn't know how to act around her now, not after he had embarrassed himself and jumped the gun.

"Yes, I will handle that, Elton," she said to the computer screen. "Both sending in the estate and property taxes. Since Ted had no debts, we'll get the beneficiaries paid off ASAP."

Gage saw she was speaking to an older man, who had to be Ted Castro's attorney.

"I'll also contact Ted's landlord. "I know I need to go down to San Francisco and clean out his place."

"He still has three months on his year's lease," Elton Briggs said. "No rush, but it will need to be taken care of."

"Can you think of anything else?" she asked. "Jackson?" She looked to him.

"No," Jackson replied. "I think we've covered everything. I'll prepare the final accounting for Sloane to send to the California probate court with the assets, expenses, and amounts to be distributed to the charities. I'll send you a copy for your records. Thanks for your time, Elton. It was nice working with you."

Jackson ended the Zoom conference call and told Sloane, "I'll e-mail you that report, as well. You'll need to sign a hard copy of it. I'll send it certified mail to the state."

"And I'll write a formal letter to the three charities involved, telling them of Ted's wishes and seeing they get their appropriate contributions," she said. Looking to Gage, she said, "Ready to talk about the pool?"

"Sure," he said, still uneasy in her company. He had never loved anyone before, at least not a woman. His love had been for the men he served with, the soldiers he considered his brothers. Romance had never been a part of his life. To have found such an incredible woman as Sloane and fallen in love, only to find she didn't return his love, was more devastating than he had guessed. He didn't know how he would be able to be in her company in the future, especially alone.

And he really didn't want to accept money from her, but he had no way to back out of their deal now. Honoring Ted's memory was very important to Sloane. He wouldn't behave like a petulant child and take that away from her.

"I've been in touch with my architect, Harry Winters," he began. "Jackson has met him and reviewed the plans, both with and without the pool. I e-mailed Harry pictures of the site I bought. He's recommended two commercial construction firms to me and has worked with both of them. I have appointments tomorrow afternoon in Portland with both of them."

"Oh, I'd love to come along," Sloane said enthusiastically. "That is, if you don't mind."

Gage did mind—but he knew she read people well and could help him make the decision which firm to go with.

"I would appreciate that."

Jackson opened a file folder and handed both of them a document. "This is what I've prepared regarding Sloane's gift to you regarding the building of the natatorium. I've kept the language simple. Basically, it awards you a set amount from Ted's estate, in exchange for the naming right to the natatorium and the guarantee of a small memorial featuring Ted Castro."

"Willow is going to speak to a few sculptors about Ted's bust," Sloane shared. "I should know more about that later today."

"Why don't we go over the particulars and have the two of you sign?" Jackson suggested.

He spent several minutes interpreting the legal language of the document. Both Gage and Sloane felt comfortable signing it when he finished, having no questions between them.

Jackson collected the documents, telling them he would get copies to both of them. He also said he would contact Gage's bank.

"It might take a few days for the transfer to be complete, but the funds will be in your business account by the end of the week, Gage." Jackson smiled. "You can start building and complete your facility being totally debt-free. That's quite an accomplishment."

Sloane beamed at him. "All your savings and hard work and savvy investing will really pay off. Do you know how long it will take to build the entire facility?"

"No. That's one of my first questions for both firms I'm interviewing," he said.

She rose. He followed suit. They both thanked Jackson for his time and then walked out together.

"Have you composed a written list of questions?" she asked.

"No," he admitted, having thought he would merely listen to both pitches and ask any questions he thought of afterward, based upon what he had heard in the presentations. "I'll need to do that tonight."

"Maybe I could come over and help you with it," she suggested.

He didn't want to be around her but wouldn't let his stubbornness override common sense. Sloane was very smart and would have excellent ideas on what to ask the construction reps.

"Sure. I'll finish my last training session around five-thirty."

"I can swing by and pick up some dinner for us and be at your place a few minutes after that."

"All right," he agreed. "I'll see you later."

SLOANE KNEW something was wrong with Gage, but she couldn't put her finger on it. He wasn't the most talkative person. She would work on him tonight and see if she could pull from him what was troubling him.

She texted Shayla that she was on her way and arrived at the realtor's office.

Shayla greeted her and produced the rental agreement. "Did you have a chance to read over it?"

"I did. It was pretty straightforward. I don't have any questions for you."

She paid for the full term of the rental and the deposit. Shayla handed over the keys.

"I have someone cleaning the house now," the realtor said. "It was pretty dusty yesterday since it had been vacant a while. It will be swept and mopped. Dusted. New linens placed on both beds. The cleaners should be out of there by noon today, so you can move in as soon as you'd like after that." Shayla paused. "Have you given any thought as to what you want in your house?"

Sloane laughed. "Not really. Off the top of my head? I hate carpet and would prefer hardwood floors. A separate room for an office. A kitchen open to the den. A large backyard, because I'd like to get a dog."

"I have a form I can e-mail you. It talks about budget, location, and space. It helps you list your wants and needs and guides you on how to prioritize them."

"Such as?" she asked.

"Aesthetics. Things like paint colors. Fireplace or not. Style of appliances—or even name-brands you're fond of. Amenities you're interested in. A deck. Pool. Landscaping. I can also provide you with information about how to become prequalified. How much to spend. What points are, and whether you should take them or not."

"I can use all the help you can give me, Shayla. As I said, I've never bought a home of my own."

She wondered what Gage would want in a home and decided to bring it up with him tonight. Just ask for his input and see where the conversation led them.

"Then I'll give you a chance to read that information and think about. Talk with your friends. Have them take you through their houses and ask them to tell you what they like and don't like about each room. What they would change if they could. And remember, you won't find the perfect house with everything you want. You can either compromise, or you can buy and then do some remodeling as Tenley and Carter did. Jackson and Ainsley did quite a bit of updates when they purchased Clancy's house. I'd start with the two of them and go from there."

"All good advice, Shayla. Thank you. Once I've had time to think about things and set my priorities, I'll be back in touch with you. Oh—the beach! It would terrific to be close to the beach or even have access to it, like at Boo's house."

"That'll cost you, Sloane. The closer to the coast, the higher the price. And for beach access? You'll pay through the nose. I'm just preparing you."

"Thanks for the heads-up. I'll be in touch."

She left and returned to Boo's. Willow was working on sketches at the kitchen table before she began painting, and Sloane made sandwiches for them. She asked Willow what she liked about the house, and Willow told her, along with some of the improvements that she and Dylan had made after Boo's death.

"That's some good food for thought," she told her friend. "I'll be checking in with everyone, trying to get ideas of what I want in a house."

"I'm sure Gage will be one of those people you consult," Willow said. "Are you sure you shouldn't tell him how you feel about him, Sloane?"

"I don't know. I'm thinking on that."

Willow frowned. "There's not a lot to think about. Just tell him."

"What if he doesn't feel the same way? I don't want him pressured into telling me he loves me just because I've told him. I also don't want him to freak out."

"I'd tell him," Willow repeated firmly.

"We'll see. I need to get over to Tenley's now. Carter invited me to watch him tape his show with Nash and Pops."

"Oh, give Pops my love and a huge hug."

"Will do. I'm going to walk over. It's less than a mile, plus it'll leave you the car if you need it."

"I'll be painting all afternoon. Take the car."

"Okay," she agreed reluctantly, adding a note on her phone to meet with Tom Presley about a car. "I was going to get some takeout and eat with Gage tonight."

"I'd already pulled a casserole from the freezer. Why don't you stop and pick it up? Better yet, when are you supposed to be at Gage's?"

"A little after five-thirty."

"Then make sure you're here by five-thirty. I'll put it on to bake, and you can take it over, piping hot. I'll even toss a salad for you. And you can take some of the bread we baked." She laughed. "For you. Not Gage."

"Thank you, Willow. You are a lifesaver."

Sloane claimed her tablet, where she had a list of ideas regarding the fitness center. She would share those with Gage tonight and also help him compose a list of questions to ask the construction firms tomorrow.

On the short drive, she called Karl, Ted's landlord, identifying herself.

"Yes, Mr. Castro spoke very fondly of you, Miss Anderson. I saw about his death on the news. I'm very sorry for your loss."

"Thank you," she said quietly. "I know I need to remove Ted's belongings from the apartment. I need to see about getting a key from you."

"I can save you a trip. After Ted's death was reported on the news, I went to his apartment. If he had furniture before, it was gone. There's an air mattress. A card table and single chair. And a carton with files and news clippings. That's it, Miss Anderson. I can mail the box to you so you can go through it. But the apartment is bare. No food in the freezer or fridge. No clothes in the closet. There was a cup in the bathroom with a toothbrush in it and a tube of toothpaste that was almost empty."

"That's it?"

"Yes, ma'am. It surprised me. Then again, I haven't been in the apartment in a good while. Ted wasn't home often. He was always on the road with you."

"Please send me the box. I would like to go through it and see if there's anything I'd like to keep."

"Will do. Again, I'm sorry for your loss."

Sloane hung up, sad that Ted's life had boiled down to a single box—and the money he'd left her. It made her more determined to see his name placed in Gage's fitness center.

Two vans were in the Carters' driveway. She supposed they belonged to the film crew. She rang the doorbell, and an elderly gentleman answered, a broad smile on his weathered face.

"You don't need any introduction, young lady. I know you're Sloane Anderson. I'm Pops, Nash's granddad. Come on in."

She stepped inside and heard activity toward the kitchen. "I assume the film crew is setting up?"

"They've been here a few hours. Lots of discussing going on. Stuff about lighting and timing. I'm just ready to cook. I eat a lot of bologna and peanut butter sandwiches and nuke a frozen dinner in the microwave every night for my supper. Might be good to know how to cook something on my own."

"What are you and Nash making with Carter?" she asked.

"Hell if I know," Pops said genially. "But I know it'll be good. Carter's food always looks good on the computer."

"I watch his vlog, too. And I'm not much of a

cook," she admitted. "He's roped me into doing a segment with him."

"You mean I have to do one with Nash when I could be cooking with you?" the old man teased. He winked at her. "I may be seventy-five, but I'm still looking. You're never too old to look, you know."

"Well, I hate to tell you, Pops, but Sloane isn't available," Nash said, joining them. "She's seeing Gage."

"Gage?" Pops shuddered in exaggeration. "That boy is all muscle. No way am I going up against him. Even if Sloane here is too good for him. Sorry, honey. I want to live to love another day. Gage can keep you."

She laughed. "You're a live wire, Pops."

"Carter says I'll make for good TV," he said proudly.

An assistant appeared. "We're ready for you."

Pops grinned. "Let's go make some TV magic. Maybe after watching me, Sloane'll dump Gage's ass for a better looking, more mature man. Me."

Sloane knew the afternoon was going to be a fun one.

CHAPTER 22

Sloane watched Trae Shepherd, the director, grimace. The shoot was not going well.

And they were only ten minutes into it.

The reason was Pops. He was jovial and delightful. A true entertainer. But that's what he was doing. Entertaining.

She looked at Carter and saw him tamping down his frustration. Nash looked bewildered. Tenley's expression was pained.

"Excuse me," she said loudly, deciding to step in.

Carter and Tenley looked relieved. Nash swore softly. Trae shot her a look that begged her to fix everything. She heard one crew member say, "Finally."

"Pops, come with me," she ordered, turning her back and moving toward Carter's office.

Sloane expected Pops to follow. He did, a confused look on his brow. She closed the door.

"Have a seat," she ordered.

"What am I doing wrong?" he said. "Nash and Carter told me this would be fun. All it is, is stop and start. Cut. Start again."

"That's because you're misbehaving. Badly," she informed him.

"Me?" Pops frowned. "They just told me to be me."

"Yes, you need to be you. In the short time I've known you, Pops, I can see you are a delight. Fun to be around. Quick-witted. Spry. But you've forgotten what you signed up for."

"Then tell me, missy," he said, obviously put out with her.

"You are a guest on this show, along with your grandson. You are not the star. *Carter* is. And you came on supposedly wanting to learn how to cook something. Not cut up and tell jokes the entire time. You are acting like a class clown out there. You are here to learn," she said firmly. "That means *listening*. Can you make a sarcastic remark? Of course. Can you be funny? Sure. But the point of the show—the reason people will be tuning in to watch—is because Carter makes cooking seem simple and fun."

Sloane sighed. "You are so busy dominating and trying to entertain and get in the last word that you are ruining everything. You're also mugging at the camera. You need to listen. Learn from what Carter is teaching you. Yes, play off him and Nash. Viewers want to see your personality and how you and Nash interact. But they won't put up with a show about nonsense. They want to learn to cook. Carter is here to share his expertise with you and Nash. Do what he says. You try something. You see if you're doing it right. Ask questions. Make a few funny remarks. Be you—but a more restrained you. Remember, you're not the star. Carter and the food are."

Guilt made Pops' face flush a dull red. "I get it. I'm sorry."

"I'm not the one you should be apologizing to.

Time is money in the TV business. I know that better than anyone. If Carter and the director can't get a great first show in the can, they may cancel it. I know you don't want to see that happen."

"No, ma'am," he said firmly. "I get it now. I know my part."

"Then let's go try it again. And look at Carter, Nash, or the food. Not the camera."

"Got it."

They left the office and returned to the kitchen, where the crew viewed Pops with suspicion. Nash looked embarrassed. Carter appeared frustrated.

Good to his word, Pops said, "I'm sorry about how I was acting. I'm here to learn something. And show others you can be seventy-five and still keep learning. Come on. We haven't got all day. Let's start at the top. No stopping this time. I'll roll with things."

Relief blanketed the room. Tenley moved to Sloane and slipped an arm about her waist. "Thank you," she whispered. "For whatever you said to him."

"No one knew how to approach Pops and get him back on track. He'll be fine now."

Pops was better than fine. He brought a warmth and his trademark humor—now in small doses—to the segment. Sloane watched the cooking lesson unfold, with Carter praising Pops and Nash for their efforts, telling Pops he was asking great questions that viewers at home also had.

When they pulled out the completed lasagna and each man took a fork to it, Carter had them talk about the flavors and then what they had learned. Both Pops and Nash gave thoughtful answers.

Trae said, "Cut! That was fantastic TV," he told them.

"Sloane, you need to try a bite of this," Pops called.

"You, too, Tenley. Hell, the whole crew needs a taste. Nash and I done good."

While Tenley found plates and served lasagna to the small crew, Sloane decided to pull the director and Carter aside.

"Thank you for saving this shoot," Carter said fervently. "I was afraid we were dead in the water."

"I don't know what you did to whip Pops into shape, but he made for great TV after you talked to him," Trae said.

"I think it did come out well," she agreed. "But will the cooking be all?"

"What do you mean?" Carter asked. "We introduced Nash and Pops and gave a brief background on both."

"You need more," she said. "Can I try something to show you what I mean?"

"I'm game if you are, Carter," Trae said.

"Okay. I need a cameraman and Pops."

Sloane went and talked to a cameraman, who told her his brother had worked with Ted at a California news station. She appreciated hearing that because it gave them a connection.

"I need you to come out on the porch and shoot some film for me," she said. "I want to talk with Pops."

"Fine with me. You worked nothing short of a miracle," he told her.

She grabbed Pops and had them both slip into jackets and go outside. She also carried a chair from the kitchen for her to sit in.

"This may be part of the show," she told the old man. "I want you to sit on the swing. I'll ask you a few questions. Look at me as you answer, not the cameraman."

"Okey-dokey."

Placing the chair directly across from Pops, she told the cameraman to shoot from behind her.

"I don't want to be in any shot," she instructed. "Just Pops."

Sloane then asked Pops a few things about himself and growing up. Taking on Nash and the things they used to do together. Then she had him talk about food and what he liked to eat. The things he learned today.

"That was great," she told him. "I'm going to do the same with Nash."

Pops went inside and sent Nash out. He situated himself on the porch swing, and Sloane repeated some of the same questions but also aimed for different ones.

When they finished, Nash asked, "Is this part of the show?"

"If Trae is smart, it will be," the cameraman said.

Inside, she pulled Carter and Trae and had them watch the raw footage. It totaled about fifteen minutes.

When it finished, she said, "I know this is way more than you could use, but you can take snippets of it. Use some at the beginning and then weave those small gems throughout the actual cooking lesson. It will bring variety to the show. It will also allow viewers a glimpse into these two men and who they are. What they mean to each other. Cut my questions out. I asked everything in a way that had them repeat what I asked them anyway. I think it will make for more than a typical, run-of-the-mill cooking show."

"You aren't kidding," Carter said. "I need you to do this for every segment."

"I agree," Trae said. "Because of your background in interviewing, you got gold from those two."

"It took me time to learn just how to ask questions

and how to get to the heart of the matter," she said. "But anyone experienced in journalism could do this. Even Carter could, now that he sees what direction I went."

"No, I want you," Carter said. "You're going to be in the Cove for a while. I want to hire you to do these segments for my show. The network won't have to pay you since they didn't budget for that. But I will out of my own pocket."

"For a friend?" Sloane asked. "I'll do it for free. It's always something I can slap on my resume," she joked.

"You would be great as a guest," Trae said.

"Sloane has already agreed to come on," Carter said happily.

"Could we shoot her episode now?" the director asked.

Her heart skipped several beats. She hadn't been on camera since the day Mwangi and his rebels invaded the school. But suddenly, she knew if she could conquer this—go back on camera—she would be the winner. Not the African gang lord.

"I hadn't talked with Sloane about what we would cook together," Carter said hesitantly.

"Anything you choose is fine with me. Whatever's in your fridge, let's go for it. I just need a few minutes to prepare. And have hair and makeup take me in hand." She glanced down at her sweater. "Turquoise should photograph well in Carter's kitchen, don't you think?"

"It's perfect," Trae assured her.

The director called over the hair and makeup people. They took Sloane in hand, using Carter's office to ready her. She asked that they leave her ponytail to keep it out of her way as she cooked, and the stylist agreed, undoing and fluffing it some. The makeup artist applied the makeup, finishing with a terrific lip color that Sloane made certain she got the name and brand of.

"You like it so much," the makeup artist said, "it's yours. You saved today's shoot. A tube of lipstick is a small price to pay." She handed it to Sloane.

The pair left and she closed her eyes, mentally preparing herself as she slowed her breathing. Then she pushed all external thoughts away and concentrated on her breath. On the gentle sound of it. On how serene she felt when she was aware of it.

When she opened her eyes, Sloane felt like a new person. Would she have a panic attack in the future? It was possible. But she knew she was in control now. She would be doing something fun with a new friend. She was eager to get on camera again and test herself.

Returning to the kitchen, Tenley met her. "Are you ready for this?"

"I am. I'm looking forward to it. Carter told me yesterday to make the most of the life I had. Those are words I plan to live by from now on."

Trae gave her a few final instructions, and they began filming. Sloane joined Carter in his kitchen, mentioning she wasn't much of a cook, but she certainly enjoyed eating a well-prepared meal and that she was trying new activities and bringing more fun into her life.

"Nothing says fun like salmon," he teased. "Sloane was one of my wife's roommates in college, so I know she appreciates good seafood because they've eaten a lot of it together over the years."

She pushed up the sleeves of her sweater. "I'm ready to tackle it. What are we making?"

"Baked salmon," Carter said. "It's simple and ready in less than half an hour. You can pair it with a green vegetable or rice. I also like to serve a nice side salad with it."

He handed her an apron, and she tied it. "Let's do this!" she said with enthusiasm.

Carter told her about the handful of ingredients, saying either chicken broth or white wine could be used on the two fillets he had waiting.

"Could we try one with each?" she asked. "That way, I'll know which I prefer when I make this in the future."

"I like your style," he said.

They patted the salmon dry and brushed it with butter before mixing a little lemon juice, pepper, and tarragon. Carter separated the mixture into two bowls and then added a quarter cup of the liquids into each and had her stir.

"Normally, we'd bake in the same pan. Since we're mixing flavors, we'll use two separate ones."

They got the salmon into the oven and sliced zucchinis and tomatoes, adding olive oil, garlic, and Parmesan cheese.

"This microwaves really well," he told her, giving her the time and power level. Sloane placed the veggies inside and got it going.

He taught her how to put a simple cashew pear salad together, finishing it off with a poppyseed dressing.

The vegetables finished at the same time the salmon did. Carter had her remove everything, and Sloane mimicked his plating of those dishes.

"You can top this off with a crisp, white wine or sparking water," he said. "Think you could replicate this, Sloane?"

She grinned. "I'm going to make this meal for my boyfriend, Gage Nelson."

Now, the entire world—or at least those who watched Carter's cooking show—would know she was taken.

CHAPTER 23

Gage had scheduled make-up sessions with his afternoon clients, telling each of them why he was bailing on them. All were thrilled that he was opening his own fitness facility and promised they would join—and spread the word.

He showered and dressed in the only sports shirt he owned. Thankfully, he had a pair of dark slacks to wear with it. Everything he owned was either gym wear or casual T-shirts and jeans. He hoped the reps from the two construction companies wouldn't judge him unfavorably because he wasn't in a coat and tie.

Last night had been eye-opening for him. Sloane had brought over a meal she had cooked on her own, from a filmed segment she did at Carter's house. She explained how she had watched Nash and Pops shoot their show and how the director had asked her, since she was already there and had agreed to be one of Carter's guests, if she wouldn't mind shooting her episode on the spot. Sloane had excitedly told Gage about it as she heated up the meal she had prepared earlier in the Clarks' kitchen as the cameras rolled.

What had thrilled her the most was she seemed to

have lost the fear which had weighed her down ever since the kidnapping at the girls' school in Africa. She told Gage about her talk with Carter. What he had shared regarding Emily's death and how he urged her live in the now and not let Mwangi steal another second from her. While she had been a bit nervous, she had done some of the yoga breathing and been able to go on camera without any sign of a panic attack.

Not only had Sloane cooked, she brought a list to him that was so comprehensive, he realized how ill-prepared he was to open his own gymnasium and natatorium. His entire focus had been on raising the capital and finding the right architect to bring his dream into reality. He had worked so hard on that portion that he'd let his foot off the gas. Sloane had given him different lists to consider, and they were comprehensive.

The first involved one-time, startup costs. While he had already chosen and paid for the physical location of the center and also worked with Jackson on incorporating and obtaining a business license, the other costs were investments necessary for the kind of facility he wanted to provide the community. She had included estimates for gym equipment, telling him her research showed he could easily get a discount if he purchased equipment in sets as a complete package, versus buying individual machines. He would need to investigate licenses and permits, as well as comply with health and safety standards in Oregon—all things he should have already been thinking about.

She had researched the kinds of certifications his staff would need and handed him folders with information from the National Academy of Sports Medicine, the American Council on Exercise, and the

National Strength and Conditioning Association, among others. She also had a list of legal paperwork she hoped he had already discussed with Jackson. Jackson had been on to Gage to meet with him again so they could create his business plan, operating agreement, and employment agreements, but he had put off doing so. Now, he realized he should be not only on top of these things but getting ahead of the game. Once they broke ground, things could move quickly. He didn't want to drag his feet and bog down the process because he was unprepared.

Insurance was another legal necessity, according to Sloane. She provided detailed notes to him about general liability, workers' compensation, and surety bonds, something he had never heard of. She also had plans regarding marketing, with a website, online advertising, and radio and TV campaigns, as well as brochures.

She stressed he would need a computer network in order to accept payment for gym memberships, handle payroll, and order new or replacement equipment. She even had thought about the way his employees should dress, giving his staff uniformity, stressing he needed to create a logo to place on the staff shirts and his website and promotional materials.

Sloane mentioned though the original plans didn't have it, he might think of adding a juice bar or place to sell merchandise such as supplements, protein shakes, and apparel. The locker rooms would need basic supplies, such as towels, soap, and shampoo in the showers. Even hairdryers were a suggestion.

And that was just the initial costs.

Recurring costs would include insurance, utilities, equipment repairs and maintenance, and permits, not to mention salaries for his staff. She thought providing free Wi-Fi would be smart, as most members would expect it. He even needed to budget for cleaning supplies or a cleaning service which would need to come in daily.

Frankly, it was mind-boggling, the thought she had put into it—and everything he needed to do.

As smart as he was, and as well as he had done playing the market and earning the money to open his dream gym, Gage realized he'd only achieved the tip of his dream. So much more needed to take place before it became a reality. Sloane was on the ball about all of this. He had taken in everything she mentioned and told her he wanted to read over all her notes before tomorrow's meetings with the contractors. Disappointment had crossed her face, and he knew she was as ready for sex as he was. Sloane left him with a brief kiss, telling him she would see him tomorrow afternoon.

But Gage felt himself pulling more and more away from her. Sloane didn't love him. She was way smarter than he was, really out of his league, if he were being honest with himself. And he couldn't help but think she would be gone soon. His heart had already taken a beating when she couldn't tell him she loved him. It would be worse once she left. He decided he needed to cool things between them. Tell her they should pull back. That he would be devoting every waking minute to the fitness center and didn't have time to handle a relationship.

It might hurt her, but then again, he was already hurting pretty badly himself. Someone with Sloane's looks and personality would easily find another man. One better suited for her. One who had the education and background and breeding to be a better match than he ever could. Not a foster kid who bounced around the system unwanted, one with a GED who would have to continue living on a shoestring if he were to make a go of his facility.

He had agreed she could come along to hear the presentations, and he wouldn't back out of it. She might hear or see something he missed. He needed her guidance. Then that was it. He would call it quits. Stand on his own. See his facility built.

He had no other choice.

Gage texted her he was on his way to pick her up and slipped into his coat. When he pulled into Boo's driveway, he thought that he would need to slowly withdraw from socializing with their common circle of friends. He would still run with the guys in the morning, but going to Game Night and other things, such as back yard barbeques, needed to stop. He didn't think he could be around Sloane and not want to touch her. Kiss her. Make love to her.

His excuse would be how busy he was. Not that his friends would buy it. But they were tactful enough not to call him out. Besides, Sloane would be gone in a few months. She had mentioned to him that her contract ran for another three months and how her boss had generously agreed to her taking a sabbatical. Gage assumed it would be through those three months—and then she would sign a new contract. She was popular with viewers. The network execs wouldn't want to lose her. And now that she seemed to have regained her equilibrium, she would go back to reporting with a vengeance. She was meant to be shared with the world—and not confined to a small town on the Oregon coast.

He pulled up to the house. The February day was chilly and windy, so it didn't surprise him that she wasn't waiting on the porch.

She must have seen his truck arrive, though, because the door opened and she came down the porch stairs, wearing a black blazer and black pants, a cream blouse beneath it. She looked like the professional she was. Once again, he worried about how underdressed he seemed. Then he decided his money was as good as any guy who wore a suit. He would select the best construction firm and hope they wanted him as much as he wanted them. Thanks to Sloane's abundance of preparation, Gage had spent half the night Googling to see what he should ask in today's meeting.

Getting out of the car, he beat Sloane to her door and opened it for her before coming around and climbing back into the truck.

"You look very nice," he said neutrally.

She laughed. "It's a *Be on TV* stateside outfit. Black and navy blazers are typical for news reporters. You can place neutrals under them or spice them up with color. To be honest, I don't own a whole lot of clothes. Just a few basic business pieces like these. The rest of my wardrobe was more suited to the places I went abroad, especially Third World countries. Lots of tans, dark blues, and sage. No jewelry. Minimal makeup, even if I was on national TV. That was because a lot of my reporting was done out in the field. I mean literal fields. Some reporters abroad report from economic summits or cover political elections. I got the war zones and weather disasters and drug lords and smuggling. Not that I minded. I don't mean to complain. I *wanted* to report on the stories I did from the places I was assigned. Even if it did embarrass my parents."

"I'm sorry that they didn't value you and your work," he told her.

"I remember getting a letter from Tish. She asked why I couldn't cover presidential balls or Nobel Peace

Prize ceremonies. She said I looked foolish appearing on television in a bush jacket and safari gear and hated that my hair was forever in a ponytail. She especially despised that I only wore lipstick and not full makeup."

"A letter?"

Sloane rolled her eyes. "My parents stopped speaking to me when I didn't become engaged upon college graduation and I accepted a news job. Thatcher cut off all communication with me, but Tish wrote a couple of times over the years, always berating me. It doesn't matter. I am like a person from another planet to them, an oddity that doesn't rate spending ten seconds thinking about." Sloane paused. "That's why it's nice to have Willow and Tenley as my friends and true sisters. They don't judge me. They merely accept me as I am."

They drove for a few minutes and then she asked, "Do you stay in contact with any of your foster brothers or sisters?"

Gage barked out a harsh laugh.

"That's a no, I take it."

"A big no," he agreed. "No matter what family, it was always a competition. From the basics, such as food or clothing, to luxuries like attention. Anything you were given, others tried to steal. Shirts. Shoes. A toothbrush. I never made friends with any other foster child. As far as I was concerned, they were the enemy."

Sloane placed a hand on his forearm. He tensed.

"I'm sorry you had the childhood you did, Gage. But it helped you become the man you are now. All on your own, you set goals, such as getting your GED and becoming a Navy SEAL. It helped you study business and stocks and save a crazy amount of money. You're reached your dream of building your own fitness center from scratch and will be running it soon. You're a good man, Gage. You'll be a good father. You will instill the right values and discipline in your kids, and you'll love them with all that love you have inside you. Love that's grown over the years and will spill out, with happiness, when you have a family."

"I don't think I'll ever have kids," he said bluntly, not believing he could be a good father when he hadn't known one himself and didn't know how to love a child.

Her hand fell away. "You don't?"

"No," he said flatly.

If Sloane wanted children, hearing he didn't would definitely push her away.

Not a word passed between them the rest of the way into Portland.

When he pulled into the parking lot, he said, "We're meeting at Harry Winters' office. He's my architect. I asked Harry to sit in on the presentations, since he designed the building. He's worked with both commercial construction firms in the past. I value his feedback."

He got out of the truck and saw Sloane quickly did the same. They walked up to the building and signed in, being directed to an elevator. Once they arrived at Harry's firm, a receptionist greeted them and took them to a conference room, asking if they wanted anything to drink. Sloane asked for water. Gage said he didn't want anything.

Harry entered moments later, his smile broad.

"Sloane Anderson? You were maybe the last person I thought I would see in my conference room. What are you doing here?"

"Hello, Harry," Sloane said. "I'm familiar with

Gage's project and asked to sit in on the presentations."

The architect looked to him. "You've been holding out on me, Gage. I had no idea you knew someone like Sloane."

He shrugged, retreating into silence.

Sloane rescued the awkwardness. "Gage and I have a few friends in common. I'm visiting my two college roommates, who live in Maple Cove. Gage is friends with their husbands. I've heard him speak about his fitness facility and found it interesting. Your plans are really well done, Harry. I was impressed by them and how you brought Gage's vision to life."

"Thank you."

"I'd move the locker rooms if I were you, though."

Harry's eyebrows shot up. "You would? Why?"

She launched into a quick discussion with Harry, sparring verbally with him, making several good points.

Harry chuckled. "You've won me over, Sloane. I agree with you. "What do you say, Gage?"

"Sounds good," he said.

Harry shook his head. "A man of few words. That's our Gage."

The receptionist appeared in the doorway. "Woods & Waters people are here."

"Show them back," her boss said. "Sloane, feel free to ask any questions. I'll do the same. Gage, I think after the presentations, we can talk about both firms, but I also believe your gut will tell you by then which to go with."

Gage listened to their pitch and an hour later, heard the second one. Both companies shared a bit of their history. How long they'd been in business and the number they employed. They both talked about various projects they had completed and who would supervise his project. One used subcontractors, while the other did all the work themselves. Each talked about the timeline for his project and how time was built in for delays, as well as how those delays would be handled.

When prompted, he asked them for contact information for past clients who had similar construction projects to his. He also inquired about the payment schedule and their company safety records. When he asked what made their firms unique—and uniquely qualified to build his fitness facility—he sensed Sloane's approval of the question.

"Do you have any questions, Harry? Sloane?" Gage asked.

"Why don't you tell Mr. Nelson about your suppliers," Harry suggested. "I'm sure he's interested in the quality of the materials being used."

Gage thought Sloane asked the best question. "Is your bid an estimate or a fixed price? Mr. Nelson would like to establish the exact costs from the start, so there won't be any surprises as the project moves forward to completion."

When the second presentation ended, Gage and Harry thanked them for their time.

The moment the door closed, Harry said, "What do you think?"

"I'd like to hear what Sloane has to say," he said. "I value her opinion."

She colored slightly, and he knew she recalled their earlier conversation in the car when he stated he was sorry that her parents hadn't valued her or her work.

"I'd go with the first firm. Woods & Waters."

"Why?" he asked.

"Both firms knew their stuff and had ready answers and could complete the project within a few weeks of each other. I liked that Woods didn't use subcontractors. They also had a firmer timeline in place and what I thought were more solid ways to address delays and make up the time if they hit a snag. While they were speaking, I checked on both companies' safety records. Woods & Waters had a better one. While their bid was slightly higher, it was fixed. No surprises. The other company couldn't vouch for their total being the bottom line."

"I agree with you," Gage said. "I want to go with Woods and Waters."

"I can contact them on your behalf now. Both knew you were eager to get the ball rolling. I'm sure they'd be happy to have you come to their offices now and firm up things. They're located only two blocks away."

"Yes. Let them know we're coming," he told the architect. "I want to break ground immediately."

Harry told Sloane how nice it was to meet her, and Gage and Sloane left the architect's office.

In the elevator, she said, "You can head over to the offices on your own. You've made your choice. It's a good one. I think they'll do a terrific job."

He frowned. "Where will you be?"

"I've got an appointment with a friend of Rylie's. Tom Presley. He's going to show me a car."

"You're buying a car?"

"Buying or leasing. Tom will help me decide."

The elevator doors opened. They walked to the entrance of the building. He felt blindsided by her suddenly walking away. It was what he thought was best, but he somehow wasn't ready to let go just yet.

"Can I give you a ride to the dealership?" he offered.

"No, I'll do a ride share. You need to get to Woods & Waters and get a start date on your project."

She took out her phone and began tapping it, scheduling her ride.

Gage stood there awkwardly for a moment. "Okay. So, I'll see you back in the Cove."

Sloane glanced up. "Yes," she said coolly.

"Thank you for coming with me today," he told her. "I really appreciated hearing your opinion. And for everything, really. The information you've pulled together for me. The lists you've made of all I need to consider and do."

"I enjoyed listening to the presentations." No elaboration. Sloane went back to typing. She finished and looked at him. "They'll be here in four minutes."

"Okay. I'll... talk to you soon."

Gage left her sheltered inside the building, feeling it had been chillier in there than when he stepped outside.

He had wanted to end things with Sloane. Obviously, his remarks about kids had definitely done that.

Then why did he feel so damned miserable?

CHAPTER 24

As Sloane waited for her car to arrive, she quickly texted Rylie.

In Portland & want to drop by your friend's dealership. Have you mentioned me to him?

Rylie answered moments later, assuring Sloane she had discussed her with Tom Presley. She numbly stepped from the building and approached the car she had ordered, climbing in and greeting the driver. He told her it would be about a twenty-minute ride, and she settled against the cushion, trying to make sense of what had happened between her and Gage today.

She had sensed something different about Gage for a couple of days now and had worried he regretted making their relationship physical. She had wanted to share with him last night during dinner about leaving Willow's and renting the former cottage Nash had when he'd first arrived in the Cove. Instead, she had directed the conversation toward his new business venture, realizing too late that in her enthusiasm, she had bombarded him with information. He had told her he needed time to read through and absorb all she had brought, and Sloane had reluctantly left and returned to Willow's, where she had packed up her belongings.

This morning, she had moved into the rental and hung her clothes in the closet and filled the dresser drawers, going through the house and familiarizing herself with everything. She had also returned Ainsley's clothing to her and then come back to Boo's, where she dropped off her friend's car and waited for Gage to pick her up for their appointment in Portland.

She doubted that Gage had even wanted her to come with him today, but she had bullied her way into accompanying him. He was too much of a gentleman to disinvite her. She had enjoyed listening to the representatives from both construction firms as they went through their presentations, and she was certain that Gage had selected the company that would do the best job on the project. If Woods & Waters stuck to the timeline they had presented and no unseemly delays occurred, Gage's fitness center would be completed by the beginning of June, if not earlier. He would need to make certain that he ordered all the equipment and supplies necessary to get up and running, as well as interview and hire the instructors needed to teach the various classes.

It seemed that would no longer be a concern of hers. Gage had pulled away from her, and her gut told her their relationship had ended. Obviously, a deal-breaker for her had been the fact he didn't see a future with children in it. She was determined to have them and be a much different mom than Tish. Sadness filled her, though. What had once burned so brightly between them had flamed out quickly.

She wished she understood what had gone wrong between them, but she was extremely grateful she had not told Gage that she loved him. She might never understand what went wrong between them because he was not much of a talker, while she was all about talking things out. She wished for them to have closure, however, and decided she would arrange one final time for them to be alone to help her understand why the relationship went south. If she could get Gage could open up to her, that is.

They arrived at the car dealership, and she thanked her driver, promising to give him a good rating via the app.

Entering the showroom, Sloane looked at a few of the models on display before being approached by a salesman. He was about thirty, tall, and with an open, friendly face.

"You wouldn't happen to be Sloane Anderson, would you?" he asked with a smile.

She tamped down her swirling emotions and returned his smile. "Guilty as charged," thinking he must not watch the news.

"I'm Tom Presley, Rylie's friend from college. She tells me you're not sure if you want to lease or buy your vehicle. Let me get you something to drink, and we can go to my office and talk about it."

She passed on a drink, and he escorted them to a small, tidy office. Tom asked her several questions, and Sloane responded, finding she liked his openness and ideas. Knowing that no matter what happened between her and Gage, she would stay in the Cove, she decided purchasing a car would be more advantageous than leasing one. Tom asked about features she wanted in her car, and then he showed her several brochures, helping her narrow down her selection.

Once she had, they returned to the showroom and looked at several models there and outside. She was now ready to test drive a couple.

"If you're looking for a bargain that has most of the features we discussed, you might want to consider one of last year's models. It's February, and we still have a few of them in stock. Their prices dropped with the new models coming out, so you can get a real deal on what is a brand-new car, except in year only."

"That sounds amazing. Could I test drive one of those?"

He took her to an area of the lot, and she fell in love with a dark-maroon compact SUV. They got inside it, and Tom explained several of the features to her before they drove off the lot and through the residential streets around the dealership.

"I really like how it handles," she told him.

"Then you should take it on the highway for a few exits so you can get a feel for its pickup and how it rides at a higher speed."

He gave her instructions to the nearest interstate, and she entered the ramp, finding acceleration extremely easy. She went three miles before exiting the freeway and then looped around so they could return to the dealership.

When they arrived in the parking lot, Sloane told him this would be her car. "No need to drive any others."

It took about ninety minutes to make their way through the paperwork and get approval from her bank. She paid for the car outright, not wanting to bother with monthly payments when she had the money. By the time they finished their transaction, the car was waiting for her, having been detailed by the staff. It gleamed, giving her the thrill of having purchased her first car.

She offered her hand. "Thank you, Tom. You were a dream to work with."

He laughed. "Tell Rylie to keep sending her friends my way. I'll let you know when your license plate comes in, and we'll exchange the paper tags for you."

Getting into her new vehicle, Sloane inhaled deeply that lovely new car smell, and quickly paired her phone to it as Tom had demonstrated. She turned the ringer back on since she had silenced it during their negotiations and now saw she had a couple of texts. She quickly read through them before heading out toward the Cove.

Calling Rylie, she told her friend she had purchased an SUV from Tom. Rylie was thrilled she had been able to throw business her friend's way.

Next, she called Willow.

"Sloane, I'm so glad you returned my message. I think I've found the perfect sculptor to work on Ted's bust. I know you've just moved into your own place and you've been in Portland with Gage all afternoon, so you haven't had time to shop for groceries. Come have dinner with Dylan and me, and I'll tell you about Maia Jarrell."

She readily agreed, realizing she would need to stock her fridge and pantry tomorrow. As she drove west toward the Pacific, her phone rang. She saw it was Carter and answered.

"Hey, Carter."

"I had to call and tell you the network has looked at the rough cut Trae put together from the show with Nash and Pops. He interspersed the cooking with the comments you drew from both of them. The execs went wild over the idea. They agreed it added a dimension to a regular cooking show, getting that insight into the guest. I wanted to call and let you know and thank you for the idea. Actually, thank you for saving that episode—and the show. I think we all were a little intimidated by Pops. Eventually, I think we could have settled him down, but you saved us a ton of time by giving it to him straight."

"I was glad to help out since I was there."

"I have to also thank you for agreeing to shoot your episode on the spur of the moment. Trae and I watched not only our cooking together but you sitting on the porch swing and talking to the cameraman. Trae said it would be easy to make the cuts and weave them in because you're such a seasoned pro." Carter paused. "Were you serious about wanting to interview my guests?"

"I really was," she told him. "I'm looking for new outlets and experiences. I've decided I don't want to go back to being an international correspondent. I want to stick closer to home." She sighed. "The Cove has become home to me, Carter. Not only because Tenley and Willow are here, but because of people like you who have extended your friendship to me."

"I'm glad to hear that, Sloane. Having grown up in the Cove, I think it's the best place on the planet. I hope also that you and Gage might stay a couple."

"I think that's over, Carter," she said quietly. "Gage has a lot on his plate, trying to continue to run his fitness business and at the same time, build his workout facility. He's being pulled in a lot of different directions now, and I don't believe he has the time—or inclination—for a relationship with me."

"Are you certain about that, Sloane?" he asked. "I've seen how he looks at you. How you look at him. You two just seem meant to be."

Her eyes welled with tears, and she blinked rapidly as she kept her focus on the road ahead.

"I had thought so, too. But things have changed between us. Gage has disengaged from me," she quipped.

"I see. Well, maybe we could get together this week. I'd like to share with you the schedule that I have so far with those who have committed to tapings. I want to make sure those times and days are convenient with you."

Sloane laughed. "Since I don't have a job and not much going on, I'm free as a bird. It would be good to get those dates on my calendar, though."

They arranged to meet the next afternoon at his house, and Sloane hung up. She drove the rest of the way to the Cove and to Boo's house.

Willow came outside. "I saw an unfamiliar car pull up and you get out of it. What's going on? I thought you went to Portland with Gage."

"I did go and sit in on the meetings he had. He's chosen a construction firm and went to their offices after the presentations to sign all the paperwork and get the ball rolling. It gave me some free time. I had discussed with Rylie about meeting with Tom Presley."

"Tom is the best," her friend praised. "He helped me choose my vehicle. Rylie should probably get a commission since she's sent so many customers his way." Willow walked around the car, admiring it. "You did really well, Sloane. It's gorgeous. You have a new car and a place to live, as well as new friends and a great boyfriend. I'm so happy you decided to stay in the Cove."

Sloane's throat grew thick with tears and she cleared it. She decided not to mention anything about Gage and concentrate on the business at hand.

"Come on in. I left Dylan tossing a salad."

They went into the house, and over dinner, Willow told Sloane a little bit about Maia Jarrell.

"I can call up her website so you can see her previous work. She's the one I had in mind from the beginning. I spoke with her this afternoon, and she sounded eager to talk with you about the project. If you'd like, you can FaceTime her after dinner. I told her to expect your call sometime this evening."

"Let me clear the dishes," Dylan offered. "You show Sloane Maia's website."

They retreated to the sitting room, and Sloane perused Maia's work.

"She's really good."

"I told you so," Willow said.

"I think what I like best is the way her subjects' eyes look human though they're cast in bronze."

"Let me give you her number, and you can call her now."

"Where is she located?"

"She recently returned from Paris and is living just outside of San Francisco."

"Good, I didn't want it to be too late when I called."

Willow left and Sloane took time to e-mail Maia a few pictures before dialing her number.

"Hello?"

"Hi, Maia. This is Sloane Anderson, Willow Martin's friend."

"Ah, Sloane. Willow told me about your friend passing and how you want to honor him. It's a very unique idea, naming a natatorium in his honor. Do you have a few pictures of Ted I could see?"

"I viewed your website a few minutes ago and found your e-mail address. I just sent you three shots of Ted by himself and two with me. They're from different angles, so I hope that would help you get a total picture."

"I'm bringing them up now. Oh, Sloane, Ted was a fine-looking man. Mid-fifties, I'd guess?"

"Yes. We were colleagues and best friends. I lost him in a very public, tragic way. I want to make sure I honor him because I don't want a good man like Ted Castro forgotten."

"Tell me about him," Maia urged.

Sloane spent a few minutes discussing Ted's work ethic. How he had a heart for children and how loyal he could be.

"Ted loved the water most of all. He swam from an early age and loved surfing, skiing, and kayaking. In fact, I recently scattered his ashes in the Pacific because I thought he would feel most at home there."

"Hmm. I may think of a way to incorporate his love of water into my work." Maia paused. "Are you set on a bust? Or would you be open to a small sculpture the size of a bust?"

"I hadn't really given that any thought. Yes, Maia, I would be open to a full sculpture. Especially if it reflected Ted's love of the water."

They discussed Maia's fees, and Sloane said she would send the deposit. Maia gave Sloane her banking information and then said, "I will text you numerous sketches once I begin. They won't be final by any means. I do sketches to explore my subjects. Sometimes, I will do between thirty and fifty before I hit upon exactly how I want to portray my subject."

"You're the expert, Maia. I'll leave things in your hands. I look forward to seeing the drawings you send me."

"It will be a process, Sloane. I may have you select a few you like best and then work on combining elements of each sketch into a single one. I'll work on some that I'd do for a traditional bust, but I'll also try a few other ideas that try to incorporate water in some way. When does the natatorium open? I'm sure you'd like to have it done by that time."

"Probably early to mid-June," she replied. "They're about to break ground on the facility."

"Okay. That gives me an idea of how I want to work this into my schedule. I'll be in touch soon," Maia said.

Sloane went and found Willow, who was watching TV with Dylan.

"I really enjoyed chatting with Maia," she said. "She'll be sending me sketches soon. Thanks for putting me in touch with her."

"I'd be happy to look at anything she sends you and give you my professional feedback. Especially since I've met Ted."

"I appreciate your input. I think I'll head home now," she told the couple.

"First night sleeping in a new bed," Dylan said. "Hope you enjoy the place. And if you don't? You're always welcome here."

Sloane knew Dylan wasn't giving her lip service and really meant it.

"I know. But I do like the place."

"At least it will give you and Gage some privacy," Willow said.

She smiled tightly. "I'll talk to you soon."

Sloane returned to her new car and drove the short distance to her temporary home. She parked and went inside. The house was quiet. A wave of loneliness swept through her. She began second-guessing her decision to remain in the Cove, now that she and Gage were no longer together. Then she decided she wasn't going to let a man and a failed relationship that had barely begun dictate her future.

Maple Cove felt like home. She had friends here. Time to decide the next direction her life would take. And enough money so that her decision needn't be rushed.

Still, when she went to the empty bed, Sloane cried herself to sleep.

CHAPTER 25

S loane rose and drank a glass of water. She would have preferred to have warmed lemon water, but she had no lemons. She had nothing in the kitchen. Not a teabag or box of cereal or piece of fruit. Shopping would be her top priority this morning. She would need to go over to Salty Point to do so since they had a large market, and she had a lot to buy. She knew Ainsley made a weekly trip to Costco for bakery supplies and might tag along to see if she could also get some items for her freezer. Salmon would definitely go on her list. After seeing how simple it was to bake after her cooking lesson on film with Carter, she planned to eat the fatty fish at least once a week, especially since she lived on the coast now, and it was a healthy choice for her.

She put aside thoughts of taking that meal over to Gage's and eating with him. He would be relegated to friendly acquaintance. The Cove was too small for her to totally avoid him. She would smile and greet him whenever their paths crossed. Thoughts of wringing an explanation from him as to why things hadn't worked out between them were gone. She loved him.

She needed to get over him. Prolonging things by questioning him wouldn't be in her best interest.

Retreating into yoga, she called up an app on her phone and set it for a sixty-minute session. The app's host led her through deep breathing exercises and then a variety of poses. When she came across an unfamiliar one, such as Garland and Pyramid, she watched the instructor demonstrate the pose before she tried it herself.

Her workout left her feeling refreshed. She hit the shower, finding the water heated quickly and the nozzle was easy to adjust. It was funny how she was already starting to take things such as an indoor shower with heated water and flush toilets and toilet paper for granted again. Her years abroad would always stay with her, but she enjoyed the perks of being an American. Indoor plumbing. Refrigerators. Readily available Internet. Cable TV. She decided her next move would be to sign up for Netflix and start bingeing on water cooler shows she had missed over the last several years.

Dressing in jeans and a cable knit sweater, she grabbed the purse borrowed from Willow, thinking she needed to go into Portland to do a little shopping for basics, such as a hair dryer and several pairs of new shoes. She would also need to pick up toiletries for her bathroom. Willow had provided everything she needed in the guest bathroom. She would need to buy shampoo, bodywash, floss, and several other similar items. Even someone as low maintenance as she was needed moisturizer.

She pulled on a jacket and was about to head out on her errands when a text came in. For a moment, her heart leaped, hoping it was Gage. Then she angrily pushed that thought aside.

Call me when you have a moment. Or drop by.

It was from Ainsley. Since Sloane was hungry after her yoga session, she thought she would reward herself with a treat from Buttercup Bakery and see what her friend wanted. She could easily eat a pastry in the car on her way to do her grocery shopping

Heading your way.

Within five minutes, Sloane was parking and entering the bakery. Gloria greeted her and said Ainsley was waiting for her in the back. She went behind the counter and through the doorway, waving to Gus and hugging Ainsley, whose belly seemed to have sprouted further.

"What's up?" she asked.

"I'm going to work as we talk," Ainsley said, beginning to ice a cake. "Willow mentioned to me that you might be interested in getting a dog."

"It was pretty hard to go to sleep last night without Shadow in bed with me," she admitted. "Yes, I have thought about it."

"I think I have a perfect one for you. Stan Shorter is our local vet. His wife was in here a few minutes ago. She mentioned how Stan had brought home a border collie last night. His owner passed away suddenly, and there was no one to take him. She told me to put out the word so that Murphy could find a good home. I immediately thought of you and told Janie I'd see if you might be interested."

"I am," she said impulsively. "Give me her number. I'd love to run by and see him after I go over to Salty Point and buy some food. My cupboard is bare. I'll need to grab breakfast here before I leave."

Ainsley put down her piping tube and retrieved the phone number for Sloane.

"Tell me if you decide to get him or not. I would

take him, but with the baby coming in about six weeks, I don't want to take on the responsibility right now."

Sloane returned to the front, ordering a coffee and a cinnamon twist. Taking both to her car, she decided to eat first instead of trying to drive while she did so. Making quick work of the pastry, she drove to Salty Point and picked up everything she thought she would need for the next month. She would have to decide if she were ready for home ownership once her lease ran out or if she should continue to rent. With the Cove being on the Oregon coast and a popular tourist attraction, good housing for the summer might already be gone. If push came to shove, she supposed she could go back to Boo's until something became available.

Carting in the many sacks of groceries took time, as did putting everything away. It was satisfying, though, to see the refrigerator stocked with fresh produce and dairy products and the small pantry filled with her favorites, such as peanut butter and graham crackers. She took her other items to the bathroom, placing them in the medicine cabinet and drawers and her bath accessories in the shower.

Finally, she called Janie Shorter, identifying herself. Janie said she was home and that Sloane could come and look at Murphy now if she were free.

The moment she set foot in the Shorters' house and caught sight of the black-and-white border collie, Sloane was smitten. She sat on the floor, petting and talking to him, as Janie looked on in approval.

"Stan tells me border collies are very intelligent," Janie said. "They have an abundance of energy, though, so you would need to make certain that Murphy got plenty of exercise."

"I love long walks, especially along the beach," she told the vet's wife, wrapping her arms around Murphy's neck and kissing his head.

"Murphy is affectionate," Janie said. "He's about eighteen months old, so you wouldn't need to do any kind of potty training. Stan said he did obedience school with his previous owner and takes commands well."

"He's a perfect size," Sloane commented. "Not too large."

"Yes, he's as big as he'll get. Up-to-date on his shots, too." Janie paused. "What do you think?"

She grinned shamelessly. "I think you already know Murphy's coming home with me."

Janie smiled. "I'm so glad to hear that. Streaky, my cat, is afraid of dogs. She spent all last night and this morning under the bed. She'll be glad Murphy's found a new home. Let me gather up his toys. He's also got a leash. I can text Stan and tell him you're going to drop by his office. He may have some last-minute instructions for you."

"Thank you so much," she said, hugging Murphy and then snapping his leash onto his collar. "Let's go, boy."

Sloane carried the sack with toys to her car, placing it on the back floorboard. Murphy jumped into the backseat, and she left him there, not knowing if she should buckle him in or not. She drove to the vet's office, meeting Sandy, the receptionist.

"I'm so glad Murphy's found a home," Sandy said, beaming at Sloane. "My husband has told me not to bring home anymore animals, otherwise I would've have taken Murphy. He's a real sweetheart."

Sandy took her back to an examination room, where Sloane met with Stan Shorter. He told her a bit more about Murphy's owner and the food she should buy.

"I prepared a list of things for Murphy's new owner to know," Stan said. "When to feed him. When he's due for his next round of shots. My best advice is walk him at least twice a day. He's got boundless energy and needs to expend it on a daily basis."

Stan got her a complimentary bag of food to get started and threw in a tin of treats Murphy could have twice a day.

He accompanied them outside and spent ten minutes walking her through commands and the tone of voice she needed to use with Murphy when she instructed him to do something.

"I've already heard through the grapevine that you've been sleeping with Shadow. I prefer crate training myself and a dog who sleeps in his crate, but something tells me that won't be happening with Murphy."

Sloane laughed. "Nope. Murphy is going to be my bed buddy."

"Good luck with him, Sloane. I hope you'll enjoy having Murphy and living in the Cove."

Returning home, she gave Murphy food and water. She hoped he would adjust quickly to her and his new home. He finished eating and leaped onto the sofa, curling up. Sloane sat beside him, stroking him, marveling at how she already loved this sweet, furry animal.

Her cell rang and she glanced at the number, seeing it was the same as the last time she had spoken to Salana.

"Hello?"

"Sloane? Can you hear me?" Salana asked, her voice sounding surprisingly strong.

"Yes, I can hear you, Salana. How are you feeling?"

"Much better, Sloane. The doctors say I am strong. That I will get better. I wanted to hear your voice."

Tears welled in her eyes. "I'm very glad to hear yours, Salana."

"My speech is fine now," her friend told her. "My vision, too. The doctors are surprised both are so much better and so quickly."

"That's terrific. Johari told me your sight was blurry."

"It cleared up. Much of my mind has cleared, too. I do not recall that day, but I suppose that is a small blessing."

"I agree. What you should concentrate on is the present—and your future. How is your leg?"

"Still broken," Salana quipped, causing them both to laugh. "But they have me up. I walk with crutches. I could not at first. I knew what I was supposed to do, but my body would not respond. It does now, though."

"Will you leave the hospital soon? Go to a rehab facility?"

"That is the plan." Salana sighed. "It will take much time, but I will get better."

"I know you will."

"Johari wishes to speak to you."

"Please, put her on. And call again, Salana. Any time."

A few moments passed and then Johari said, "Hello. I hope we called you at a convenient time."

"I will always make time for Salana and you, Johari," Sloane said fervently. "Would you update me on things?"

"The doctors are shocked at my sister's progress," Johari revealed. "They say since she is young and had good health, that has helped. Her speech has improved rapidly. She does get frustrated when she wants her body to do something, and it does not respond quickly enough. She is working with a therapist now on thinking and reasoning. Her vision has cleared up. She has no sense of smell, though. That may never return."

"It sounds as if Salana has made remarkable progress in a very short period of time. That's encouraging."

"It is," Johari admitted. "But she still has a long way to go. I have talked to her of her childhood, trying to spark memories. We also talk about things going on in the world. She has a few gaps in her memory, but nothing severe. More than anything, she wants to return to teaching."

"I hope that will be possible. Is there anything I can do? Can I help pay any of her medical bills?"

"You should not feel guilty for what those men did to her." Johari paused. "At first, I blamed you for their coming to the school. I thought your reporting had brought unnecessary attention to my sister and the girls. I realize now those men were pure evil. They would have come sooner or later to burn the school and take its pupils. I am sorry, Sloane."

"Don't apologize. Mwangi and his gang are responsible. Hopefully one day, Africa will be free of such vile men."

"We can only hope. Would you be kind enough to write to Salana? I can give you my e-mail address. If you would mention to her the names of the different girls. What was being taught. What the two of you spoke of as you built a friendship. I believe it would help."

"I will do that, Johari. I will send several and keep them short. You can have Salana open them one at a time, maybe once a day, so that she won't be over-whelmed."

They exchanged e-mails and the minute they hung up, Sloane reached for her tablet. As Murphy sat next to her, she composed an e-mail to Salana, reminding her of how they met and mentioning several of the girls, especially Akachi's poems.

She then composed a series of e-mails, numbering them. Sloane talked about many of the students and all the things Salana had been teaching. She reminisced about how they would talk after classes ended for the day, Ted often joining them. Sloane also told Salana about her new life in the Cove. She described her friends, both old and new, and told about Pops and how she had scolded him as Salana might one of her pupils, assuring her that Pops rose to the occasion.

Her last e-mail shared how she had just adopted Murphy. She took a picture of the sleeping dog beside her and attached it to the final e-mail. There were ten in all, and Sloane thought they would last for at least a week. By then, she hoped to have heard from Salana and Johari again.

Nudging Murphy, she said, "You've slept enough. Let's go take a walk."

Apparently, the collie knew the W word. He bounded off the couch and trotted to the door. Sloane could have sworn he was smiling at her. She collected his leash and attached it to his collar. She would try and walk him early in the morning, after she had completed her yoga session. Today would be a later start. He would also need a walk later in the day, either late afternoon or early evening.

She set out for Willow's, thinking she would stop and see if her friend and Shadow wanted to join them on their walk. As she led Murphy down the road to

Boo's, Sloane was grateful she now had a furry companion in her life. Murphy wouldn't replace the hole in her heart left by Gage.

But having the collie would be the first step to helping her heal.

CHAPTER 26

G age complimented his last class of the day,
thanking them for their efforts today. He had
pushed them hard, thanks to his growing frustration,
and he felt guilty for doing so.

"I'll take it a little easier on you next session," he
promised, saying goodbye and loading equipment into
his truck.

He drove home and rummaged in his refrigerator
for something to eat, pulling out hummus, olives,
grapes, and a container of stew. While the stew heated,
he munched on the rest, spreading the hummus on
pita chips. Restless, he wandered the small space,
feeling like a caged tiger.

When the stew was hot, he ladled it into a bowl
and splurged, popping open a beer, a rare treat. Usually, the only beers he drank were at Game Night. He
didn't think he would be attending one of those anytime soon, especially because Sloane would be there.

As he ate his dinner, Gage realized he just wasn't
frustrated.

He was deeply unhappy.

He had always tried to keep his emotions in check,

from his early days in foster care. He never wanted anyone to know how he was feeling. The same was true during his SEAL days. Emotion swings could affect a mission, which is why he tamped everything down, from fear to anxiety to jubilation once a mission was completed. He possessed the ultimate poker face.

Now, though, he was downright miserable.

If he were going to feel this terrible, he should have soaked up every minute with Sloane while she was still in the Cove and been depressed after she left. Instead, he had pushed her away as a proactive measure, one which had ultimately failed.

Would she consider taking him back?

They hadn't truly broken up. He'd merely given her a tiny shove and drifted away, like George Clooney had detached from the tether in *Gravity* and floated into space, sacrificing himself to save Sandra Bullock.

Sloane Anderson didn't need saving, though. She had confronted her fears and the panic attacks and pushed through them. True, she might still face panic attacks in the future, but she had equipped herself with the tools to manage them. She was moving on with her life.

Gage decided he had to take a chance. He would rather have a short amount of time with Sloane before she left than never be with her again. She was one feisty, strong-willed woman, however. There was a good possibility she wouldn't take him back. But if she did, he would do anything—anything—for one more minute with her. One more hour. Another day.

Another night...

Quickly rising, he left the rest of his meal uneaten, not bothering to rinse his dishes. He tore off his clothes and got into the shower, washing away the day's sweat and grime from the many workouts he had participated in. Gage dressed and grabbed his coat, putting it on as he raced down the stairs of his apartment. Behind the wheel of his truck, his heart pounded against his ribs in anticipation. He tried to prepare himself for Sloane slamming the door in his face. If it happened, it happened. At least he was making an effort. Maybe in vain. Maybe not.

Then he thought showing up unannounced might not be wise. He pulled out his phone and texted her, trying to open a line of communication.

Would like to talk. Can I come by?

Gage stared at his screen, waiting for those dancing dots to appear as she typed a reply. He waited one minute. Five minutes. Ten. His spirits sank.

Maybe her phone was on the charger and she was downstairs eating dinner with Dylan and Willow. He decided to go straight to Boo's and see.

When he arrived, he noticed Carter's truck in the driveway and assumed he and Tenley had been invited to dinner. Of course, Sloane would want to see her friends as much as possible, especially since she was no longer seeing him.

With trepidation, he left his truck and went to the front door, ringing the bell.

Dylan answered. "Hey, Gage. Come on in. We just sat down to dinner. Join us."

Without a word, he followed Dylan to the dining room, immediately spying Willow, Tenley, and Carter.

No Sloane. Maybe she was with Rylie. Or Ainsley.

Or maybe she'd up and left the Cove.

"Have a seat," Dylan said. "I can get you a plate."

"No, thanks. I had texted Sloane and hoped I could see her."

An odd look crossed Dylan's face. "She moved out, Gage. I thought you knew."

Dylan's words crushed him. He grabbed onto an empty chair's back, his knuckles growing white.

He had missed her. She had left, truly left, without a goodbye.

Dylan's hand gripped Gage's shoulder. "Are you all right?"

"No," he admitted, tears forming in his eyes. He had never cried. Ever. But the thought of Sloane gone from his life caused them to spill down his cheeks.

"Sit," Dylan told him.

Moving to the chair, he collapsed in it. Gage placed his arms on the table and buried his face in them, sobbing. He had Dylan's hand on one shoulder. Another, lighter, feminine one touched the other.

"It's all right, Gage. We're here," Willow said, squeezing his shoulder.

He didn't know how long he cried, but it seemed forever. Regret filled him. If he could do things again, he would act so differently. He would be more open with Sloane. He would let her in more. He would soak up their time together and cherish it when it was done.

Raising his head finally, he brushed his forearm against his eyes. "I'm sorry," he apologized. "I made some pretty awful mistakes."

"With Sloane?" Carter asked.

Gage nodded. "I... I launched a preemptive strike against Sloane before she could attack me."

Tenley frowned. "You mean you tried to hurt her before she could hurt you?"

"Yeah." He shook his head, disgusted with himself. "I blew it. And now she's gone."

"No, she's not," Willow said. "Sloane moved out of here. Not from the Cove, Gage."

"What?"

Willow smiled. "Sloane is still here, Gage. She rented the same house Nash did when he arrived." Her smile faded. "I thought she would have told you, though."

Carter spoke up. "She thinks you've ended things with her. I talked to her yesterday afternoon. She was pretty upset. She said things were over between you. That you had disengaged from her. Those were her exact words."

He winced. "I did."

"Why?" Tenley demanded. "You two are terrific together."

Carter slipped an arm about his wife's waist. "Gage doesn't owe us any explanations, babe."

He looked at the circle of friends around him. "I appreciate your support. But right now, I need to get to Sloane. I hope you understand."

"We do," Willow assured him.

He hurried to his truck and checked his phone again. Still no response from Sloane. Was she so mad —or hurt—that she refused to answer a text from him?

Starting his engine, he drove the short way to the house Sloane now occupied. He wondered why she had left Boo's.

Gage hoped to get that question answered—and provide Sloane with the answers which she deserved.

He turned into the driveway, seeing a lamp burning in the window, and an unfamiliar car sitting in it. It must be the car she had leased or bought yesterday. Parking behind it, he got out and made his way to her front door, riddled with anxiety. Despite all the missions he had completed as a Navy SEAL, the bravest thing he had done in life up to this point was raise his hand and knock on this door.

When she didn't respond, Gage knocked harder. Then he beat on the door with his fist, willing her to open up to him.

He stepped back, waiting, defeated. He hadn't thought Sloane to be a coward. If anything, he believed she would have confronted him. Chewed him out. Hell, even slapped him for the way he had treated her. Not answering her door and speaking with him, though, let him know how truly hurt she was.

Turning, he started back to his truck and halted in his tracks.

Sloane was coming up the driveway, a black-and-white collie leading the way.

She froze, seeing him. "Gage?"

He moved toward her, stopping six feet away. The dog sniffed at his boots.

"Can we talk?" he asked, a lump in his throat.

"I suppose," she said, a wary look in her eyes.

He knelt and rubbed the dog's head. "Hey, buddy. I'm Gage."

"This is Murphy," she said.

"Good boy. Good Murphy," he said, stroking the dog and then rising. "Yours?"

"Yes."

She moved past him and to her front door, unlocking it, bending to unhook the leash from the dog's collar.

"Come in," she said stiffly.

Gage did, and she closed the door. Murphy moved to the sofa and jumped up, sitting on the middle cushion. He looked right at home. Sloane went and sat beside him. Gage joined them, sitting on the dog's other side. The animal served as a barrier between them. He knew he was going to have to make the first move.

"When did you get a dog?" he began.

"Today. Ainsley told me about him. His owner passed away suddenly, and Stan Shorter was helping to find Murphy a new home."

"Owning a dog is a lot of responsibility," he said.

She frowned. "You don't think I'm responsible?"

This was going badly.

"I just thought... well, with you traveling for your job and all... it might be hard to have a pet."

"I'm not traveling now," she snapped.

"I meant when you do go back to work." He swallowed. "When you leave the Cove." The lump in his throat grew bigger. His eyes began misting with tears again. "Dammit, Sloane."

She crossed her arms defensively. "What is wrong with you?"

Gage dropped his head, raking his hands through his hair. "I'm sorry. I'm frustrated and angry and upset."

"And I'm not? I thought we had something, Gage. Something special. At least I felt it and you didn't. You cut me off at the knees. You weren't man enough to communicate and tell me that you didn't want to see me anymore. Just shoved and split."

He raised his head, his gaze meeting hers, tears falling. Her jaw dropped.

"Gage?"

She stood and nudged Murphy so that the dog moved to the cushion she had been sitting on. Sloane took his hands in hers. "Talk to me. I know you're this stone-faced, silent type. But I need you to talk. I'll listen. I'm good at it." She smiled.

"I fucked up everything with you," he lamented,

tears flowing freely now. "I've never cried in thirty-four years—and I've broken down twice tonight."

Her fingers squeezed his gently. "Why?"

He blinked several times. "I fell hard for you, Sloane. I've never done that before. It was so foreign and new. I was unsure how to act. I thought we might try to make it work when you went back to your job. I hoped—"

"I'm not going back," she said, her gaze pinning his. "Ever."

"What?"

"I'm not returning to the network. I called Steve, my boss, this afternoon and told him. He wasn't happy, but he understood." Sloane took a deep breath and let it out slowly. "I had a successful career, but I want to do something different now. Whatever it is, I'll be staying in the Cove. This is home to me now, Gage, with or without you."

"I thought you would leave. Leave here. Leave me. And when I told you that I loved you, you—"

"You what?" she cried. "When the hell did you say that? You didn't. I'm the one who loves you. My gosh, all our friends know. I confessed it to them. But I was too afraid to tell you. I thought you would think it was too soon and run like crazy from me. Instead, you turned cold and aloof. We went from burning hot to icy cold. You didn't use words to tell me we were done. You just froze me out."

She pulled her hands from his. "I was hurt, Gage. Really hurt. So don't say you told me you loved me because you didn't."

"But I did, Sloane. And you didn't say it back. You didn't say anything. I thought your silence meant you didn't love me. That you knew you were leaving sooner or later and didn't want to give me your heart."

"When did you tell me you loved me, Gage? When?" she demanded.

"After the last time we made love," he said. "You were lying in my arms. I thought it was way too soon to tell you—but I did so anyway. I whispered in your ear that I loved you. That I would forever." He paused. "You didn't say a word. I knew right away what a terrible mistake I'd made. What a fool I was for thinking you could love someone like me."

Tears brimmed in her eyes. "You idiot," she said softly. "You did make a mistake. You said you whispered?"

He frowned. "It was loud enough for you to hear," he insisted.

"No, it wasn't. You said it into my bad ear. The one I lost hearing in."

Everything crystallized in that moment. Gage could see himself standing with his friends, ordering for them to shut off the TV they had been gathered around, listening to reports of Sloane's kidnapping. He heard Tenley mentioning how Sloane had lost thirty percent of her hearing in one ear. How she was disillusioned with her job.

"You didn't hear me. You didn't hear me," he repeated, understanding dawning.

Sloane shook her head. "No. I didn't. If I had, Gage, I would have told you that I loved you, too. That yes, it was too soon to be feeling everything I did, but I knew you were my soulmate." Tears cascaded down her cheeks. "I'm sorry. So sorry. We let a tiny misunderstanding blow up. It almost cost us everything."

"That's on me," he said. "I do keep too much inside. I should have talked to you about it."

Gage captured her hands in his. "I let my ego and lack of communication skills get in the way. It made me lash out and push you away before you could do that to me."

He looked at Sloane with all the love he felt and spoke from his heart. "I promise I'll keep the lines of communication open. You may have to teach me how to do that. We can fight—and we will. We'll disagree on things. But I will not let our spark die. I will not bail on you when things get tough," he promised. "I am committed to you now and forever, Sloane Anderson. I may let you down, but I will never let you go. I'm all in. Always."

She tore her hands from his, reaching for his face and yanking him down. Their mouths collided. Instant heat ensued. Gage kissed Sloane as if he were parched from wandering in the desert a thousand years. He couldn't get enough of her. She kissed him back, lighting a fire within him that threatened to consume him.

They began tearing at one another's clothes, wanting—no, needing—bare flesh to touch. Once their clothes had been shed, their mouths fused together as their hands roamed each other's bodies hungrily, greedily. Gage lifted her into his arms.

Tearing his mouth from hers, he hoarsely asked, "Where's the bedroom?"

"That way," she pointed, kissing him again, causing desire to flare through every limb.

He carried her to it and they fell on the bed together—and brushed against fur. Immediately, they both laughed as Murphy's tail thumped on the bed.

Releasing her, Gage fumbled until he found the light switch on the nightstand's lamp. The room lit, and they saw Murphy at the foot of the bed, paws stretched in front of him.

Wearing a huge grin.

"Is that dog *smiling* at us?" he asked, returning to Sloane and slipping his arms around her again.

"I believe so. But I don't think one medium-sized dog can stop us."

"Hell, no," Gage said.

He made love to her frantically, desperately, all his recent frustrations releasing, allowing the tension to escape his body. They climaxed together, calling one another's names aloud, the pleasure greater than anything he'd ever known.

Gage collapsed atop her. "I can't move," he moaned. "You've drained me."

"Good," she said cheekily, her arms entwining his neck. "Because I don't want you going anywhere. You're stuck with me, Gage Nelson. You're giving up your garage apartment and moving in here with Murphy and me. I'm going to help you open the business of your dreams. We are a team. Now and forever."

"You probably should run the place. You know as much about it as I do," he told her.

"We'll do it together," she promised.

He moved from her and pulled her to her feet, tossing back the covers so they could climb into bed. Gage held Sloane close.

"Tonight is the start of a beautiful future together," he told her, kissing her softly. "I love you, Anderson."

Her eyes sparkled. "I love you more, Nelson."

Murphy curled upon against their feet and Gage said, "Don't get too comfortable down there, Murph, because I plan to keep the love of my life up all night."

And he did.

EPILOGUE

FIVE YEARS LATER...

Sloane entered Buttercup Bakery and waved to Gloria before heading to the back.

Ainsley saw her enter. "Hey, girl. I've got the cannolis you requested. And I'm finishing up the cake now."

"Carter loves them so much. I thought the cannolis could be for him, and the cake could be for the crew and his kids. It's hard to believe today's taping will be episode one hundred."

Carter and Tenley had a four-year-old girl who had been born on the same day as Willow's and Dylan's first boy. The couples had traded two years later, with Tenley producing a boy and Willow giving birth to a girl two days later.

Ainsley finished piping and motioned Sloane over. "What do you think?"

She looked at the cake. "It's perfect. You're still the best around."

Ainsley had been the first of their group of friends to have a boy five years ago. She and Jackson had added twin girls three years later. Jackson split his time between being an attorney and serving as the mayor of the Cove, while Ainsley had cut her hours considerably, working from nine to three. She allowed her staff to prepare the pastries for the morning rush, and they also did all the breads and cookies. Ainsley handled all the specialty cakes for birthdays, weddings, and graduations, as well as producing the more difficult pastries such as eclairs, Napoleons, and baklava. Her reduced hours allowed her to drop the kids off at preschool and pick them up and still allowed her to make magic in the kitchen.

"Let me box the cake up for you," Ainsley said. "Are we still good for Game Night tonight?"

Game Nights had been cut to one Friday night every six to eight weeks. Though they all loved their children, it was fun to have strictly adult time with treasured friends.

"Yes. At Boo's. Gage and I will be bringing the pizza."

"And I'm about to make the chocolate poke cake since you and Gage were victorious last time. It's rich and decadent, with hot fudge sauce and topped with chocolate whipped cream Perfect for a chocoholic."

"My husband will be in heaven," Sloane said. "Me, too. See you tonight."

She left the bakery and flipped on the radio as she headed to the Clarks' house. *Cooking with Carter* had run for five seasons now. Sloane had gone from interviewing guests to producing the show the past three years. Carter also had written a cookbook a year during that time, and he and Elmo Nichols, his agent, were in talks for Carter and her to create a cooking show for a children's cable network.

"And this is the latest song from Nash Edwards which is burning hot on the charts, written by his wife, Rylie. Here's *Will She Come Back?*"

Sloane turned up the volume, still getting a thrill that her friend had written two songs which had won Grammys. Nash had also won seven Grammys over the past few years and been named the Country Music Awards Entertainer of the Year twice.

As she sang along, she rolled the windows down, enjoying the cool of the mid-May morning. She arrived and a production assistant greeted her, taking the cake inside while she grabbed the cannolis for Carter.

"Happy One Hundred Shows!" she told him, giving him a hug.

"It doesn't seem possible, does it?" he asked, opening the box and snagging a cannoli. "Mmm. Ainsley makes *the* best."

Tenley appeared and slipped a cannoli from the box. "I know they're yours, but I need the sugar rush. I'm at a crucial scene and could use the extra boost."

Tenley's first trilogy had eventually expanded to seven books over the past few years, with films being made of the first three. She was now working on a new fantasy series.

"Wow, these are good," Tenley exclaimed. "Keep me away from them. I'm headed back to my computer. See you at Boo's tonight, Sloane."

She decided to corral everyone. The crew had little turnover, and everyone knew their jobs well. Today's guest was Liz Freeman, Gage's former landlord. The feisty widow was eighty now and showed no signs of slowing down. She had told Carter she liked a little spice in her life and in her food, and the pair made taco bowls today, the first a chili lime sweet potato bowl with chipotle ranch, and the second a chicken burrito bowl with black and mango salsa.

Since Liz had a sweet tooth and lived alone, Carter

also taught her to make a single-serving apple crumble, which had only four ingredients and could be assembled and microwaved, ready to eat in ten minutes.

After the cooking segment had been filmed, Sloane took Liz outside and interviewed the widow. It amazed her how every person had an interesting story to tell or something in their background that viewers enjoyed hearing about. In Liz's case, it came out that she had worked on a pit-racing crew and had been a flight attendant on a crew whose route was to the Far East.

"That was some great stuff, Liz," she praised.

"I had fun," Liz admitted. "And I'm definitely going to make that apple crumble tonight."

Sloane checked in with Trae, who said he had all he needed to cut the segment.

"Then I'm off," she said, telling everyone goodbye and heading to her car.

She drove the short distance to Boo's and rang the bell. Willow answered, smiling.

"I'm betting you've already finished reading your essays."

Laughing, she said, "Of course. Here they are." She handed Willow several file folders. "I don't want to influence you, but if Jenny Jacobs doesn't win this latest Boo Martin scholarship, I just might have to help put her through college or art school myself."

Willow had continued holding an annual contest and awarding a scholarship in her grandmother's name to a local high school student. Her friend also had continued to paint while being a full-time mother, still holding a yearly show at the Runyon Gallery in New York. Dylan had won reelection as the town's sheriff and accompanied Willow to New York each fall for the show's opening before returning to keep the household running in her absence.

"I've got to run," Sloane said. "I'm heading to NFC now to show Gage a new social media campaign before I pick Mason up at preschool. I'll be back tonight with pizzas in hand."

Willow sighed. "Boy, I need Game Night tonight."

"I think we all do. Later."

She hugged her friend and return to her car, driving to the Nelson Fitness Center. Gage handled everything dealing with numbers for NFC, from keeping the books and dispersing the payroll, to ordering and maintaining the equipment. Sloane had taken on all PR and marketing for the work-out facility, along with running its various social media accounts. Somehow, she had found time to also write two non-fiction books about her reporting days. Her life was busy and very full—but she wouldn't have it any other way.

Arriving at NFC, she parked and went inside. She officed at home, but Gage kept an office here. They had agreed not to talk shop at home and for all business decisions to be made at work.

She waved breezily as she passed the reception desk and glanced inside the childcare center. That was one thing their original plan had lacked. When they became parents, they realized other parents still wanted to work out and often were prevented from doing so due to childcare issues. They had converted one of the exercise rooms to a daycare center and hired two workers to staff it. The care was free and limited to two hours at a time. Having it had led to a thirty percent surge in memberships.

Sloane reached the doors to the natatorium and paused a moment, admiring the sculpture of Ted

Castro cast in bronze. Instead of a more formal bust, the sculpture showed Ted on a surfboard as a wave crested. Maia Jarrell had captured joy on Ted's face, and the water looked real. The plaque told briefly of Ted's professional career. She glanced above the door and saw the words *Ted Castro Natatorium*, which still give her a thrill all these years later.

Making her way past the indoor pool area, she went to Gage's office. He sat behind his desk, wearing the uniform she had designed, a black T-shirt with NFC on its pocket and athletic pants.

Glancing up, his frown became a smile and he rose, meeting her and enveloping her in his arms for a nice hug and an even better kiss.

"You taste like cake," he said.

"I had a piece at Carter's. We were celebrating getting one hundred shows in the can."

His arms still around her, he said, "Then I guess you won't have any room for dessert at Game Night tonight. I suppose I'll have to eat your piece."

"It's a chocolate poke cake, and it sounds divine," she told him.

He gave her a lingering kiss. "It does—but you taste divine, Anderson."

She entwined her hands about his neck. "So do you, Nelson."

They kissed again, and Sloane marveled how much she loved this man.

Breaking the kiss, she said, "I was going to show you a new campaign, but you don't really care to see it, do you?"

Gage grinned. "Not really. I like everything you do. Just run with it. You don't need my approval."

"We make a pretty good team, don't we?" she pressed.

"You bet. Running NFC. Parenting Mason."

"I have a new project in mind for us," Sloane told him.

"Hmm, sounds intriguing. What's involved?"

"Oh, a lot of late nights. Some crying. Pumping. Rocking. And definitely changing diapers."

His eyes lit up. "Mason is going to be a big brother?"

"Yes. Probably around Christmastime."

Gage lifted her in the air, swinging her around. Sloane laughed freely, happiness spilling from her.

He set her on her feet again and pulled her close. "Just when I didn't think things could get any better for us, they have." He framed her face in his hands. "I love you, Sloane. You and Mason and Little Nelson."

"I love you, Gage. Always."

They kissed again, a kiss that united them in purpose.

And love. Always, always in love.

ALSO BY ALEXA ASTON

A Bit of Heaven on Earth

A Knight for Kallen

SECOND SONS OF LONDON:

Educated by the Earl

Debating with the Duke

DUKES DONE WRONG:

Discouraging the Duke

Deflecting the Duke

Disrupting the Duke

Delighting the Duke

Destiny with a Duke

DUKES OF DISTINCTION:

Duke of Renown

Duke of Charm

Duke of Disrepute

Duke of Arrogance

Duke of Honor

MEDIEVAL RUNAWAY WIVES:

Song of the Heart

A Promise of Tomorrow

Destined for Love

SOLDIERS AND SOULMATES:

To Heal an Earl

To Tame a Rogue

To Trust a Duke

To Save a Love

To Win a Widow

THE ST. CLAIRS:

Devoted to the Duke

Midnight with the Marquess

Embracing the Earl

Defending the Duke

Suddenly a St. Clair

THE KING'S COUSINS:

God of the Seas

The Pawn

The Heir

The Bastard

THE KNIGHTS OF HONOR:

Rise of de Wolfe

Word of Honor

Marked by Honor

Code of Honor

Journey to Honor

Heart of Honor

Bold in Honor

Love and Honor

Gift of Honor

Path to Honor

Return to Honor

Season of Honor

NOVELLAS:

ABOUT THE AUTHOR

A native Texan and former history teacher, award-winning and internationally bestselling author Alexa Aston lives with her husband in a Dallas suburb, where she eats her fair share of dark chocolate and plots out stories while she walks every morning. She enjoys travel, sports, and binge-watching—and never misses an episode of *Survivor*.

Alexa brings her characters to life in steamy historicals, contemporary romances, and romantic suspense novels that resonate with passion, intensity, and heart.

KEEP UP WITH ALEXA
Visit her website
Newsletter Sign-Up

MORE WAYS TO CONNECT WITH ALEXA

CPSIA information can be obtained
at www.ICGtesting.com
Printed in the USA
BVHW08327110922
646700BV00005B/231